The Gods of Our Time

The
GODS of
Our Time

Cothburn O'Neal

CROWN PUBLISHERS, INC.
NEW YORK

Any similarity between the characters in this book and real persons living or dead is purely unintentional and coincidental; but a strong resemblance between the people in the story and real people who might have lived and died is an end most to be desired.

The Gods of Our Time

CHORUS

IT WAS A natural mistake. Like any one of us could have made it. Maybe we all goofed, and then maybe it wasn't such a shuck after all. We're still searching it. That's what we do all the time—search. We're dedicated to truth.

Anyway Teresina took this cat in. She runs a secondhand book and record shop down by the pier, with a hospitable, roomy pad upstairs. She's a Venus-built variosexual in her forties, about halfway in and halfway out of our colony here. Sometimes she's with it and sometimes she's not; so you never can tell what she'll take up with, or shack up with, next—man, woman, or child. But she's right. She can smell fuzz a mile away, the same as she can smell pot; so she's a good watchman at the gate, if anybody is holding or pushing junk in the neighborhood.

A lot of squares trying to make the scene come by way of Teresina. And some real gassers have stopped off with her on the way in. We all like her. She's welcome in any pad in the district. And, as the squares say, any friend of Teresina's . . .

He was in his middle twenties and stood at least six feet two in sandals, all muscled up under his sweat shirt and well hung in his dungarees. His hair and beard were flaming red, and as curly as fresh pine shavings. We would have tagged him "Barbarossa" even if Teresina hadn't beat us to it. But there the brute stopped. His face had a beatific radiance about it that was positively seraphic; and his eyes, of a pastel blue like Foulard's

9

Brittany skies, were the gentlest ever seen this side of innocence.

We got hung up on his eyes. We weren't held by them, not like the Wedding-Guest, nothing like that. We just looked that far and somehow rested our gaze there of our own volition and got some peace or thought we did and felt a little better, like we had turned on to a new vision.

We talked about it at some length before he ever said more than three words to any of us, but we asked no questions of him or of Teresina. Like it's their business. Anyone can tell all he knows in one of our all-night talkfests and we listen. We don't mind questions. We answer them and we ask them when we know they're welcome. After a few bennies or a stick or two of tea to break down the inhibitions, we communicate absolutely, relate basically. It's all part of the search. Until we all know what we all know we can't know anything. We're nowhere.

"Like Barbarossa has either flipped or he's the new shaman," Dick Ferguson said. We were sharing a gallon of wine in his pad, waiting for his wife to come in from the office and cook up some eggs for supper.

"That's strong, man, strong," Foulard said. He was painting one of his pale Brittany skies over a mural which a former tenant of the pad had left unfinished.

"Strong, I mean strong," Dick said. "You look at him and you know he's with it or he's an idiot. I mean there's no guile and no search in those eyes or that face. He's a child or he's the wisest old man on the West Coast. Wise, I mean hip, real hip. Dig? He's not even trying to make the scene."

"That's good," Foulard said. He put the paint brush between his teeth and scratched his crotch thoughtfully. "Or that's bad."

"Another pair of opposites," Kay said as she came into the pad and stepped over Dick's legs, which took up most of the floor that wasn't already littered with scrap metal that Dick was assembling for a piece of sculpture.

"Barbarossa," Dick said.

"Yeah, he's a bundle of opposites," Foulard agreed.

"Or he can find an opposite in just about any pad around here," Kay said on her way to the kitchen. "As soon, that is, as Teresina let's him go."

"Or brings him," Foulard said. "What's his kick? Can't we lure him somewhere?"

"Teresina," Kay called from the kitchen. "She's his kick. You know that. She'll keep him off pot, horse, or anything else that might take away his nature."

"Yeah," Dick said. "That's what bugs me. I mean like he's cool, like he's hip, all the way."

"Zen, maybe?" Foulard asked.

"That's a better bet than Teresina, though she's a far-out partner if sex is his kick."

"Poetry, maybe?" Foulard guessed again. "He's a mick. They're all poets."

"Let's have a reading somewhere tonight." Kay came out of the kitchen. She kicked off the shoes she had worn to work and padded across the floor barefoot. "Kurt will read anytime at his pad." She stubbed her toe on a railroad spike which was lying on the floor, but merely rubbed her foot for a moment and made no complaint.

"Yeah, let's do," Foulard said.

"Got any bread?" Dick asked.

"Sure, I got paid today," Kay said. "There's thirty or forty dollars left after groceries. Want it?"

"Yeah. I'll go get some more wine and a can of tea if I can make a connection."

Kay looked around to see where she had thrown her purse. She pointed to it and went behind a screen to change her clothes. Dick got up, rifled her purse, and started out the door.

"Later," he said from the hallway.

"I'll see Kurt," Foulard volunteered, and he too cut out.

11

News of the reading session spread rapidly, and by ten o'clock Kurt's pad was filled to capacity. Foulard brought his bongo drums, and Clara Bergson carried a pearwood recorder under her arm. It being Friday night, no other musicians showed up.

Teresina and Barbarossa came in a few minutes before Kurt started reading; and they, of course, were the guests of honor, though only three or four of us knew it. We four, however, managed so that we could keep an eye on Barbarossa. A good many others had the same idea. By some magic, or mystique, the bodies, packed though they were, arranged themselves so that every pair of eyes could see Kurt, seated on a stool behind a homemade lectern, as well as Teresina and her guest squeezed up tight on the edge of a pallet.

Kurt was in the throes of alliteration just then; so he read his *bound by the bastards* to a bongo beat.

> bound by the bastards
> big business bosses
> bankers brokers
>
> bound by the busybodies
> betterment bureaus
> bossy old biddies
>
> bound by the bitches
> busts bosoms
> butts bottoms
>
> bound by the billboards
> buick barbasol
> big bad b o
>
> bound by the buck
> better buy
> better buy

                    bound brother break
                         break away
                        bound away
                          brother!

Foulard did very well on the bongo drums, but Clara never seemed to get with it on the recorder. Kurt sounded a loud and colorful opinion of her jazzmanship, with some wonderfully pointed remarks about her virtue and ancestry. Although she deserved the criticism, Kurt's eloquence really stemmed from fast-rising jealousy. Both Kurt and Clara were trying to make it with a recently arrived bull-fiddler from Haiti, but he was shacking up with a canary singing in the same combo with him.

Dick Ferguson produced the pot he had bought, and so eased the tension. While we ringed ourselves in circles of five or six and started passing the sticks around, Kurt put some jazz discs on his hi-fi. Then we settled down for a solid séance.

It was apparent from the first that Barbarossa dug jazz, whatever his reaction to Kurt's poetry might have been. He fell right in. He never said a word, never even closed his eyes, just sat there, took a puff or two each time the reefer passed his way, and *saw* those cats swinging through the decibels—Thelonious Monk, Jimmie Giuffre, Old Satchmo and Charlie Bird. Like he *saw* it, man, saw it! He saw everything, his face like a little boy's at the county fair. Only once, when Foulard added his bongo drums to one of Bessie Smith's old songs, did Barbarossa change his expression. Then that cherub face of his took on a chiding look—but gentle, more in sorrow than in censure, love, all love. It was beautiful to behold. And Barbarossa was right, hip all the way: there was no place for bongo drums in Bessie's music.

After a few sides, the party reached the talking stage—the confessional, the truth-ritual of our search. And it turned out to be a ball, a real gasser that lasted all night. Teresina, who might

13

have been as curious as we were about Barbarossa, began a long truth-talk all about her girlhood with a lecherous stepfather and two foster brothers as well as a spinster neighbor who had a yen for dark-eyed Latin girls.

"Yes, yes, yes," echoed several old-timers whenever Teresina struck a familiar chord.

"What we remember is what we are. What we learn is what we shall be," Kurt pronounced solemnly when she had finished. He was composing.

"Who are you? What are you, Barbarossa?" Teresina asked rhythmically, swaying to the pulse of the pot.

"Who am I?" Barbarossa asked.

"What do you remember?" Kurt coached him.

"Where shall I begin?"

"From in front, man, from in front!" It was all poetry, with the beat.

Barbarossa began from in front. I remember well how he related to us that first night. He didn't even speak our language. Yet he did speak our language, a tongue we remembered nostalgically from our childhood. He communicated. We dug him. The obvious paradox bugged no one for the next hour.

It was his voice that turned us on. Big, soft, low, powerful, and loving, it was that voice man has always heard during his tribal rituals—the voice from the mountain, the voice in the Shekinah.

I can hear it now, as Barbarossa said, "That would be . . ."

SARASOTA, 193—

WHERE DOES memory begin? In the womb? In a dream? In ecstasy? In shock?

There may be an earlier half-world shrouded in mists, but suddenly, from somewhere, comes that first full-blown image, clean-cut and everlasting, which in time may take on many meanings or may remain forever one bright vision floating free in the consciousness, haunting, puzzling, frightening—or comforting and consoling—in its mystery.

Mine is always there, to be recalled at will or to intrude itself, unsummoned, into my restlessness, that sun-washed picture of the baby Ella naked in the playpen beside me on the shining sand. Ella is my twin. I knew then that she was there. But did I know that I was there? Does memory precede self-consciousness? Did I know Ella before I knew me? Is my memory older than my *self*? Anyway, I knew that Ella was there.

Mama was there, too, dark and beautiful and naked. And Daddy was there, naked beside her as Ella was beside me. They played on the beach, their sea-wet bodies glistening in the sun as they plunged into the surf and rose again, dripping, laughing. Mama strangled on the brine. Daddy beat her on the back —brutally, frighteningly—until she laughed again and ran away from him, toward the playpen, toward me. One of the babies gurgled in delight.

But Daddy chased her, caught her, held her, and threw her

15

down roughly—too roughly—on the blanket spread nearby. They struggled. Their laughing subsided. Daddy seemed to be biting Mama. She moaned softly and clung to him, then held her breath for a time and released it in a long shuddering sob, louder than the soughing of the sea.

I heard it all. I can still hear it. Ella heard it, too—maybe she still does—and we both began to cry.

They looked our way and Mama said, "Oh, Al, for shame!"

Ella, and I suppose I, wailed louder and louder, our terror rising with our voices.

Mama rose first and came to the playpen. Daddy followed. She picked me up and hugged me to her.

"*Va bene, bambino mio,*" she crooned. I was happy again. That is all. There is no more.

That is, there was no more at first. Time has put the scene in context, placed it in perspective, filled it with meaning. The place was a sheltered beach near Sarasota. It was morning or early afternoon, for Gina, who is six years older than Ella and I, must have been in school. And it was winter. Otherwise the circus would have been on tour. When? How should I know? Ella and I were babies, but how old I have no idea; and of course I could never ask, not even Ella—not until now, and there is no need to ask her now.

Ella probably remembers everything I remember, knows everything I know, and more. Is there stronger rapport between twins than between other siblings? Ella says there is. We know many things together without being told. We always have known, she always more than I.

We knew what it meant when Colonel Strongforth, the ringmaster, came to tell Nonna, our grandmother, that she should leave the Bounding Bercellis and join the Living Statues.

"It's for your own good, Mrs. Bercelli," he said. "It's time we old folks let the youngsters do the hard work." He was handsome in his top hat, cutaway, and immaculate white riding

16

breeches. Or is that the way I remember him, compositely, from the many times I watched him in the ring?

"He'sa right, Mama," Avolo said. "It'sa time you took it easy."

"We need you in the Statues," Colonel Strongforth said. "It's hard to get experienced circus people who know what the public wants these days."

"I don' know," Nonna said slowly. Tears were in her eyes when she turned to Mama and asked, "What you think, Nestra?"

"You'll make a beautiful Statue," Mama said. "Could I come too, Colonel?"

"Well, now, Nettie," he said, "of course you can. But with both you and your mother in the Statues I doubt that I could keep my eyes on any of the other rings. Could Nettie be spared from your act, Mr. Bercelli?" He turned to Avolo.

"No, Nestra, you stay," Nonna said hurriedly. "You besta girl we got in our act now. I go to Statues for Colonel Strongfort'. You stay wit' Papa anda boys."

We all looked at the ringmaster.

"Well, Nettie, that settles it," he said. "We could sure use you in the Statues, but I guess you had better do as your mother says. We wouldn't want to rob the Bounding Bercellis of all their beauty."

That settled it. My grandmother went to the Living Statues. Everyone was sad—Mama, Avolo, Uncle Tony and Uncle Mario and their young wives, recently arrived from Sicily. We all knew what had happened. Nonna had lost caste. She was being reduced from a talented acrobat to a chalk-white female body, retired from action, drained of life, relegated to the rock pile.

I say we all knew what was happening. But how could Ella and I have known then? The Living Statues were discontinued after 1935, when Ella and I were only three years old. I cannot remember ever having seen them posed.

We know *now* what was happening then. After that first bright vision, memories blend and fuse into one another and we cannot keep them ordered in time or fixed in their context. They crowd us. They crowd one another, devour one another cannibal-like, and tantalize us with their phantasmagorial parade. Yet they form the slender thread which holds us together.

Big cats, high-school horses and liberty horses, Ponderous Pachyderms, chattering little monkeys, the bandwagon, the Man on the Flying Trapeze, the catcher, the teeter board and the understander, popcorn, peanuts and chewing gum, sweet fresh hay, huge hunks of horse meat for the hungry lions, the Grand Entry, silks and plumes and long silken legs, the Bounding Bercellis in the center ring with Mama, beautiful Mama, as the main attraction—and towns, an endless string of towns, all alike, all different.

Some of the phantoms falter in passing, stabilize for a moment, long enough to be fixed and filed away, to be bottled. Pull the cork and out they come, like Aladdin's jinn—jinn from a lamp or, better still, jinn from a gin bottle—to plague or pacify.

There are the bright ones, when we all sat at home in the evening, in the soft, moist night of Sarasota, and Mama studied the lessons along with Gina, with Daddy's help, and later went through them all again with me and Ella, learning, as we learned, to speak the language like a native, to be a Good American, which was Avolo's dream for all his line in the new country.

There were better nights, on the circus train, when Mama took me into her berth with her and Daddy took Ella with him, and Gina slept with some other circus girl small enough to share one of the narrow bunks comfortably. Mama and Daddy divided us twins between them, as they shared Gina, sometimes generously, sometimes jealously. I was at peace then, lulled by the clackety-clack of the Pullman trucks, soothed by Mama's soft crooning of lullabies which Nonna had sung to her in a gaudy caravan creaking its way along the rocky roads of Sicily.

My peace was sometimes broken when Daddy chose to share Mama's berth and left his to Ella and me—two unhappy, bewildered outcasts, clinging to each other in our misery, sobbing ourselves to sleep—or, in some of those nights remembered, Ella playing Mama and singing to me or I playing Daddy and petting her until, our tears dried by make-believe, we found peace together.

Good times, too, were those when Nonna cooked highly spiced Sicilian food, out of doors on a clay-lined furnace, for all the Bercellis. Other troupes, lured by the rich aromas, dropped by to sip a glass of dago red and to repeat old circus lore—gruesome stories of flyers falling to earth, of the time the circus train ran into the rear of a troop train during the war, that other war back in 1918, of fires and floods and hurricane winds which ripped the canvases to shreds. Gay stories, too, of sunny days and mixed romances—and sad ones, of broken-hearted clowns and freaks who loved beyond their reach.

On such mellow occasions Daddy always told how he met Mama. Did he always tell, or do I remember only those times he did tell the story? And did he have to tell it? Did someone always ask? Someone probably did. It must have seemed a marvel that any man could have won her. She was the most beautiful woman who ever lived, with the kind of face the Italian Renaissance artists never tired of painting, and the lithe, sinuous body which kept the Bounding Bercellis in the center ring long after Nonna had retired and Avolo was an old man faking his part in the routine.

That Daddy, the son of Danny Meaghan—top banana of big-time burlesque, Primo Bozo of the Minsky houses—should have aspired to her must have been a source of wonder.

He stood as he talked, so he could gesture freely. He was over six feet tall, almost as tall as I am now, with the same shock of red hair, the same blue eyes, and the same damned sprinkling of Van Johnson freckles across the bridge of his nose—every mother's little boy grown big.

It was Mama, of course, who had caused him to forsake his song-and-dance routine in vaudeville and become a circus clown. He let no one forget that point.

"There I am," he said, "standing in the wings at the Palace, waiting to come on in the second spot."

He always began with a disparaging preface, reminding us that tumblers and jugglers and acrobats and animal acts were used to open the show, to quiet the house, to prepare the way for the better performers who came later. No one, except me perhaps, objected to his insinuations. The Bounding Bercellis carried such excellent billing as circus performers that they could well afford to put up with a few snide remarks from a soft-shoe dancer during the thirteen weeks in winter when they played a vaudeville circuit.

"I'm wearing my flashy blazer and a straw hat and carrying a cane." Daddy then danced a step or two and pantomimed his hat and cane. "I look out on the stage and see this doll, this gorgeous brunette in a G-string and a couple of spangles, coming at me in a back-flip routine."

"I was wearing tights," Mama interrupted modestly. She prided herself on never revealing her navel.

"Tights don't hide what you've got, baby," Daddy said. He called her "baby" then, but as Gina and Ella grew up he began to call them "baby" and to call Mama by name.

"Anyway," he went on with his story, "I see that she's coming all the way off stage. Do I get out of her way? Not me. I drop my cane and catch her from behind. She squeals and spins around in my arms to see who's got her.

" 'Perdoni, signorina,' I say brightly in my best Bostonian accent, and tip my hat politely. 'I thought you might lose your balance.'

20

" 'Lose my balance!' she says, shooting fire out of those big brown eyes, and whirls back onstage for bows. She exits off the other side and I hear my intro from the pit.

"That's the only time in my life I ever muff my patter or louse up a soft-shoe routine. I'm gone, I tell you, gone! I even cut my encores and strike out to find this doll again.

"She's left the theater; so I have to buy the low-down on her from the doorman. For three weeks I make my pitch, but she won't leave the act and team up with me in a double.

"Well, I get my agent to match the Bercellis' bookings for the rest of the season. It works out O.K. in the long run. So here I am with a rubber ball for a nose and a fright wig covering my crisp Irish curls."

He laughed. Everybody laughed. I laughed at first, though early I began to resent his manner of telling the story. He had made no sacrifice. Mama was too good for him, too good for any other man I ever knew—too *womanly*, too sensuously feminine, too completely the embodiment of what all men cherish and dream about to belong to any man, least of all to a scion of the Big Wheel.

How many times did he tell his story? Once? A thousand times? Too many times, as many times as Avolo took Ella and me on his knees and held us while we listened to Mayor La Guardia read the funny papers over the radio when the circus was playing in Madison Square Garden.

The Little Flower was his idol, proof positive that an Italian could become a Good American, a great American, mayor of the biggest city in the new country.

"Listen to him? Ain't he funny?" Avola said and laughed— always the same.

Ella and I laughed. We always did. We loved Avolo. There was much love among the Bercellis while we were all together.

There were gray scenes too. Avolo died, then Nonna. Gina left the circus to study in New York—voice and ballet—as soon as she showed true signs of talent. Our arc of the circle was broken.

But it was not all bad after that. Mama and Daddy had more time for Ella and me. We rehearsed acrobatics with the remaining Bercellis in the winter quarters. We practiced long hours on the piano, with Mama hovering near, her perfume scenting the very music that we played. We studied our homework together, too. Then came bedtime, and Mama kissed me, leaving me tingling and longing for the circus train to pull out again, longing to share the sweet intimacy of her Pullman berth.

Through the years I have ridden many trains, listening to the wheels rattle over rail joints, invoking again that peace I once found there. I have pulled the cork many times to release the jinn from the bottle, to conjure up those precious images.

There is a filter. There must be, to select a few from the many, a few that fall into a pattern—or there is no logic, no peace, no sanity. But which of these shall be chosen, which selected? And how? Which of these constitute the ecstatic moment? Which would each of us capture for his life on earth, which project into eternity, as the red man has projected his Happy Hunting Grounds, the fair-haired Nordic his Valhalla, the desert wanderer his Zenana of seventy-two houris, the polyglot his Golden Streets and Pearly Gates? Which shall I choose? Or have I a choice?

If I can find which of these rule my consciousness I shall know who I am and what I am.

CHORUS

HE REALLY sent us. It was square, homey, full of Mama and Daddy, Avolo, and the funnies. It was careful talk, clean talk, the kind we were taught in grammar school—no jive, no inside hipster.

But it was cool too. It searched. It was poetry.

       where does memory begin
            in the womb
                in shock
                     in ecstasy

     suddenly
         from somewhere
    comes that first full-blown image
         clean-cut and everlasting
    which in time may take on many meanings
               or
   remain forever one bright vision
       floating free in the consciousness
           haunting
              puzzling
                frightening
  or comforting and consoling
               in its mystery.

It was the "ecstatic moment" that stoned us. We went frantic. Happy Hunting Grounds, Valhalla, Golden Streets and Pearly Gates! Everybody sounded at once.

"Orgasm!"

"Fix!"

"Moment of truth!"

"Far out, swinging wide!"

"The aesthetic moment," Kurt proclaimed, and the pad took on an awful silence. It was as though we had all fallen out of our frenzy at once. But we rose again.

We searched. We explored Lessing's *Laocoön*. Crazy, man, crazy! Barbarossa was no idiot. He was wise, the wisest old man on the West Coast, the high shaman, the newborn babe. And he looked it. He sounded no more, made no more contributions to the search. He had searched already, and he had made it. His placid infantile face was full of what we all sought in our ecstatic moment.

Except ye turn, and become as little children, ye shall in no wise enter into the kingdom of heaven.

He had only begun to talk.

. . . and a little child shall lead them.

Wolf and lamb, leopard and kid, the calf, the young lion, and the fatling. They shall dwell together and lie together.

Teresina disengaged Barbarossa from the other arms and legs on their pallet and cut out with him. The rest of us stayed on, all day Saturday and all Saturday night. No one felt like breaking the mood. No one could afford to. Barbarossa was the only one who had made it. We waited for his second coming. Now and then someone went out for more beer or wine or pot or food—or other cats fell in, bringing supplies with them.

By Sunday noon the party had grown so big that Kurt's pad would no longer hold it; so we moved down to an oceanside warehouse where Dick Ferguson gigged part time as night watchman. It was against his principles to accept money for his

24

labor, but he had a satisfactory arrangement with the regular watchman to pay him off in scrap metal. It worked out well for all of us, especially on week ends, when the warehouse was closed all day.

"We ought to be waiting on a mountain," Clara said reverently, but it was no real objection.

"Or in the bushes," Kurt said. We recognized incipient jealousy in his tone. Barbarossa was on his way in, the Haitian on his way out.

Our excitement rose as the sun set in the Pacific. A few of the more frantic ones who couldn't stand the strain gave up and cut out to do themselves up with heroin. Dick made them leave the warehouse. If anyone was caught holding horse there Dick would have to scrounge his own scrap iron.

We had to risk marijuana, though, when Barbarossa arrived. Teresina had let it be known that he talked not at all until he started potting up.

"Like maybe it's the only time he remembers," Teresina said. "He talks very little around my pad. Just takes walks, works me when the shop isn't busy, jots down notes in his Sacred Writings."

The hint at Sacred Writings put us on edge. Frenzy! We dispensed with poetry that evening and started from in front with the ritual of the stick. As the fumes of pot began to sweeten up the warehouse, Clara Bergson led off the truth-talk. Hers was no sordid childhood in a broken home. She was short cars and Wellesley all the way, with a little too much of the nymph in her to make the square scene. She usually accepted calls on the week end to keep her pad warm for the cats who really sent her, mostly musicians or hairy poets. Barbarossa was good and sufficient cause for her to welcome chastity and poverty for a while, however.

Her search that night made some very strong points on why she kicked the square acres for the Village and ultimately came to the West Coast. It was all right with us for her to suggest a pattern for Barbarossa's séance. Whatever broke up that good life of his—the love circle rooted deep in the warm soil of Sicily? Clara all but asked the question.

"It came—" Barbarossa began to blow. Words—sonority!

Man, like how prophetic can you get? *It came!* His first words did us up in a fix. Exploded! High from in front.

"It came in—"

HARTFORD, 1944

AFTER MADISON SQUARE GARDEN the circus played Boston and then worked its way back south again into Connecticut. I remember New England in the spring—wide lawns and clover-scented meadows, bordered by lacy fern and sumac, guarded by trees of every shade and size—green, all green, from the Sound to the foothills of the Berkshires. So it was in Hartford the first week in July.

Gina came up from New York to spend a few days with us. She was almost eighteen then, Ella and I just turned twelve. We were happy that morning, as we made the rounds with Gina. Everyone, animals and all, loved her. The Bercellis were proud of her, and their pride overflowed into all the circus people. She was our bid for respectability, our candidate for diva or ballerina, that fine lady who stands on the peak of the professional pyramid, followed in order by actresses, ordinary ballet dancers, talented performers such as aerialists, bareback riders, tumblers, contortionists and wirewalkers, all honorable enough because they *do* something besides expose themselves, thereby entitling them to look with scorn upon the lower echelons of chorus girls, show girls, nautch dancers, and the so-called "exotics" of burlesque.

How had Ella and I acquired this snobbishness, this nice judgment based on the caste system of show business? Indeed, had we acquired it then or is it something that has crept into our memory since that bright green morning in Hartford?

Whether or not we knew all that then, we felt privileged to go from troupe to troupe and share the warmth accorded our big sister. Big, I say, though I was as tall as she then; but Ella was still a little girl.

And I say Bercellis, too. Of course Gina and Ella and I are Meaghans, and I look like a Meaghan, but somehow Daddy seemed not to belong. He was an alien among us, as I am an alien in the presence of the Good American, that magnificent amalgam which is the envy of all first-generation immigrants— or was before *Yanqui* became a dirty word throughout the Old World and the Latin portion of the New.

Certainly it was as Bercellis that we renewed acquaintances on the circus lot. It was as the Bercelli kids that we approached Colonel Strongforth near one of the dressing tents.

"Welcome home, Madamigella Diva," he boomed in his powerful ringmaster's baritone. He stretched his arms toward Gina and she ran to him and hugged him and kissed him.

"It's only me—Gina," she protested when he held her away from him to look at her appraisingly.

"So I see," he said. "Or is it Nestra I see? I do believe you're going to be as beautiful as your mother some day."

"Oh, Colonel, I couldn't possibly be," Gina said, and she meant it. Gina was the best one of us all, the most generous, the most talented, the most promising.

"I didn't say *more* beautiful," Colonel Strongforth said gallantly, for Mama was standing nearby. "But I'll wager I have to declare a draw when you fill out a little more. Have you been working too hard?"

He frowned. Gina was as tall as Mama, but her face was a little thinner, her figure slighter.

"Not working at all," Gina said and laughed happily. "My studies are really play. That's what I like about show business. We *play* here this week—we *play* there next week—always play, never any work."

"I guess you're right, Gina," the colonel agreed. "It has to be play. If we worked as hard as we play, we'd all be worn out before we reached my age—just a bunch of wrecks for the doctors to practice on." He brightened at the thought. "Doctors don't work either, you know. All they do is practice, practice, practice!"

He laughed at his own witticism and let go of Gina. He looked old and tired, dressed as he was in a shapeless tweed coat and slacks. Come two o'clock, the colonel, decked out in the elegant dress of a ringmaster, would be playing again, young and handsome.

"It's good to have you back," he said, "even for a few days. Too bad for us you're going to be a diva—a great loss to the circus—but I'm sure your grandfather would have been proud of you."

Mama and Daddy and the entire Bercelli troupe were ringed around Gina now, basking in the discerning old ringmaster's approval of her. Ella and I stood outside the circle, a little way off, backed up against a hot canvas sidewall. I felt her hand slip into mine. I held it, found comfort in it. It was sometimes like that with us when Gina was around.

Gina belonged to Mama and Daddy. I belonged to Mama, Ella to Daddy, and we were never jealous of each other; but when both our parents gave their attention to Gina, we sensed their preference for her, their first-born. Perhaps we could feel their tension, their unconscious struggle for her undivided affection, their fear of which one would win if ever her loyalty were put to a test.

We could not blame Gina. We loved her too much. Nevertheless, we felt unloved on such occasions. It was as though we had been cast out of their hearts as we were cast out of the berths on those nights when, for reasons unfathomable to us, Mama and Daddy preferred each other to either of us. After

29

such a night we were irritable, and usually ended up by being spanked soundly before the day was over.

I think we wanted to be spanked, to be reassured that Mama and Daddy were aware of our existence after they had neglected us all night. Maybe we wanted them to hurt us and know they were hurting us. It is terrible to suffer a slight from someone who does not realize that he is slighting you.

I could not ask Mama if she loved Daddy or Gina more than me, or if she loved me simply because I was Daddy's son. Nor could Ella ask Daddy if he loved her more than Mama or Gina. Some children can ask that; but Ella and I never could. I suppose that we are more alike than anyone would suspect. We certainly look nothing alike, not like twins, or brother and sister—or even distant relatives—no more alike than Mama and Daddy. But we unconsciously sought each other whenever Mama and Daddy seemed to have forsaken us for Gina.

Gina saw us standing apart from the others. Her face clouded for a moment; then she smiled at us.

"I have to do some visiting," she said brightly to Colonel Strongforth. "Will you excuse me, sir?"

"Reluctantly." The colonel made an elaborate bow.

"Come on, kids," Gina said and beckoned to us.

We came running. Gina casually put her arm around Ella. She considerately allowed me to walk along unattached, now that I was too big to be holding a girl's hand.

"Are you kids having fun these days?" Gina asked.

"Sometimes," Ella said.

"Sure," I said.

Gina wore a light-green circular skirt and a white blouse, open at the neck. She carried a purse and handkerchief in one hand and smelled good, grown-up good. She used Mama's cologne.

"How were your lessons last winter?" she asked.

"Fine," Ella said.

30

"Fair," I said.

"And your piano, Rusty?"

"Oh, all right, I guess," I said. Actually I was doing very well, but I considered it sissy to admit it.

"Hi, Tom," Gina called to a crippled peanut-vender who was firing up his roasting wagon.

"Hi, Gina. Mind if we whistle at you?"

"Not at all. I'd be flattered."

He tooted the steam whistle on his wagon in imitation of a wolf call.

"How about a bag of peanuts for Superba?" Gina let go of Ella and started to open her purse.

"Sure thing." Tom handed her a bag of peanuts but refused her money.

We started toward the herd of elephants standing by to help the set-up crew when needed.

"How long you gona be with us, Gina?" Tom called.

"About a week, I guess."

"Good. Be seein' you around."

Superba hoisted her trunk in greeting as Gina approached.

"Hello there, you ugly old mountain," Gina said. She emptied the peanuts into her free hand and began feeding them to the elephant. When the peanuts were gone Superba lowered her trunk, and Gina was lifted onto the elephant's head.

Gina curled one leg under her and extended the other one gracefully, as she had been taught to do when she rode Superba in the parade.

"Want to go for a ride, Gina?" the trainer asked.

"No, thanks, Ab. I have a lot of visiting to do. Put me down, Superba."

Back on the ground Gina led us through the animal tent, petting other of her favorites, and then for a casual stroll around the rest of the lot. We stopped at the calliope.

"Could Rusty play for us, Professor?" Gina asked.

"Sure, if he wants to."

Not that I particularly wanted to, but I did sit down and play a simple minuet by Bach. I could have played something more advanced, but I liked the way that one sounded on a calliope, Herr Bach's intentions notwithstanding.

"Ach!" the professor said in despair. A fine pianist, and my first teacher, he loathed having to play the calliope for a living.

"Now, Professor," Gina said. "If Bach were alive you know he would write a prelude and fugue for a well-tempered calliope."

"Heaven forbid. 'Swanee River' is for the calliope." The professor grinned, however, and we went on under the big top, where various performers were checking their rigging and testing the earth on which they were to work that afternoon.

My uncles were feeling out the footing in the center ring while a bareback rider put her mount through his paces in a wide circle around them. She waved to Gina, who called back a compliment on her work.

Mama and Daddy came in from the cook tent. Daddy had already put on his big red nose and begun making up for the afternoon performance.

"How about singing for us, baby?" he asked.

"I really don't have anything ready—and no accompanist." Gina said.

"Sure you have. Come on over to the bandstand."

Gina looked at Mama, who nodded and smiled.

"Oh, all right, if you insist," she said.

Daddy hastily rounded up eight or ten bandsmen; and after a brief consultation with them, Gina stepped to the front of the bandstand and sang "Il Bacio" with a purity of coloratura that surprised me. She gave "Giannina Mia" as an encore, to the delight of the rapidly increasing audience—the taste of which she had unerringly satisfied in her choice of songs.

Daddy, always the exhibitionist, took up the role of emcee.

32

"How many of you would like to see our little girl dance?" he asked.

His answer was a unanimous affirmative.

"But I have no costume," Gina said.

"We'll fix that. Hey, Gabrielle, how about the loan of your dress?" he called to the bareback rider, who had sent her horse away and joined the crowd.

"*Oui*," she said.

The women quickly raised a canvas screen around Gina and Gabrielle, who exchanged costumes in less than a minute. Then, with sure-footed grace, even on the tanbark, Gina danced two numbers from her classic repertoire and a modern routine introduced by Sono Osato in *One Touch of Venus*.

It lasted only a few minutes, but it was a revelation of artistic and physical development. Gina's voice was all that could be expected at this stage of training. Her dancing was even better, her figure perfect—slighter than Mama's but promising as much in maturity, and provocatively alive in every curve and muscle.

"More," Daddy urged.

Gina looked pleadingly at Mama.

"She's done enough, Al," Mama said. "Besides, we have a show to do."

"Anyway, you were wonderful, baby," Daddy said.

We all started out to the dressing tents. Daddy left us just outside the big top.

"How was I really, Mama?" Gina asked anxiously. "Daddy thinks anything I do is wonderful."

"Your voice is lovely," Mama said. "Of course you need more training, much more."

"I know that," Gina said.

"You dance exceptionally well. I would like you to concentrate more on your singing—Avolo, Nonna—"

"Oh, I intend to," Gina cut in hurriedly, eagerly. "I know what they wanted."

"I'm glad to hear that," Mama said. Daddy was out of earshot now. "I was afraid you might be tempted to go into musical comedy. You've had offers, I'm sure."

"Yes—chorus, a bit part or two—but I didn't really consider them."

"Well, don't. Don't start too soon. Wait until you're ready. Then—well, I think the Bercellis may have a diva in the family at last."

"Honestly, Mama, do you? Really?" Gina hugged Mama happily.

"Yes, honestly." Mama kissed her on the cheek. "You kids eat something," she said to us. "I have to change."

"I'll see you at the cook house as soon as I get my dress back from Gabrielle," Gina said, and entered the dressing tent with Mama.

Ella and I started toward the cook tent. She did not take my hand, but she managed to touch me as we walked.

"Gina's good," she said. "I mean singing and dancing."

"Yes."

"And pretty."

I grunted agreement.

"But I look more like Mama than she does," Ella said. "Don't I?"

"I don't know." Ella was a little girl. Gina was, as I had seen for the first time, a woman—or almost a woman, grown up anyway.

"Well, I do," Ella insisted. "And I'll look more like Mama when I'm bigger, exactly like her. So much like her that even Daddy can't tell the difference."

"Humph," I said.

"Or you either, Rusty." She edged away from me. "And then everybody that loves Mama will love me just as much as they do her."

We had reached the cook tent. The cook did not ask us what

34

we wanted to eat, but gave us what Mama would have ordered for us. We took our plates and ate in silence. Gina joined us in a few minutes and chatted gaily with everyone who came by.

The lot filled with people, a shrill crowd composed mostly of women and children—a typical matinee audience. Soon the band began to play under the big top. When they struck up "The Entry of the Gladiators," Gina rose hurriedly, her meal only half eaten.

"Come on, kids," she said. "I don't want to miss the Grand Entry."

We ran to the roustabouts' flap nearest us. Gina spoke to the guard, who raised the flap and let us inside the tent. We clambered to the top of some vacant bleachers near the end and sat down. Gina inhaled deeply.

"I love the smell of the tanbark and the animals," she said. She watched the gaudy parade as eagerly as any of the paying customers. We all waved to Mama and laughed at Daddy's sidesplitting antics. Al Meaghan was not Danny Meaghan's son for nothing. He knew every trick of pantomime used in burlesque as well as what he had picked up in his twenty years with the circus. He was funny. I had not then learned the derogatory connotation of *clown*. By the time I could appreciate that shade of meaning, it too fit Daddy perfectly.

But that afternoon we enjoyed the circus, at least until the Bounding Bercellis had done their stint and relinquished the center ring to Dainty Diana Dietzel, Performing on the Roman Rings, High above the Ground, WITHOUT A NET.

The drums rolled while Diana was being hoisted to the very peak of the big top. The crowd was quiet, tense, as Colonel Strongforth awesomely pronounced the dangers of the act, the daring and courage bound up in so dainty a little bit of femininity as Miss Dietzel.

No one smelled the smoke at first, but we all saw the flames at once, licking up the sidewall behind the bleachers opposite us. We saw panic, too, spread with the fire.

"Out, kids," Gina said calmly and grabbed each of us by the hand. She led us down the empty bleachers carefully, slowly.

I was fascinated by the sight across the rapidly emptying rings. The crowd seemed to melt into one huge, formless body, screaming in one voice and flailing myriad arms and legs about aimlessly. It flowed like a giant jellyfish, tentacles waving and sucking for air. It slithered, fluid and viscous, down the bleachers, folded itself over itself, cried out in anguish as one fold smothered another, one tentacle stung another, one gelatinous blob absorbed another, then merged and dissolved in the horrible heat.

"Rusty!" Gina shouted, to break the spell, and tugged at my arm. I let her drag me out through the opening we had entered by originally. Outside she jerked us into a run and rushed us to the edge of the lot, well away from the burning tent. The smoke raised a towering column, red and searing at its base, black and bulbous as it puffed into the sky. Some of it drifted our way, burning our eyes and stinging our nostrils. I smelled burning flesh. I knew what kind of flesh it was—the animals had all been herded clear of the fire—and it made me sick.

Ella whimpered and Gina hugged her tight.

"Mama. Where's Mama?" I asked feebly. I do not know whether I was crying or my eyes were merely smarting from the smoke.

"Mama's all right," Gina said. She held onto my hand, to keep me from running to look for Mama, I suppose.

"Daddy!" Ella was really crying.

"He's all right, too. We'll find them as soon as things clear up." Gina had to shout. Fire sirens, ambulance sirens, police sirens were screaming everywhere. People were screaming. Animals were roaring and trumpeting and squealing and whinnying, each after its kind.

36

I thought of a band, a choir, a song: *I went to the animal fair/The birds and beasts were there,* and I laughed.

Gina let go my hand and slapped me. I stopped laughing and stared at her in astonishment.

"Just don't laugh, Rusty," she said, grabbing my arm. "I'm not mad at you and I didn't intend to hurt you. But don't laugh, and don't try to run away."

I felt sick again, but I sat down on the grass beside my sisters and stared at the horror before me. We were calmer now. Only Ella kept sobbing, her face buried in Gina's lap. I reached over and clasped one of her hands.

That is the way Mama and Daddy found us some minutes, or hours, later. Mama still wore tights, her face flushed and smudged, her hair—free of its bandeau—falling in loose curls around her shoulders, a wild, beautiful sight, a pagan priestess out of a Tarzan movie. I ran to her and she hugged me so tight it hurt both of us. Over her shoulder it was as if I could see the green of Connecticut again, no longer burnt out, seared, and scarred by the fire, as it had been before she came to find me.

"Thank God, we're all safe." She sobbed and squeezed me tighter still.

Daddy held both of the girls to him. They kissed his clown's face, smearing grease paint on themselves.

"How are Uncle Tony and the others?" Gina asked at last.

"All right. We're all safe now," Daddy said.

Safe for the moment, he meant, safe from the fire. Why did I discount what he said then? Or *did* I discount what he said then? True, he looked grotesque—a painted-up clown in baggy pants and oversized collar, with a rubber ball for a nose, and two Bercelli beauties hanging onto him hungrily.

Why could I never give him credit for anything he said or did? He had courage of a sort, bravado at least, and an ingrained stubbornness which might have been considered admirable in some quarters. We were reminded of his courage later that evening when Colonel Strongforth made his rounds to tell the performers how things stood with the circus after the fire.

The colonel was unofficial liaison officer between the management and the performers; so it was to him that the troupes of bewildered foreigners looked for explanations. The Bercellis were gathered in a family group, one of fifty similar companies, speaking in low tones but awaiting further word from the higher-ups before making any plans. We sat on trunks and campstools in one of the dressing tents. The whole lot still smelled of burning canvas and hay and flesh. We held sandwiches, which no one had any stomach for; and my uncles and their wives passed a straw-covered bottle of Chianti among themselves while Daddy drank rye whiskey from a paper cup. Mama, wearing a long gypsy robe over her tights, sat on a campstool. I sat on a coil of rope beside her and rested one elbow on her lap. No one had much to say until Colonel Strongforth joined us.

"No performance tonight," he announced unnecessarily, with a forced laugh.

Uncle Tony offered him the Chianti bottle. He shook his head. He still wore his smudged white breeches and cutaway, but he looked as old and tired as he had in his knockabout tweeds at noon.

"A shot of rye?" Daddy asked.

"Well, yes," the colonel said. "Just a nip to drink to your heroism this afternoon, Al."

Daddy poured two or three fingers of rye into the paper cup and handed it to the ringmaster.

"You saved a good many lives today, Al," the colonel went on. "I've heard a number of tributes to you from officers and firemen as well as our own people. Here's to your stellar performance." He lifted the cup level with his eyes before he drank.

"Thanks, Colonel," Daddy said in the same manner in which he would have acknowledged a compliment on his clowning.

"There'll be a bonus for you," Colonel Strongforth said after he had sipped a drink.

"In fact, there'll be a bonus for all of you," he added, addressing himself to the entire troupe. "The management is proud of your behavior this afternoon and happy that none of you were injured."

"Where do we go from here?" Daddy asked.

"Well, now, that's still a problem. We may go back to Sarasota."

"Yeah," Daddy said. "There's another tent there."

"I'm afraid it'll be quite a while before we play in a tent again," the colonel said. "The public will remember this fire for a long time. They won't trust a tent this season, or maybe the next."

"I guess that's right," Uncle Tony said.

"Does it mean we'll close?" Mama asked.

"I can't say, not right now." Colonel Strongforth looked at Mama and then at the contents of his paper cup. "We can play in aircraft hangars, and in coliseums and ball parks and stadiums around the country—change our bookings. Then—well, there's another hitch. It looks like some of the top management may be indicted for negligence. There may be injunctions. Nobody can tell right now what we'll be able to do."

He spoke slowly, sorrowfully.

"We can all live in the winter quarters. The management will take care of us. We can be sure of that—but we'll just have to wait and see what plans can be made for the rest of the season. I'll let you know everything I find out." He looked apologetically around at the eyes focused on him and handed the cup back to Daddy.

39

"Thanks," he said and moved away to carry the bad news to the next group of performers.

"Sure," Daddy said, and then after a quick swig of rye, "that's a hell of a note—ball parks and football stadiums. We might as well quit."

Uncle Tony cleared his throat and looked at Uncle Mario for support.

"We've been thinking about leaving the circus for a while anyway," he said hesitantly. "That is, if you and Nestra and the kids can get along without us."

Daddy looked up in surprise.

"We can damn well get along without you," he said, belligerently, his face flushed with anger or whiskey. "But just what the hell do you think you can do outside the circus?"

"Join the army," Uncle Tony said.

"Join the army! That's for the birds."

"The army needs interpreters for the occupation of Sicily," Uncle Tony said. "Papa would have wanted us to do our part. This is our chance—we've already talked to a recruiting officer."

"And maybe they can help our families," Aunt Lisa said boldly. She clung to Uncle Tony's arm. "We haven't heard from them in a long time."

"We could help all our people," Uncle Mario said. His wife stood by him also. They still looked upon Sicily as their homeland.

Daddy glared at the four of them.

"Go ahead. Be chumps if you want to," he said. "I can take care of my family."

The others looked at Mama.

"Do what you want to," she said, nodding, "what you think Mama and Papa would have wanted you to do. We'll be all right."

They shifted their attention back to Daddy.

He nodded too, angrily.

"There are some good jobs in defense work," Uncle Tony suggested.

"Defense work, hell," Daddy said. "There's a public for old burlesque comics. Look at Milton Berle. I'm as good as he is, and he's doing all right in New York."

Gina and Ella hugged Daddy eagerly. They believed him.

"Can you put us up in New York, baby?" he asked Gina. "Just for a few days?"

"Yes, Daddy. That is, I have some room and there's a vacancy or two in the building where I live."

"Pack up, kids," Daddy said, rising hurriedly. "We're going to New York."

We went to New York the next day. I suppose we had money. At least we got new clothes and settled in an apartment down in the Village. Gina kept up her voice and ballet lessons, and Daddy started making the rounds of agencies and managers. He came home with glowing accounts of reunions with friends he and his father had known in burlesque—Ed Wynn, Bobby Clark, and others who had made good in the big time.

He was happy and boozy for a while, then despondent and boozy as the summer waned and most of the shows were cast for fall openings. He almost got a spot in a variety show featuring Frank Fay, but lost it to Professor Lamberti, the xylophonist, and a bump-and-grind artist who worked with him. He substituted a week in a Jersey burlesque house for a drunken bozo, but he had such a large personal following that he took over again as soon as he sobered up.

"I have 'em rolling in the aisles," Daddy reported, "but this banana comes back and I have to give up to him. Anyway the job don't pay nothing. The servicemen come to see the strippers—they're the ones who make the big money. Skits and blackouts just fill in between them. Burlesque ain't what it used to be."

As a last resort Daddy began calling up some smaller circuses and finally landed a job as a clown with a one-ring outfit that

41

wintered in Peru, Indiana. The owner agreed to let Mama and us twins live on the circus farm while the show was on the road; so we took the train to Peru and Daddy went down to Sarasota to pick up our car and some personal belongings.

In a week or so, Daddy joined us at the circus farm. As soon as he saw us settled, he left the car with us and joined the show, which was playing small towns in Ohio at the time. Gina stayed on in New York. To help keep her there, Mama got a defense job in a bearing plant in Kokomo and put Ella and me in school in Peru.

It was the first time the family had ever been so widely dispersed. Ella and I, though in the same grade, were in different rooms, and saw each other only during play periods. Mama left the farm before we did in the morning and got home an hour after the school bus dropped us at the gate. We never saw Daddy or Gina. But we all considered it a temporary arrangement. Mama, who considered holding the family together the most important thing in life, told us every night that we would all be together again as soon as the war was over.

"Will Gina come back to the circus?" Ella asked. I doubted that she really wanted Gina back.

"Maybe not Gina," Mama said. "She will be our star, but the rest of us will be together, and not necessarily with the circus." She smiled knowingly.

"Not the circus?" Ella asked. I knew what she meant. She missed the circus train, and sharing a berth with Daddy, just as I missed Mama at night, now that I had a room and bed of my own.

"I think not. When things settle down after the war we should think about you kids. Avolo meant for us to leave the circus and live like other people. You know how proud he was of Mayor La Guardia, how he used to take you twins on his knees and laugh with you when the mayor read the funny papers on the radio?"

"Yes," Ella said without enthusiasm.

"Well, he wanted his children and grandchildren to have a chance to become somebody in America. Gina will be a diva or a ballerina some day. She won't come back to the circus. And you, Ella, you don't want to be an acrobat, do you?"

"If you and Daddy stay with the circus, I do," Ella said.

"But Daddy and I will settle down somewhere. Then what?"

"Well—then, I guess I want to be a lawyer, a lady lawyer, and live with you and Daddy."

Mama laughed softly. We had just seen a movie in which a woman lawyer had been depicted glamorously.

"And you, Rusty? Have you decided what you want to be?" Mama asked me.

"No," I said. I really did not know.

I told the principal of our school the same thing when he called me in for routine counseling on my choice of a career. I suppose I looked apologetic because I could not answer his question.

"Well, I wouldn't worry too much about it, if I were you," he said. "What studies do you like best?"

"I don't know," I said. "None in particular." The only thing I really enjoyed was music, my piano especially, but I did not want to tell him that.

"That doesn't matter too much, either," he said congenially. "The big thing for you to learn in school is life adjustment, to get along with people, to become well rounded."

"Yes, sir," I said, without comprehension.

"You're a big good-natured boy. You'll be a big easygoing man, I think, and that counts for a lot in this day and time. It isn't given to all of us to be an outstanding success as a professional man, but as long as we become adjusted to life and fit into our community we can be happy." He beamed on me as though he were forgiving me for something.

"Yes, sir," I agreed again.

"So, if you have a little trouble with some of your subjects now and then, just don't be envious of the boys, or mostly the girls, who find things easy for them. Just remember that each of us have our place in the community."

I remembered my English teacher's drilling us on saying, "Each of us has his place, etc.," but I let the thought drop as the principal went on.

"You might have qualities of leadership which will come to the fore. All of our leaders were not superior students, you know."

I remembered, "Not all of our leaders, etc.," but I also let that pass. I saw no point to the counseling, but I was sure that it was important. I knew certainly that the principal was my English teacher's boss and consequently deserved a hearing.

"Is your father in the service?" he asked.

"No, sir," I said. "He's traveling with a circus. He's a clown."

The principal appeared to be somewhat taken aback, but only momentarily. There were several circus farms near Peru and a number of circus people who were considered substantial citizens, very well adjusted to life in the community.

"And your mother?" he asked.

"She works in a defense plant in Kokomo."

"Well, that's fine. Doing her bit. Glad to have you in school. If you have any problems, just bring them to me."

"Thank you, sir," I said; and sensing that the counseling period was over, I rose and left his office just as the class bell rang.

Ella was anxiously waiting for me in the hall.

"What did he want?" she whispered belligerently. "What

did you do?" She grabbed my arm and placed herself between me and the office door.

"Nothing," I said and laughed. "It was just my counseling period."

"Oh, life adjustment and all that."

"Yes. Has he counseled you already?"

"Oh, sure. He started with our room and is working his way around. He told me not to get smart-alecky just because I'm smarter than other kids. What did he tell you?"

"I don't know." I laughed again. "I think he was telling me not to worry because I'm not as smart as other kids."

"Why, the old stupe! You're as smart as anybody—smarter, just like Daddy." She threw her arms around me and hugged me impulsively.

The principal opened his office door just then and saw us standing in the hall.

"What goes on here?" he asked, his face going stern. "A petting party?"

"She's my sister," I said, "my twin sister. She was worried— thought you were punishing me for something, sir."

He stared at us for a moment. Ella let go of me.

"Oh, yes, I remember," he said at last. "Al and Ella Meaghan. You don't look like twins—or even brother and sister." He smiled.

"Well, we are," Ella insisted, too forcefully perhaps.

"Yes, yes. I just have never seen you together, but I do re-member your personal record cards—in different rooms, I believe."

"Yes, sir," I said. "Ella is smarter than I am."

"Well, don't let it worry you, Rusty. Seems she'll look out for you." His smile was sarcastic as he went on down the hall.

The second bell rang and we hurried to get our books and catch the school bus.

We found Mama waiting for us in the bus area. She honked

at us and we got permission from the bus driver to ride home with her.

"My section earned an E this month and got off at noon today," Mama said. "So I thought I'd pick you kids up and we'd celebrate."

"Goody," said Ella. "Let's eat out."

"I intend to," Mama said.

We all piled into the front seat of our yellow Buick convertible. It was a flashy car—Daddy liked flashy cars—and, with its Florida license plates, brought a clamor of whistles and shouts from the children on the buses as Mama drove out of the parking lot. We laughed and waved and whistled and shouted back at the kids. Mama took us to Amy's Tea Room for dinner and then to a movie. At home we found letters from both Gina and Daddy. It was a good day for us.

Monday was not so good. That was the day I began to learn what the principal meant by life adjustment. It happened at the first play period. We were choosing up sides for a game of passball as usual, but I suddenly found myself surrounded by a gang of colored boys.

"Why didn't you tell us you was from Florida, Rusty?" asked Willie, one of the leaders.

"You never asked me," I said.

"You said you came from New York," another boy piped up.

"I did come from New York."

"But your mama's car has Florida license plates."

"Yes. We lived in Florida in the winter."

"Where was you born?"

"Florida," I said.

"Then you're from the South. You was afraid to tell us that."

"Why should I be afraid to tell you that?"

"'Cause white men in the South segregate colored people and you was afraid we'd segregate you." Willie approached me menacingly.

46

"Segregate?" I repeated. "I don't even know what *segregate* means."

"He don't know what segregate means," Willie said and glanced around at his circle of friends, who laughed raucously. My own friends had backed away from the group.

"Well, I'll tell you what segregate means," Willie said. "It means cut your balls off. You're lucky we don't segregate you right now, Southern boy."

He lunged at me. Another boy had got down behind me on his all-fours. I fell over backward. I scrambled to my feet and started swinging.

"Don't hit him, Rusty!" one of the white boys warned.

He was too late. I landed a hard right on Willie's jaw and sent him reeling. Willie sat up and rubbed his jaw but made no attempt to stand up. Instead he grinned broadly.

"You're sure in trouble now, white boy," he said with obvious satisfaction.

I was. The playground supervisor suddenly grabbed me by the scruff of my neck.

"What do you mean fighting on the school ground?" he demanded.

"Willie—they started it. They ganged up on me." I pointed at the circle around me.

"Did Willie hit you?"

"No, sir," I said. "He pushed me over somebody else."

"And you hit him for pushing you?"

"Yes, sir. He said they were going to segregate me."

"He tried to segregate us first," one of Willie's boys said.

"Shut up," Willie commanded.

"Come with me to the principal's office," the supervisor said and started marching me toward the school building. Everyone on the playground was watching.

My captor ushered me into the principal's office.

"This boy has been fighting," he said and left immediately.

The principal did not invite me to sit down.

"Fighting, huh, Rusty?" he began. "Who with?"

"Willie—I don't know his last name."

"Willie? That would be Willie Jackson."

"I guess so. He started it."

"Now, Rusty," he said, smiling at me. "Don't lie to me. I realize that you're from the South and are not used to our Yankee schools, as I suppose you would call them. But you must become adjusted to conditions here in Indiana.

"That's part of the life-adjustment program. You mustn't pick on another person just because you feel superior to him."

"I didn't pick on him," I said. "He threatened to—to segregate me and then pushed me over somebody squatting behind me."

"He threatened to segregate you?" The principal laughed. "That's a good one. We don't segregate anyone in Indiana."

"I never heard of people in Florida segregating anybody either."

"Now, Rusty." The principal's smile faded. "I said don't lie to me. You know very well that segregation is practiced all over the South."

"Well, I never heard of it," I insisted. "I didn't know what it meant until Willie started picking on me."

"Do you know what it means, now?"

"Yes, sir. It means—it means—" I blushed and looked down at my feet. "It means to cut your balls off."

"Willie told you that?"

"Yes, sir." I looked up again. The principal seemed to have shrunk up in his chair. His eyes were tired as they studied my face to make sure that I was not lying.

"Willie is somewhat mistaken in his definition," he said wearily. "Did he hit you after you hit him?"

"No, sir."

48

"You shouldn't have hit him. He took your abuse without fighting back. You must learn to do the same, not to strike back. It's part of life adj—"

He had been speaking in a dull monotone. His voice trailed off and he looked out the window.

"For punishment, you must spend your play periods in the library for one month," he said.

"And Willie?" I asked.

"You may go, now," he said. "To the library."

Ella was waiting for me in the hall. Miss Forrest, our English teacher, was with her. We were not allowed to come into the building during a play period unless there was a teacher with us.

"What did he do?" Ella asked. "Did he hurt you?"

"No. He says I must spend my play periods in the library for a month."

"What did he do to Willie?"

"Nothing," I said.

"That isn't fair," Ella said, raising her voice. "I saw it all."

"Sh," Miss Forrest cautioned. "The principal wouldn't dare punish Willie, one of our lily whites—"

"Lily whites!" Ella exploded. "Why, he's as black as—"

"Sh," Miss Forrest said again. "You're a bright girl, Ella. You'll have to become as well adjusted as our principal if you expect to get along in Indiana. Run on back to the playground. I'll take care of Rusty."

Ella left us reluctantly.

Miss Forrest walked with me to the library.

"Rusty," she said, "you are very fortunate to have a sister like Ella, but she can't help you with your present problem."

"No, ma'am," I agreed.

"But don't feel downhearted. A sentence to four weeks in the library is no punishment at all. In fact, it's a privilege. You'll enjoy every minute of it, I promise you."

I did enjoy my month in the library, especially after the weather turned cold and the first snow fell. I was accustomed to Florida winters; so for me it was a privilege indeed to stay inside and read while the others had to wade around in the icy slush and endure the cold damp winds blowing down from Lake Michigan.

Miss Forrest picked some good books for me. I remember *Visitors to Hugo* till this day, though I have forgotten who wrote it. It was about a boy who was in an accident, I believe. Anyway Hugo had to stay in bed, longing for his father, who never visited him because he thought Hugo hated him for causing the accident or something. I have forgotten the details, but at the time I thought how terrible it would be if Mama thought I hated her and was afraid to visit me when I was sick in bed—not that I cared whether Daddy ever came to see me or not.

He did come in off the road about Thanksgiving, however, when the circus went into winter quarters. Gina came home for Christmas, and we had quite a reunion. It was almost like old times—the animals, circus people, Daddy clowning, and Mama cooking up the old Sicilian dishes which Nonna used to prepare at Christmas time. But it was not Sarasota, and it was not a very large circus farm.

Daddy felt the difference more than any of the rest of us; and when the holidays were over he could stand the place no longer.

"Another week with these Hoosier rubes and I'll go nuts," he said to Mama. I could hear them talking in their room next to mine.

"Now, Al," Mama said. "You'll get used to it. I have a good job. The twins are getting along well in school. It's time we started thinking about settling down somewhere."

"I don't want to get used to it," Daddy said, "and I certainly don't intend to settle down in a hick town like this."

"I've met some nice people at the plant."

"Rubes, every one of them," Daddy argued. "I'm going to Chicago in the morning. I'll find something there, something fitting my talents."

I was glad to hear that. He was just upsetting Mama. She had hardly any time for us kids when he was around.

"I wish you'd stay. You can probably get a job at the plant," Mama said.

"For the birds!"

They argued nearly all night, but the next morning Daddy went to Chicago. Ella cried when he left, and Mama grew quiet and sulky. He left me happy. I loved Mama when she was dark and sullen. She seemed more mysterious that way, almost like a stranger, or a reluctant goddess—remote, apart from men, to be wooed and worshiped and sacrificed to in some heathen rite.

I heard her crying in her room the next night. I got out of bed, slid my feet into my new fur-lined house shoes—a Christmas gift from Mama—and went to her.

"What's the matter, Mama?" I whispered.

"Oh, Rusty, is that you?" she asked.

"Yes," I said, shivering.

"Well, get under the covers," she said and sniffed back her tears. "You'll freeze standing there."

She raised the covers and I slipped into bed beside her. She hugged me to keep me warm.

"What's the matter?" I repeated.

"Oh, nothing. Only I wish we could all stay together like other families."

"You mean Gina and Daddy and all of us?"

"Yes."

I was quiet. I did not care if Daddy never came back. Mama was warm, and she smelled good. Suddenly I hated him. He did not deserve her.

"But we can't," Mama said. "Not Gina. She must have her chance. Whatever happens, she must have her chance to be a great diva or ballerina. And you must have yours—and Ella hers."

"What do you want me—us to be?" I asked.

"I don't care. You'll decide in time. Just so you have your chance. Mama and Papa came to this country so their children and grandchildren could have their chance. I must see that they do—whatever happens, whatever it costs. That's all they lived for. That's all I have to live for now."

I had heard Avolo and Nonna say the same thing when I was small, but never with the vehemence, the near desperation, that filled Mama's voice that night. I was a little frightened, but I was comfortable. I felt like a child again. I could almost hear the clacking of the Pullman trucks as they rolled over the rail joints.

"I'll see that all of you get your chance," she continued softly, almost to herself. "I'll do everything—anything I can—and I'll kill anyone who stands in your way."

I knew she did not mean what she was saying, but I thrilled to hear her say it. I felt her body go tense with her passionate resolve. I shared the ecstasy of her determination as her arm tightened convulsively around me.

The best part was that she was telling *me*, not Daddy. I was sure that she had never talked to him that way. He would never have understood. So Mama was treating me as an equal, sharing confidences with me. She would not have said those things to a child. The thought that she no longer considered me a child disturbed me at the same time it delighted me—and frightened me further.

"Sing to me, Mama," I said, impulsively, before I thought.

"All right, Rusty—*bambino mio*," she said with a chuckle, and softened into a cloud of delicious mother-warmth. "There's no reason why I should burden you with my troubles."

52

She kissed my cheek and started crooning in my ear with just enough voice to give pitch to her lullaby. I did not hear the end of the song. I was dreaming long before she finished. I dreamed of Mama as she looked that day after the circus fire —in tights with her face smudged and her hair falling about her shoulders. I dreamed that she was a jungle queen, priestess of some primitive cult, dancing wildly around a boiling cauldron, conjuring, ordering someone's destiny. I dreamed that I was a white hunter who discovered her and tamed her, and then my dream broke off abruptly.

She was already up when I awoke the next morning.

Daddy was back in a week. He came in, disheveled and bleary-eyed, soon after Ella and I got home from school.

"Oh, Daddy, Daddy!" Ella screamed when she saw him. She ran to him and hugged him. Then she backed away and looked at him.

"You'd better shave and take a shower and change clothes," she said. "Mama will be home in a few minutes."

"That might be a good idea," he said, taking a quick look at himself in a mirror.

"I'll lay out your clothes," Ella said. "Hurry."

They went into Mama's room. I heard Ella opening drawers and closet doors. A few minutes later the shower started running. I went down into the basement to stoke the furnace. Then I brought up a scuttle of coal and built a fire in the kitchen stove. Mama arrived about the time I got it going.

"Daddy's home," Ella announced. She took Mama's coat.

"He is? When did he get here?"

"Just a minute ago," Daddy said. He came out of the bedroom and met Mama in the hall.

He started to kiss her.

"You smell like a distillery," she said and offered her cheek instead of her lips. "Did you get a job?"

53

"In Chicago? What a crummy town! Clip joints. Strippers. No job for a comic with talent."

Mama went into the bathroom and washed her hands.

"Met an old friend of yours," Daddy said when she came out again.

"Yes? Who was that?" Mama crossed the hall toward the kitchen. We all followed her.

"A guy named Ricardo. 'Justice' Ricardo they call him."

"Ricardo?" Mama repeated. She tied an apron around her waist and started to prepare supper.

"Said he knew the Bercellis in Messina."

"Oh, yes," Mama said. "The Ricardos had a café in Messina, with a garden. We played there a number of times. I remember now. That was a long time ago."

Daddy sat down at the kitchen table. I leaned against a door jamb, and Ella began peeling some potatoes.

"He remembers too."

"How did you meet him?"

"Well, I'm sitting in this club, talking to the manager. I'm telling him the things I can do, trying to get him to let me build a show around me.

"He's got a line of eight ponies and a couple of strippers. 'Let's give them some real old-time burlesque,' I say.

" 'I don't know,' he says. 'I'll have to talk to the boss. He goes for class.'

" 'I got class,' I say.

" 'Yeah, but burlesque—'

"About that time this Ricardo character comes in.

" 'Here's the boss now,' this guy says and introduces me.

"So I make my pitch to Ricardo. Naturally I tell him who I am, what I do, and mention the Bercellis."

"And he remembered us?" Mama said.

"He remembers you."

54

"He does? I couldn't have been over fourteen or fifteen the last time we played Ricardo's place."

"Well, he remembers you, says he's very fond of the Bercellis. Asks about your papa and mama and the little boys. Laughs when he realizes that Tony and Mario are grown up and married."

"But he didn't give you a job."

"No. Says he can't quite see burlesque in one of his clubs. Wants class. Well, I'm not begging anybody for a job. I don't want a friend of the family to think I really need one; so we talk about the Bercellis for a while and part company."

Mama took some steaks out of her special marinade and put them on a griddle on top of the stove.

"What else?" she asked.

"That's all. Seems Ricardo is the big shot in the syndicate. Controls everything. Makes all the decisions. He's the *don,* if you know what that means."

Mama stopped and looked at Daddy for a moment, suspiciously, and then went on with her work.

"I know what that means," she said.

"Well, I don't. Damned greasy wop. Everywhere I go I run into this, 'Gotta talk to the boss. Gotta see what Justice thinks.' So I tell them all to forget it and I come home—back here anyway." Daddy tore the heel off a loaf of French bread, which Ella had put on the table, and took a bite of it.

"Why don't you try to get on at the plant?" Mama asked.

"Not me," Daddy mumbled, his mouth full of bread. "If I have to work in a defense plant I'll try Allison down in Indianapolis. No use living in the sticks. I've got some leads down there anyway. I'll follow them up tomorrow."

That sounded good to me, but Ella looked sad and Mama began to sulk again. Daddy did most of the talking during dinner. He had run into some friends of his in Chicago, of course. It was the same old story. None of the burlesque comedians were doing any good unless their wives were strippers.

"Do you want me to start stripping?" Mama asked.

"You'd have to show your navel," Daddy said, teasing, but not being funny.

"I'd even do that," Mama said, "if we could get good enough bookings."

"Chicago's a crummy town," Daddy said. "Everybody's working for peanuts except the featured exotics, and I think Justice Ricardo takes a big cut out of theirs. Let me try Indianapolis."

Daddy tried Indianapolis, and to the surprise of everyone—except Ella, perhaps—he came back with a job.

"Guess who's recreation director at Allison?" he asked enthusiastically. He found us all in the kitchen again.

"Who?" Mama asked.

"Bert Marks, fellow I know from the old days in Boston. Used to be producer at the Howard."

"So?" Mama said. She kept right on preparing dinner.

"So he hires me as his assistant, and when I tell him about your experience in the bearing factory he gets you a job on the line. So we're moving to Indianapolis."

Daddy beamed at all of us.

"We'll be out of this dump as soon as we can pack," he said.

"Not so fast," Mama said. She was still sullen, in one of her beautiful dark moods. "I'm not leaving my job on short notice, and the twins aren't changing schools in the middle of the term."

"But the term's over in two weeks," Ella said. She always sided with Daddy.

Mama looked at me.

"Is that right, Rusty?" she asked.

"I—I guess so," I said. I hated to see Daddy win, but the semester *was* coming to an end, as Ella said.

56

I was sorry for Mama. I went over and stood beside her while she worked, just to show her how I felt.

Again Daddy monopolized the dinner conversation. He had big plans for us. Mama lost the argument before the meal was over.

CHORUS

"THE PREJUDICED black bastard. That white-baiting spade," Paul Patterson said in disgust, after Teresina and Barbarossa had cut out for her pad.

Paul is a Negro himself, though we hadn't thought about it until he spoke. Like we're not race conscious. We're *race-conscious* conscious. We're beyond racial tolerance; we have love. Everyone is everyone's brother. That's how it is with us. And Barbarossa was our favorite brother then.

"Love him, Paul. Love Willie Jackson," Paul's chick piped up. "He digs not what he makes."

"Square," Paul said generously. "Square." He shook his head in sorrow for Willie Jackson. Love!

"Do you cats know what Barbarossa's name adds up to?" Clara sounded us. Her eyes were bright, her cheeks glowing.

There was no answer.

"Nobody was listening—nobody but me was digging him when he made his revelation," she went on. "Rusty Meaghan?" Her words were ecstasy.

The joint went still. The quiet was holy. Reverence filled the temple to the point of pain.

"Rusty Meaghan," some chick whispered hysterically.

"That's what he said," Clara repeated. "Rusty Meaghan."

"Can't be," Kurt argued in awed tones.

Rusty Meaghan was just a name to us, a name and a sound. But what a name and what a sound! None of us had ever moved

59

in his circle. None of us, except Clara perhaps, had ever had the chance.

"I never thought he'd be like this," Kurt said.

"I did," Clara insisted. "Just like this. O-o-oh! And he's here. He's come to us."

"I'm not so sure," Kurt said.

"Me either," Dick Ferguson said. "Like he's either this or that."

"A bundle of paradoxes," Foulard said. "From in front we said he's flipped or he's the new shaman. It's still the same. Like he thinks he's Rusty Meaghan when he's potted up. He's having hallucinations."

That broke up the session. The thing was too big for us. It shook us up, every one of us.

We left the warehouse quietly, by two's and three's and four's.

"We'll have to communicate with some cats in the Village and Chicago and North Beach," Foulard said as we neared his pad. "I mean like some cat somewhere can pick us up on Rusty Meaghan."

"We can ask Barbarossa," Kay suggested.

"No!" Clara said. "We're sounding him enough. He's searching. We can't bug him with questions before their time. Anyway, I know he's Rusty. He has to be. It's just the gay boy coming out in Kurt. Fags are the most jealous-hearted creatures in the world. He doesn't want Barbarossa to be Rusty Meaghan. He couldn't stand it. It's wishful thinking."

"We'll find out," Foulard said. "We'll have a jam session somewhere."

"Tomorrow night," Clara urged. "None of the jazzmen gig on Monday. We'll have a jam session in my pad. Keep it small, intimate."

Clara was requesting the impossible. We arranged the jam session, all right, but there was no keeping it small. Like we're

60

not stupid, none of us. When the jazzmen left their pads carrying their axes, the cats started following them as if they were pied pipers blowing down the side streets of Hamelin.

The big Haitian brought his bass, Pants Jackson his tenor, Clyde Murdock his horn, Foxy MacIntosh his armload of drums. Clara had a piano. We tried to get Harry Vought for piano, but he was too high on horse to be of any use; so we sent word to Manny Fitch. Like, man, it was a combo you dream about.

They were really with it that night, too. The joint was jumping, swinging way out, when Teresina brought our shaman to us. Barbarossa was quiet and polite, asking everybody's pardon as he stepped over feet and legs stretched out on the floor.

"Rusty Meaghan," Clara said as casually as she could when she introduced Barbarossa to the jazzmen.

"Hi, Rusty," Manny Fitch said. "Wanta sit in awhile?"

"Hi," Barbarossa said, but shook his head and smiled that beatific smile of his as he wedged into a corner beside Teresina.

She scowled at us and hung onto Barbarossa as we all studied him. He beamed joyously at the cats blowing their hearts out for him. We could tell that he was with them all the way, or he was wearing the most stupid look that ever crossed the face of a grown man. We love everybody, but it bugged us a little that he showed no inclination whatever to fall in with the ritual.

For all our subtle invitations he might as well have been a four-cornered zombie up until teatime. Then he turned on, however, and we forgot our pique as soon as his big voice began to fill the room with an account of—

INDIANAPOLIS, 1945

CAN I CHOOSE what I will from those five hundred days in Indianapolis, or is there a mechanism within me which sorts and shuffles, picks and rejects, discards many and brings only these to the surface of my consciousness? Could I begin with those thrilling hours in our warm green back yard, or must I first feel the chill of that cold morning when Mama took Ella and me to enroll in our new school—and it *was* a new school, built especially to accommodate the hundreds of junior-high students living in the defense housing project.

The principal might have been the same one we had in Peru. Indeed, the two turned out to have been classmates in a summer session somewhere.

"Good man," he said of his colleague. "Progressive. We subscribe to the same educational philosophy. Your children will rapidly become adjusted to our fine school here, Mrs. Meaghan, I assure you. We'll round out their whole personality."

He beamed on us, when he could take his eyes off Mama.

Mama thanked him and took us across the street to a home where Professor Alonzo Winship taught private piano lessons during his pupils' free periods.

"He looks exactly like a piano teacher," Ella whispered while the lady of the house was introducing him to Mama.

And he did, I suppose—long black hair, a thin sensitive face, "artistic" hands, and a well-cut Oxford gray suit just shabby enough to attract attention. I pinched Ella to keep her from laughing at him.

"I could be on the concert stage, of course," he told Mama, "but I just love children. I really feel that when I've taught a hundred children I've multiplied my talent a hundredfold. Don't you agree, Mrs. Meaghan?"

"Yes," Mama said.

"He's done wonders with my Judy," the lady of the house said enthusiastically. "She just adores Mr. Winship, and we are delighted to have him teaching in our home."

Either Mr. Winship or Judy's mother was mimicking the other. They spoke the same language, with exactly the same inflections. By comparison, the vestiges of Sicilian accent in Mama's speech sounded more charming than ever.

"Now, Mrs. Watkins," he said self-consciously. "Really I'm quite selfish. I love Judy, and I continue to teach because I'm such a homebody at heart. I have my little apartment, just as I want it—with my books and pictures and things. I think I'd die if I had to leave them.

"But why am I telling you all this, Mrs. Meaghan? You probably love the road. I believe you said yours is a theatrical family?"

"Circus," Mama said. "But my oldest daughter, Gina, is studying in New York for a theatrical career."

"How delightful! I would love to meet her sometime. But our present business is with—"

He looked at Ella and me and waited for Mama to supply our names.

"Ella and Al," she said. "Or Rusty, as we call him."

"And I can see why." Mr. Winship giggled. "That red, red hair!"

"Shall I play for you?" he asked. "I really should show my wares, you know."

"Please do," Mama said.

Mrs. Watkins seated us variously on her matched living-room suite and stood, soprano-like, in the curve of the apartment grand to observe the effect of Mr. Winship's performance. After carefully adjusting himself on the piano bench, Mr. Winship looked up at the crown mold on the opposite wall, kneaded his hands for a moment, and then looked down at the keyboard, with a sort of nod, and began to play a rather tinkly bit of early Mozart.

When he finished we clapped softly. He played very well indeed, though he acknowledged our applause as if he doubted that any of us could have appreciated the quality of his performance.

"Lovely, Mr. Winship, just lovely," Mrs. Watkins said.

"Thank you." He turned and faced us. "Now you must play for me. Ladies first." He rose and bowed to Ella.

She slouched over to the piano unenthusiastically and played the fairly simple Chopin Prelude, No. 7 in A Major.

"Delightful," Mr. Winship said above the thin applause of the rest of us.

"Thank you, sir," Ella said, and curtsied as the Bercelli women had been taught to do; and not even Mama realized that she was kidding the professor.

"Your turn, Rusty."

I was serious about the piano even then; so I placed myself almost as carefully as Mr. Winship had done and played a Prelude and Fugue in C Major by Bach. I had not taken a lesson for six months, but I had been practicing all the time we were in Peru, and I had worked the piece out to my own satisfaction at least. When I finished I received the usual applause, but Mr. Winship said nothing until I turned around on the bench and faced him.

He had dropped his salesmanship smile.

"You play very well, Rusty," he said soberly. "Your inner

voices were coming through nicely, and your pedal work was almost professional. Do you like Bach?"

"Yes, sir," I said, "I guess so."

"Then we'll go right on with *The Well-tempered Clavichord*. Nothing is better than that to familiarize you with the keyboard.

"And Ella, we'll polish up your Chopin a bit. Shall we?" He was smiling again.

"Chopin, Carmichael—they're all the same to me."

I did not know why she said it; but I remembered every time she was flippant or malicious, as I remember now.

"Who is Carmichael?" Mama asked after she had made arrangements for our lessons and joined us in the street.

"Hoagy," Ella said. "He wrote 'Stardust.' "

"Well, you had no call to be rude to Mr. Winship."

"He's a drip."

"He can teach us a lot about piano," I said, defending Mama more than my new teacher.

"You, maybe. I'd rather study voice. Gina was under a good voice teacher when she was thirteen. I'll be thirteen soon—in the summer, anyway."

So Ella wheedled Daddy into letting her drop piano and go twice a week to a woman who taught "personality singing" at a dancing school downtown. While she was there, Daddy saw no reason why she should not take dancing lessons as well; and since Ella was going to be a lawyer anyway, Mama could not put up a very strong argument for her sticking to a more conservative concept of the fine arts. I did not care one way or the other. Ella's business was Ella's business; at least it was in those days.

We were like any one of a thousand other families in the defense housing project. Mama and Daddy worked at the plant. We went to a progressive junior high school. We were Good Americans, doing our bit to win the war.

66

But war is a fickle mistress. I was a boy going on thirteen back in 1945. Mama was an intelligent but socially naïve immigrant woman, and Daddy was a clown. We could not have been expected to know that we were becoming adjusted to a wartime economy, a transitory thing. We thought that we had put down our roots and could expect to thrive normally in the fertile Hoosier soil.

Daddy was well liked at the plant. He had been trouping so long and was so versatile that he kept the swing-shift workers well entertained during their free hours between midnight and dawn. He slept all day but had dinner with us and stayed with us until bedtime. He was gay and cheerful at home. With Mama busy, having to do her housework at night, and with Gina out of the way, Ella had Daddy largely to herself. I would practice on our rented piano while Daddy sat on the sofa with Ella cuddled up to him. He would tell her how he had wowed them at the plant the night before and she would giggle and they would whisper like a pair of conspirators. Then Mama would come in and the three of them would sit through my performance of the latest piece I had mastered. Sometimes Ella would sing, not so well as Gina, but passably, whatever was popular at the moment.

Daddy especially liked "Don't Sit Under the Apple Tree" and "Juke Box Saturday Night," which Ella and I had taken off records. He would supply instrumental effects for the latter. It was usually our grand finale, when Mama called time at eight o'clock. Then Ella and I would do our homework in our rooms, and leave Mama and Daddy to themselves until time for him to go to the recreation hall at the plant.

Mama liked our way of life. She would be humming or singing when she came in to check our lessons. I missed her dark moods. I know that her happiness should have pleased me, but I knew that I was not the sole cause of her happiness. She never confided in me when she was happy, although she always

67

hugged my shoulders and kissed my hair when she stood behind me and looked over my schoolwork. She was a necessary aura to my existence, whatever her mood.

She was proud of her brothers when they finished their training and shipped out to join the occupation forces in Sicily. I learned later that both of them left their wives pregnant, and so had further dimmed the possibility of the Bounding Bercellis' ever rejoining the circus. I learned this from Ella, however; Ella seemed always to have access to sources of information closed to me.

Only occasionally did Mama mention the one flaw in our life.

"If Gina were only here," she would say when we were having a particularly good time together. "But we'll all have to go our way sometime," she would add and look at the rest of us wistfully.

When April came—the time the circus went on the road—it was probably that same wistfulness or a feeling of nostalgia that prompted Mama to bring out our rehearsal clothes and spread tumbling mats on the fresh young grass in our back yard.

"It's good exercise," she explained to Ella and me, unnecessarily, for I was as eager as she to practice the routines we had been learning since babyhood.

But I was a big boy now, strong enough to work as an understander, husky enough to support Mama and Ella, as Avolo and then Uncle Tony or Uncle Mario had done. I thrilled to be so near Mama again, to catch her, to hold her, to balance her expert body, to savor her grace as she floated to me from the spring of a teeter board, to feel her supple muscles glide over my own as I eased her to the mat from a handstand on my shoulders or a scissors-lock around my waist. There never was so much exquisitely vibrant life embodied in another human form.

68

Although Ella was beginning to view our rehearsals some-what cynically, as juvenile gymnastics far beneath the dignity of a budding personality singer, she kept her place in the act and acquitted herself creditably. She tolerated us principally because Daddy was pleased.

"Just what I need for my recreation program," he said when he came outside early one afternoon to see how we were doing.

Mama demurred but was soon won over, and we performed two or three times at the plant after school let out for the summer. Actually she enjoyed the performances, and she heartily approved of the musical numbers which Ella and I presented by ourselves. The two of us appeared on Bert Marks's programs.

Mama was delighted when Gina wrote that she would spend the month of August with us. So was Daddy. He and Bert Marks were rehearsing a spectacular water pageant for plant employees, and he hurriedly wrote Gina to prepare a specialty act for the occasion.

"We'll show these rubes what real talent is," he said enthusiastically. "With Gina starring, it will be our show, and one these Hoosiers will long remember, if I do say so myself."

Gina arrived in time for the last two rehearsals. She had filled out since we had last seen her. I could tell that when we met her at the railroad station. Colonel Strongforth would probably have considered her as beautiful as Mama if he had seen her then.

Anyway, she got into Indianapolis late Sunday afternoon. We all went to the Canary Cottage for dinner and then home. Gina had brought presents for all of us: a scarf for Mama, a tie for Daddy, a purse for Ella, and an Earl Hines record for me.

She was as full of experiences as Daddy was of plans, and they vied for monopoly of the conversation. Ella and I found ourselves sitting side by side on the piano bench facing Daddy and Gina on the sofa. Mama sat in her usual chair and beamed. I saw her dab at a tear now and then with her new scarf, which

69

she had been clutching jealously ever since Gina had given it to her. For the first time in a long time Ella was holding my hand in a tight moist grip.

"Let's hear what you kids are doing in the pageant," Gina said to Ella and me. "What are you playing, Rusty?"

"Bach," I said, "and a couple of pieces I've taken off Art Tatum records."

"Well, let's hear them."

"All right," I said.

Ella got up and I pushed the bench back a little and flexed my fingers. Then I played my three selections.

Everyone was quiet until I finished.

"That's good, Rusty. I mean really good," Gina said seriously. "Your Bach sounds solid to me and you seem to be developing into something of a popular stylist on your own."

"Thank you," I said, facing the sofa again.

"Now, Ella."

"I'm in the act with Mama," Ella said. "I don't think I ought to sing now that you're here, Gina."

"Sure you must. Go ahead."

Gina playfully pulled Ella out into the middle of the floor.

I turned around on the bench and played an introduction to "Don't Sit Under the Apple Tree." Ella somewhat reluctantly sang two choruses with personality gestures.

"Why, that's cute," Gina said. "I couldn't have sung it half so well."

"Now sing 'Juke Box Saturday Night,' " Daddy said. That gave him a chance to get into the act.

Ella and I started out, and Daddy joined her in the middle of the floor and started clowning and mimicking Harry James's trumpet. I watched him over my shoulder. I could see Gina out of the corner of my eye. She was having a ball. I looked the other way at Mama. She too was enjoying the performance.

70

Daddy began a soft-shoe routine. I deliberately tripped him up by faltering in my rhythm. He scowled at me.

"I'm sorry," I said. "I guess I'd better watch what I'm doing."

I looked back at the keyboard and did not glance up again until the piece was over.

Gina jumped up and hugged Daddy and Ella, bringing all three of them together. Well, Mama had her family intact. I hoped she was satisfied.

The next day we all rehearsed the pageant. On Tuesday night we had the dress rehearsal with orchestra, lights, and everything. There was a water ballet made up of assembly-line girls, who worked in the center of the pool. The deep end was given over to high diving and fancy diving. At the shallow end a hurricane deck provided a bandstand and a stage for performers like Mama and Gina and Ella and me.

Daddy paddled around the pool on a trick bicycle which some mechanics in the plant had mounted on pontoons. He was dressed like a clown and acted as master of ceremonies. As a running gag, the bicycle was rigged to lose parts and seem on the point of collapse just as Daddy finished an announcement and started to the area where the next act was to be presented.

The effect of the gag was to steal a little attention from every other performer on the bill. I recognized that; and so did Bert Marks, a bald-headed, keen-eyed, slack-jawed promoter who never missed a trick. I saw him smile wryly to himself at some of Daddy's antics. And I watched his jaw tighten and his eyes narrow shrewdly as they studied Gina. She sang first, beautifully, but I suppose not perfectly. Later she came out in her ballet costume for a classical number and then in a sleek slitted skirt for a jazz routine. Her body was maturing more exquisitely than her voice.

I was momentarily jealous for Mama and, although I was beginning to despise the man, I wished I could have been near Bert Marks when Mama came on in tights earlier, to see his

71

reaction. He knew his business. I sensed instinctively that he was a connoisseur of woman's attractiveness to man, and I felt a compulsion to find out how he would evaluate Mama; at the same time I was sickened by the thought of his being privileged to make so expert an appraisal of her.

We were scheduled to play three days, August fifth, sixth, and seventh, at different hours to accommodate the various shifts at the plant. The show went well. It might have been one long remembered, as Daddy had predicted, but for the fact that August sixth brought the greatest fireworks display ever seen on earth—the A-bomb over Hiroshima.

At first we could not believe the news. The bomb was the talk of the plant, the sole topic of radio commentators, the only thing we could think about over the week end. Daddy especially was skeptical—it was all propaganda, he said, completely unbelievable; and he reminded us that he was close enough to some of the top engineers at the plant to be in a position to know. They all said that the A-bomb was an impossibility. Three days later, when the second bomb was dropped on Nagasaki, however, we had to face it. The thing was real. The war was as good as over.

The initial reaction was one of joy, the expected one. Then gloom began to settle over our war-adjusted housing development. Women began hanging over back fences and sharing their fears about what they would do now. Few wanted to go back where they had come from. Men grew glum and apprehensive. Rumors of an immediate shutdown at the plant spread; war hysteria gave way to peace hysteria.

Daddy celebrated the war's end with a fifth of rye and then tried to drown his despondency in two more fifths. He left one night for the recreation hall and failed to return the next morning. Mama waited breakfast on him until ten o'clock. Then she fed me and the girls, but none of us ate much.

"I wonder what's keeping him," Mama said as she rose reluctantly from the table.

"Business," Gina said. "Maybe he and Mr. Marks are planning something." She rose also and began clearing off the table.

"I wonder if he's been laid off." Mama was on vacation and we had learned that her section of the assembly line would probably shut down before she was to return to work. She frowned as she went into the kitchen. Gina followed her. Ella and I just looked at each other.

"I guess I'll practice awhile," I said. It seemed that there was nothing else to do.

"I'll go outside and watch for Daddy," she said.

So we got up awkwardly and left the dining room. We were thirteen then. Something had happened to Ella. She seemed strangely shy, even with me; and since Gina's arrival she had taken to sitting on the front porch alone or reading in her room. I thought it might be the bomb, or worry about what would happen to us if the plant closed, or resentment toward Gina. Women baffled me. But I forgot Ella as soon as I sat down at the piano.

I do not know how long I practiced, an hour or so, I guess. Anyway, Daddy came home while I was at the piano. He was in high spirits, and he brought Bert Marks with him.

"How about a drink while we talk, Bert?" he boomed as they entered the house.

"I'll drink a beer if you have one," Bert Marks said.

"Sure thing. Nestra, a beer for Bert," Daddy called. He went on into the kitchen and poured some rye for himself while Mama opened a can of beer for our guest. Then we all assembled in the living room, as if Daddy had called a meeting.

"Well, Nestra, we've got it licked," Daddy said with a show of forced enthusiasm.

73

"What?" Mama asked.

"Our financial problem."

"I didn't know we had one."

"Well, we have, or did have. We may as well face it. The plant is going to close down. Anyway, we been working for peanuts. Me and Bert have a much better idea."

"What is it?"

"Bert's going back into burlesque—producing. I'm going along as top banana, and we figure we've got a gold mine in our little girl here." Daddy threw an arm around Gina's shoulders.

Mama was quiet for a moment.

"You don't mean Gina?" She asked slowly, as though in disbelief.

"I sure do mean Gina."

"Not Gina! Not in burlesque!" Tensing, Mama stood up and all but screamed her words.

"And why not?" Daddy asked. "She's got everything—talent, looks, and me to look after her and coach her."

"That's just it," Mama said. "Gina has everything, everything to look forward to. In a few years—"

"In a few years!" Daddy cut in. "We need money right now, to keep the family going, to keep the twins in school; and me and Gina can make a lot of money in a hurry. With millions of servicemen returning to the seaports and separation centers, all of them hungry for the sight of a girl like Gina, we can make a fortune right quick. Ain't that right, Bert?"

We all looked at Bert Marks. He finished swallowing a mouthful of beer, wiped his lips on the back of his left hand, and glanced around at us.

"They'll love her in burlesque," he said—tauntingly, it seemed to me.

"But she can't do it," Mama said. "She's going into opera or ballet." She was trembling.

74

"A lot of big stars came up through burlesque," Daddy said. "Milton Berle, W. C. Fields, Red Skelton—"

"Lily Pons didn't come up through burlesque," Mama countered. "Pavlova didn't come up through burlesque." She was blazing, magnificent. I thrilled all over at her anger—but she was calm.

"Gypsy Rose Lee, Margie Hart, Evelyn West, Lili St. Cyr—they make more money than them ladies," Bert Marks said evenly.

Mama glared at him.

"Money is not the point," she said. "Gina shows real talent. She might make the Met. I want her to have that chance. If burlesque was the best Gina was capable of, I wouldn't stand in her way for a minute. I just want my children to have a chance to do their best, whatever it is. Do you understand me, Mr. Marks?"

"Sure, sure. I know what you mean." Bert Marks sat where he was, relaxed, unmoved. "I agree that the little girl has talent, and right now we can peddle that talent on the Big Wheel for ten times what she can get on Broadway."

"Al, I'll go into burlesque with you," Mama said, pleadingly. "I'll strip if we can make so much that way. Then we can keep the twins in school and let Gina continue her studies."

She turned to Bert Marks.

"It's not that I have anything against burlesque, Mr. Marks," she said to him. "I—I am an acrobat. I've had my day, I suppose. It doesn't matter what I do any more if I can give my kids their chance. How would that be?"

"Sit down, sit down, Nestra," he said, waving his hand as though he owned the house. "It'll take a little explaining."

Mama sat down beside me, tense, erect, on the edge of the piano bench.

"It's like this," Bert Marks went on. "Of course men come to the burlesque houses to see naked women. Now we got all kinds of strippers. Fat ones, thin ones, tramps, good-looking dames with no talent, *et cetera.*" He waved his hand vaguely.

"But a star, a little girl that makes big money, has got to have some special appeal. Now, you take the average man in bald-head row. He likes looking at all these strippers, but he knows they're a dime a dozen—he can have all of 'em he wants. He's used to 'em. They're his kind.

"Then here comes a girl that can sing like Gina, beautiful voice, poise, charm, a build like Gina's, though he ain't seen it yet. She dances, really dances—like Gina. It don't seem possible that he's gona get to see her strip down, see? She's something special, see? Well, sure enough, she ends up in a G-string and a couple of spangles. He still can't believe it, see? It's an illusion. And he keeps coming back night after night and paying good money. That's what makes burlesque profitable."

"You're saying that Gina is too good for them and still you're willing to sell her to them in your stinking burlesque houses," Mama said angrily.

"I'm saying Gina is good enough for me to pay her and Al five or six hundred bucks a week to start." Bert Marks narrowed his eyes and tightened his jaw as he mentioned the salary.

"And old women like me are a dime a dozen. Is that it?"

"Now, now, I didn't say that, Nestra. You're a good-looking woman, and you're built. You got as much that way as Gina has. And you got talent, acrobatic talent. You'd do all right in burlesque. We use acrobatic dancers. But you'd come on in tights. They'd see all you got at once. See what I mean?"

Mama saw what he meant. So did I. I do not know when I acquired the knowledge. Men want the unattainable, the woman beyond price. That is why a diva or a ballerina or a first lady of the legitimate stage brings such a premium. In the first place it is unbelievable that a woman can attain such grace, such appeal beyond that of the everyday female. Such are the nymphs, our precious dream women, outside the reach of all save the wealthiest of men. That is why a theater patron will pay box-office prices to watch these creatures for two or three hours in a darkened theater, and then envy the lover she goes home to for the rest of the night. To have one of these, or an approximation of one of these, strip down to nothing and bounce and grind her way across the stage and down the runway of a burlesque house—yes, Bert Marks knew his business.

But he did not know Mama—not as I knew her. Acrobat or no acrobat, she was the most beautiful woman that ever lived, the most desirable, the most unattainable, the most remote from all men—a pagan priestess, a creature of dreams, too good for mortal man. A dime a dozen!

"What could Al and I make in burlesque?" Mama asked.

Bert Marks shrugged his sagging shoulders.

"Couple of hundred maybe. A little above expenses," he said.

"We couldn't keep the kids in school or pay for Gina's lessons," Daddy said. "With good luck and good billing, me and Gina could make maybe a thousand a week. Gina can save hers and go on with her studies after a little while. It'll put us on our feet."

"Save hers!" Mama seemed to be screaming but her voice was low. "Al, I know you. It's not the twins or Gina you're thinking about. You're still listening to those yuks at you and your silly bicycle, or whatever you call it. You want a job in burlesque, which wouldn't pay you any more than a job in a factory, and you want Gina to pay your way—all our ways!"

That was where Mama made her mistake. She should have known better. Daddy bristled, and I thought for a moment that he was going to explode. Then he smiled, a hard, tense smile.

"Gina should have a voice in this," he said. "How do you feel about it, baby?" He half turned and faced Gina.

I saw it then. The time had come. The struggle for Gina had reached its climax.

77

"I don't know, Daddy." Gina's face was troubled, unhappy. "How much money do we have?"

"None," Daddy said. "We've just been making expenses for the last year."

"And I suppose I've used up our savings," Gina said. "I know how expensive it is to study with my teachers."

Daddy was silent. Gina looked at Mama.

"Don't even consider it," Mama said. "We'll do all right. We'll find some way to keep up your training."

"Then we do have a financial problem?" Gina said.

"We certainly do," Daddy agreed.

"In that case, if we can make as much money in burlesque as Mr. Marks says we can, I don't see why we don't accept his offer. I don't mind stripping if Mama doesn't. I mean, an artist can keep her integrity—we've been taught that always."

"Sure you can," Bert Marks said. "Your father will be with you."

"Yes, your father will be with you," Mama said bitterly and slumped beside me.

"Oh, Mama." Gina flared up in defense of Daddy. "It isn't as though I were sacrificing myself."

"That's exactly what you're doing," Mama said angrily. "Sacrificing yourself, your career, and not for the twins either. I can see them through school. You are sacrificing yourself for your father's vanity! The big clown. I forbid you to do it."

Mama stood up again, her face burning and her eyes blazing. She was like a wild thing. I rose and stood beside her, just touching her, to show how much I loved her.

"You forbid it!" Daddy jumped to his feet. Now it was his turn. "You forbid it? As long as I'm head of this family I'll do all the forbidding. I say if Gina wants to make a fortune in burlesque she will do so.

"You decide, baby," he said to Gina. "And don't let your

78

mother intimidate you. If you feel a greater family responsibility than she does, speak out. What do you say?"

"I'll do whatever you say, Daddy."

"I won't say. You decide."

"Well—if I have to give up my studies anyway—if I can help give the twins their chance—later I can—"

Gina looked at Mama, who met her gaze but said nothing. Mama could not wheedle. She never learned how.

"I guess we should take Mr. Marks's offer," Gina ended unhappily.

"That's my girl," Daddy said. He gave Mama a triumphant look and lifted Gina up in a tight hug.

Ella sat in one corner of the sofa, small and frail. She glanced around the room with hatred for everyone in it. I felt Mama go tense again.

"I believe this is all the business we have with Mr. Marks right now," she said softly, pointedly.

Bert Marks rose and stared at Mama before he smiled insolently.

"I guess that's right," he said.

"Sure, Bert," Daddy said with forced heartiness. "We'll draw up a contract tomorrow and be on our way." He let go of Gina and hurried his new producer out of the house.

"Don't be angry, Mama," Gina said. "We—Daddy is doing what he thinks is best."

She came to Mama and tried to put her arms around her. Mama shrugged her off and started toward the hall door. Daddy was just coming back into the house.

"You, too, can be on your way as soon as you like, Al," Mama said. "Once you're out of this house you are no longer head of it. You've made your last decision. You may ruin Gina's career, her life for all I know, but you'll not ruin Ella's or Rusty's chances if I can help it, and I think I can."

79

"Aw, Nestra," Daddy said. "Nestra, baby, you're just upset. We're doing the right thing. I'm sure of it."

"You're always sure—sure of everything. And just about everything has gone wrong."

"You'll see," Daddy said, coming on into the living room. "Gina and I will support you and the kids in a way to which you've never been accustomed. Fine house, school, college, everything. We're in the money."

Mama stopped in the doorway.

"You can send half of *your* salary to support the twins," she said. "I'll take care of myself."

Mama was probably the first of the Bercelli women to declare her independence. What she might have done a few years earlier or a few years later I have no way of knowing. Her life was, by accepted standards, glamorous or notorious—unusual, to say the least. But during that time in Indiana she was closer to the American Way than she was at any other time. Only then did she associate freely with ordinary women, share their views, speak their language, learn their ways. And she was quick to learn.

Her courage was inborn, natural, like her beauty. It was a combination of the two which saw us through the next year in Indianapolis. After Daddy and Gina left and Mama got her notice not to return to the plant, she started out immediately to find another job. There was, however, no more demand for an accomplished tumbler than there was for a factory hand; so she applied for all kinds of unskilled jobs, few of which would pay enough to support the three of us.

She could have had a number of them. It would have been hard for anyone to refuse her after interviewing her. The perfection of her facial features, supported by an equally striking figure, a healthy body trained to grace and discipline from childhood, gave her precedence over all other applicants except for work so menial or degrading that no one could visualize her performing it.

Anyway, it turned out that she did have a choice of positions even in those uncertain times. On the day we got Daddy's first letter explaining that getting started was quite expensive but that a money order would surely be included in the next missive, Mama took a job at Ayres Department Store. She worked regular hours behind the cosmetic counter, and modeled underwear at the semiweekly style shows.

She was ideally suited to both. Her thick, velvety skin, impervious to blemish, glowed with the wholesome vitality of her entire being. The sheen of her hair, black like her long upcurling eyelashes, reflected the same perfection of body-tone; and her natural coloring was the fashionable suntan promised by Caribbean cruises and a dozen brands of lotion.

That she could say honestly to her hopeful customers, "I use this cream myself," was all she needed in the way of sales talk. Likewise her mere modeling of lingerie convinced thousands of shapeless women that the intimate wear would flatter them as Mama's loveliness flattered the garments themselves.

It was more than good business that prompted her to let Ella and me meet her at the store once or twice a week and go to lunch with her, though I am sure the floor manager encouraged our visits for purely commercial reasons. It certainly did not hurt sales to let it be known that the enviable Nestra Bercelli (she, unintentionally perhaps, used her professional name when applying for jobs) was the mother of two teen-age children—three, in fact, the eldest nineteen. Would you believe it? Other women her age might hope to be just as attractive.

Actually Mama was trying to keep our spirits up until school opened. It was dull at home. I practiced several hours a day on the piano. Ella practiced, sporadically and halfheartedly, whatever she was supposed to be doing, but mostly she read or sat outside and brooded.

"Go away," she would say when I tried to interest her in a game of some kind.

"What's eating you?" I asked her once when I was bored beyond endurance.

"I've got the furies," she answered without looking up from her book. She was curled up in Daddy's place on the sofa.

"The what? Never heard of them."

"Everybody's heard of the Furies," she said condescendingly. "Alecto, Megaera, and Tisiphone. Now, go away before I sick them on you."

She never did look up. I could not see what she was reading. I left her alone; and it was ten years before she sicked the furies on me.

Gina's letters, sometimes containing money (which Mama promptly returned), were bright spots. Daddy's letters, seldom with money in them, left Mama gloomy for several days, though Ella read them and reread them, finding pleasure in their patently false optimism. Once Daddy sent large gloss prints of his and Gina's lobby-board pictures. Mama frowned darkly at the photographs of Gina but dutifully pasted them in her bulky scrapbook as part of the Pictorial History of the Bercellis in the New World.

It is difficult for me to single out any specific episode during that year. Even the many pleasant winter evenings we spent at home have merged into one long, perfumed twilight. I was happy. Ella could have been. It did become increasingly clear, however, that we had lost Daddy and Gina. I should have realized that once the circle was broken we would dwindle one by one until each of us was left alone.

It was clear from the way Mama was acting that she was worried about something. I should have known that it was money. Daddy was either making much less than he had expected or he was far more extravagant than he admitted in his letters. Mama frowned as she worked over her accounts. She frequently counted the money in her purse before she took us swimming or to a movie. In July she sold our automobile. Her face lost some of its radiance and set into a disturbing grimness when we received a letter from Daddy saying that he and Gina would soon stop off to see us on their way to St. Louis.

I doubt that Ella noticed the change in Mama. She was so excited by the prospect of seeing Daddy and Gina again that she could think of nothing else. For a week she primped and tried on every combination of clothes her wardrobe afforded. She interrupted my practice and pestered me into spending most of my time working out accompaniments for her songs and dances. One would have thought that she was going to join the act.

Mama's mood somewhat damped my enthusiasm, but I am sure that we were all noticeably excited for one reason or another when we met Daddy and Gina at the railroad station. Ella, of course, crowded the barrier when the train was called. Mama and I waited a little way behind the crush of passengers. And Ella saw them first. She ran to Daddy, who swung her clear of the floor and laughed with her as she hung onto his neck.

Gina came directly to Mama. They embraced, Mama a little coolly, I think; and Gina turned to me.

"What on earth have you done to your hair?" Mama asked.

"Dyed it," Gina said, apologetically, after she kissed me. It was as red as mine and it hung in heavy curls around her shoulders. Gina had changed perfumes, too.

Daddy came up then and kissed the cheek Mama deftly placed in his way when she refused to give him her lips.

"Redheads are all the rage in the East now," he said, in defense of Gina. "The burlesque houses are so full of wops and Puerto Ricans that it takes a blonde or a redhead to attract any attention. So we chose red and changed Gina's professional name to Flame O'Dare. How do you like it?"

"I don't like it," Mama said. "But we wops have no taste."

"Now, Mama," Gina said. She did not look any of us in the eye.

"I'll get our bags," Daddy said, "and meet you at the taxi stand."

"I'll go with you," Ella said.

We went to the taxi stand. As I remember, we talked very little on the way.

When Daddy joined us, Mama said, "I've reserved rooms for you and Gina at the Lincoln. We'll take your bags there and let the children go on home."

So we kids got into one taxi and Mama and Daddy into another. Ella sulked all the way home, leaving Gina to carry the burden of the conversation.

As always, Gina was kind to us. She asked about our schoolwork, about our music, about Mama; and when we reached our house she gave each of us a hundred dollars and told us not to mention it to Mama. But in spite of our gratitude, we could not get close together. Gina, for all of her goodness, was a stranger now.

I played for Gina, who complimented me and very ably compared my improvisations with the popular records I was copying. She knew what I was doing or trying to do. That was encouraging.

Ella saved her talent until Daddy arrived. Then she really put on a show—every song and dance she had learned the past year plus a new routine, which explained an arrangement she had coached me on but had never used before.

"What are you doing, Ella?" Mama asked in horror.

I looked over my shoulder in time to catch Ella giving her interpretation of bump-and-grind, a childish travesty on all the

84

burlesque queens who ever peeled in public. Daddy laughed. So did I.

"Stop it!" Mama commanded.

Ella stopped and began to cry.

"What's wrong?" she asked. "Gina, will you teach me how to be a burlesque dancer?"

"No," Gina said, "I will not, and I'll spank that fancy little bottom of yours if I ever hear of you trying to learn."

"But I want to learn. I want to be with you and Daddy."

"I thought you were going to be a lawyer."

"No. I want to help you and Daddy take care of Mama and Rusty."

"Stick to the law," Gina advised soberly. "Daddy and I may need a lawyer in the family, someone to keep us out of jail some day."

Obviously the performance was over. As we ate dinner and then settled down for our visit, I had a chance to observe Daddy and Gina at rest.

Daddy was fatter than I remembered him. His face was puffy, his eyes shifty with soft pouches under them. Gina looked tired, and when she let her smile drop, her face looked older than Mama's.

We were awkward together. We talked around things. Mama and Daddy had already had their conversation, downtown at the hotel alone. There was nothing more to say.

Finally, about ten o'clock, Daddy looked at his watch. He stood up.

"Well, Gina and I had better go," he said. "We have to catch an early train."

"No, Daddy, don't go yet," Ella said. She still clung to him, as she had all the time they were sitting side by side on the sofa.

" 'Fraid we must, baby," Daddy said.

No one else raised any objections; so Daddy called a taxi and we sauntered outside to wait for it. When it arrived Gina hugged Ella and me.

"Be good to Mama," she whispered. "We'll never come home again, not to live, I mean."

She was crying when Daddy helped her into the taxi.

Ours was a droopy household for several days. Ella had a bad case of the furies. Mama's face was grimmer than ever. I mirrored all their moods.

Then Mama came home one day with a determined lift to her shoulders. She had made some sort of decision.

"I've been offered a good job in Chicago," she explained, "as a demonstrator for one of the cosmetic firms. Will you kids be all right for a few days while I go up to see about it?"

"Can't we go, too?" Ella asked.

"No, we—we can't afford it."

"I can, I—"

I pinched Ella, who I was sure was on the verge of telling Mama about the money Gina had given us.

"Sure, we'll be all right," I said quickly.

"I'll get somebody, one of the neighbors, to stay with you at night," Mama said.

It could not be said that we got along all right while Mama was away, but we got along. At least nothing bad happened to us.

She got the job, a very good one, it seemed, because we had no more money troubles.

"He—they gave me a thousand dollars' advance," she said.

"Goody," Ella said. "When do we leave?"

"We'll stay here until September and then—well, I've made arrangements for us all. As a demonstrator I'll have to travel a lot, so—well, you won't be able to live with me for a while."

"Where'll we go?" I asked. I was appalled by the idea.

"Rusty, I'm entering you in Highcastle Military Academy. You know it, don't you?"

86

"Yes," I said. "Mr. Winship teaches down there one day a week. He's mentioned it."

"That's one reason why I'm sending you there. It isn't far from here."

"What about me?" Ella asked.

"You're going into a convent."

"Oh, Mama, not a convent! Where?"

"In St. Louis."

"St. Louis?" Ella caught herself before she burst with enthusiasm. "Oh, well. O.K., I guess," she said casually, too casually for her.

I could see her mind working. I almost forgot my own despair as I imagined her trying to wheedle some of the sisters into taking her to a burlesque show to see Al Meaghan and Flame O'Dare.

CHORUS

It was Teresina who bugged us for a while after the jam session. Like Barbarossa would do anything she asked of him. There was never a more co-operative cat in the colony than he was. He was eager to please everybody. But he had to be sounded, sounded directly, dig? He was beyond guile or subtlety himself. He just couldn't dig anything except direct action. He expected of us exactly what he was willing to give of himself. But Teresina forced us to be devious in our approach.

"You try to hustle Barbarossa, any one of you, and you'll answer to me for it," she warned us. "Like I'm hip to all your shucks, every one of them.

"He's searching. He's laying all he's got in his truth-talk. Let him alone. Let him search in his own way. He's used to searching—you can tell that. Maybe he's searching all the time, when he's out there walking all by himself or loafing on his surf-board—all the time."

"What about his Sacred Writings?" we asked.

"They're his. But don't try to shuck me, either. You really want to find out if he's Rusty Meaghan. Now, I don't care whether he's Rusty Meaghan or not. I love that boy. And that's what he is right now—a little boy just entering a military academy. That's where he is in his search; so that's where he is with me, and that's O.K. by me.

"If he says he's little Rusty Meaghan, age fourteen, then he's little Rusty Meaghan, age fourteen, as far as I'm concerned. Dig?"

"Yeah," we said. She could tell we were drug. We couldn't go over her or around her.

"That's all he's said so far. Clara jumps at conclusions. If the time comes and he says he's *the* Rusty Meaghan, then he's *the* Rusty Meaghan."

"If he can prove it," Dick Ferguson said.

That sounded square, coming from Dick. Like if we all had to prove who we are, then we would all be nowhere. Like that's not search. Like we search *being,* not *is* or *am.* Foulard says we are really searching *becoming;* otherwise we would be hung up on *being,* just as stagnant as if we stopped on *is* or *am.* We're always *going,* never *gone*—unless Barbarossa was gone, as he seemed to be with that holy vision in his eyes. But as far as we could be sure at the moment he was still going—searching, searching.

We've learned that we have to go along all the way with any cat if we expect to dig him when he really lays it for us. Whatever his kick, we can't force him. Like you don't turn on to Zen with one deep breath and a quick glance at your navel.

But Dick said it, right in front of Teresina, and she took it upon herself to discipline him for it. Like we said from in front, sometimes Teresina is with it and sometimes she's not. She held out on us for over a week, keeping Barbarossa completely out of circulation. She even took him to a pad she keeps on a remote stretch of beach up the coast line a few miles to get him away from us.

Dick took it personally, that jazz about proving who you are. He stole a small torch from the warehouse one night while he was on duty and started to work on the piece of sculpture he had in mind. Kay threw a party for him, celebrating the end of his scrounging period and the beginning of his creative period.

90

She was proud of him that night. There weren't more than a dozen of us—those real gone on symbolism—crowded into her pad for the party. It was all sculpture that session, no pot, no horse, no hi-fi, just enough beer and wine to oil the bearings.

Dick sat cross-legged in the middle of the floor, surrounded first by a ring of scrap metal and then by a circle of cats draped on pallets and old car cushions pushed against the wall. In his left hand he held the hub of a tugboat propeller with one fan still attached; his right hand rested on the discarded blade of a disk harrow. He was meditating on the symbolism of his piece.

"This propeller hub is obviously the Eye of Fate," he said, "and the disk is the sun or the world or the universe. Dig? It's not nicked anywhere, just worn down, still a perfect circle."

He picked up a rusty worm gear from the junk pile beside him and furrowed his brow as he studied its corkscrew threads.

"This worm gear can't be anything but a phallic symbol," he said. "Now I must decide what I want my statue to say: 'Screw Fate,' or 'Screw the Whole Damn Universe.'"

We picked up on his problem immediately. Dick was the kind of artist who believed in knowing where he was going before he started. That was, of course, a wide-open question. It came close to violating the code of our movement. Most of the cats with work in progress believed otherwise, in beginning in a vacuum and following the muse wherever she led them. It was this contrary aesthetic principle that had prolonged Dick's scrounging period for something over three years and made the beginning of his creative period a moment of such great import in our colony, especially for Kay.

We pondered with him most of the night, hoping that he would fire up his torch and make the all-important first weld on his statue. He never did, but he inspired several of the rest of us to go back to our pads and get to work seriously on our creative projects.

You realize that all this stemmed from the influence of Barbarossa spreading among us. Since Dick had made the mistake of openly challenging Teresina to make Barbarossa lay his true identity at once, we had the uneasy feeling that he might do just that. If he did, if Rusty Meaghan was really our new shaman, we would have an influx of cats from everywhere, and there was still enough of the square in some of us to make us feel we should stack up worthy of him. Like if he was really gone, if he had made the big scene, then we ought to be way out there with him when the cats came swarming in on us.

So we eased off the pressure and let Barbarossa proceed in his own way, on his own terms—or Teresina's terms, since he was as docile in her hands as a pet kitten. But she was fair. After she felt that we had been disciplined sufficiently, she gave a tea party in her own pad and encouraged Barbarossa to tell us the truth about life at—

HIGHCASTLE, 1946

HIGHCASTLE Military Academy stands on a bluff overlooking the White River some thirty miles south of Indianapolis. The main building is indeed a castle (why does the word "formidable" come to mind whenever I think of a castle?), a huge fortress of gray stone fashioned after the insignia of the Army Corps of Engineers, with crenelated battlements and turrets rising sternly from its flat roof.

The barracks behind it, built in a quadrangle around the well-kept parade ground, are less imposing but no less grim. They probably house thousands of memories for illustrious alumni who return each fall to praise dear old HMA for the start it gave them toward becoming what they are today. What can I, a disappointment, maybe even a disgrace to the corps, say for my *alma mater?* To me it was a formidable bastion, which I never stormed, though it paid me homage in my heyday there. Its sons, all-American boys all, have one face, one gait, one gray West Point uniform, one *esprit,* one long finger forever pointing at me. If this were the story of Rusty at Highcastle I no doubt could fill a volume with academic trivia; but I would have to search, rack my memory, perhaps return to the bend in the White for authentic color.

I will not delve there. Surely the significance of Highcastle has been filtered, distilled, rendered into an essence which is ever present in my mind, or so near the surface that I have only to relax and permit its entry into my consciousness. Highcastle is a room in the barracks, or four rooms exactly alike, in four different barracks, each with four pairs of stacked bunks, eight study tables, eight chairs, eight foot-lockers, and an adjoining bath with four showers, two urinals, and two commodes—and down the hall an abandoned guardroom into which they moved the piano Mama rented for me against the better judgment of Major Swann, the cocky little superintendent.

Highcastle is Major Swann, five feet six of military discipline, with a shiny, black-rimmed pate, a stubby mustache, and a strip of USO ribbons from World War II pinned above his left breast pocket. It is Ruby Swann, his overripe wife who always wanted a son like me. It is Coach Wijiecski, too, who was grudgingly proud of me and then ashamed of me, though it was I who got his college job for him. It is a corps of uniformed cadets passing in review on a bright spring day, or more precisely a boys' chorus cheering from the bleachers across a cruel frozen gridiron, across the slush and mud of the first snow, falling too early in the season to be of any lasting beauty.

Better, it is Pop Horner, the athletic trainer—a roly-poly man past middle age, completely bald and as pink as a Kewpie doll.

"You must be Red or Rusty," he said to me when he met me and Mama at the bus station in Martinsville the day I enrolled. "You're too big to be called Pinky."

It is Captain Bob Hammer, the officer-in-charge of the freshman barracks. Most of all it is Captain Hammer.

He checked me in when I came to stay. One other little freshman and I arrived a day before the others, and Pop Horner delivered us to A Barracks. Captain Hammer, a big man, fit and trim, with clear gray eyes and a blond crew-cut, sat behind his desk and filled out our forms for us.

"That's all here," he said. "Now I'll show you to your quarters."

He picked up a pair of metal crutches, which had been hidden behind his desk, and stood up. He must have sensed my

94

shock at the incongruity of his crutches as he hobbled around the desk on stiff, unwrinkled shoes.

"I'm not like other men, Rusty," he said with a smile. "I have no feet. You'll have to get used to me."

Once clear of the desk, however, he moved quite smoothly, and had no trouble at all getting us settled into our quarters. He went to dinner with us in the almost deserted mess hall, and quite unobtrusively kept us clear of the sprinkling of upperclassmen who had also arrived early.

After dinner he sat with us in the common room of our barracks and puffed on a fat, short-stemmed pipe.

"Do you teach, too, sir?" I asked by way of making conversation after my shy classmate and I had exhausted our stock of questions about the academy in general.

"Yes," he said. "History."

"Do you like to teach history?" I asked.

"Yes, very much."

"Would you rather teach history than anything?" The question sounded rather childish after I had asked it.

"I don't know," he answered thoughtfully. "I might prefer philosophy."

"What's that?" my companion asked.

"Oh, it's the study of ideas, an attempt to find the answers to the big questions—like who are we, where did we come from, where are we going, why are we here."

"I know why we're here," the small boy said.

"Why, Jimmy?" asked Captain Hammer, a smile of amusement curling around his pipe stem.

"Because our families don't love us." Jimmy sniffed back his tears.

"Well, now, that wasn't exactly what I meant. I don't mean why are we here at Highcastle, but just why are we here—here in the world. And we certainly wouldn't be here if it weren't for our mothers." Captain Hammer spoke gravely. "Your mother no doubt has good reasons for sending you to Highcastle, one of them being that she loves you very much."

Jimmy had nothing to say to that, probably because he did not trust his voice just then. I felt a little like crying myself; but it was homesickness, not doubt, that was saddening me. At least I think it was. Anyway our conversation was running out. The captain yawned.

"You men may turn in whenever you like," he said.

"Could I practice a little while?" I asked.

"Practice?" He was puzzled.

"On my piano. It's here, isn't it?"

"Oh," he said. "So you're the boy with the piano."

"Yes, sir," I said. I knew then how he felt, the man with plastic feet. He felt like the boy with the piano.

"Yes. It's here. The delivery men put it in the guardroom at the end of the hall. Sure, you may practice for a while, until ten if you wish." He reached for his crutches.

"I can find it, sir," I said, rising before he was put to any further trouble.

"Can I come and listen?" Jimmy asked eagerly.

"Sure, come on."

We said good night to the captain and went off down the hall together, the smallest freshman in the class and the boy with the piano. I forgot Jimmy as soon as I sat down at my piano. He listened quietly. I think he cried some. My own eyes were misty at times, as I played pieces I knew well and remembered when and where I had learned them.

I played from memory that first night for I had not yet unpacked my music. The next morning I began to unpack all my things and stow them away according to the instructions in my cadet handbook. My most treasured possession was Mama's scrapbook. I lingered long over its pages when I came to it in my luggage. From it I took my favorite picture, a large professional glossy print of Mama in tights, one knee bent slightly in, her right arm down, held gracefully out from her side, her left hand up, palm inward, a few inches to the left of her face in a kind of salute or acknowledgment of applause, the broad wedding band on a level with her smiling eyes. Her hair, unbound for the picture, tumbled around her shoulders and framed her happy young features. It was the most beautiful photograph ever taken.

When I went to the post exchange to get my uniform, I bought a frame for the picture and put it on my desk even before I tried on my new day uniform of West Point gray. But I was properly dressed and had my living area in order by the time my roommates began pouring into the barracks. We were all shy at first, making awkward introductions and trying to appear worldly wise in spite of the fact that it was probably the first time away from home for most of us.

I have forgotten many of the boys who shared my room in A Barracks. I seldom remember people unless I have some special reason to do so. Of course I remember Cadet Morton, a stupid, gangling, pimply-faced hillbilly from somewhere in Missouri. He had been sent to school by a successful uncle who no doubt was ashamed of the Ozark branch of the family. I had reason to remember him—he was the one who stole Mama's picture while I was practicing on my piano that second afternoon at Highcastle.

When I returned to my bunk after an hour in the guardroom, the first thing I noticed was the empty frame on my desk. I wheeled around and looked suspiciously at everyone in the barracks.

"What's wrong, Paderewsky?" some smart aleck asked.

"There's a thief in here," I said angrily.

"Where?"

"In your bunk maybe," I said and grabbed the smart aleck by his arm. I pulled him out of his bunk and hurled him into

97

the middle of the floor. He fell sprawling. I put my knee in the small of his back and began twisting his arm.

"Either you stole my picture or you know who did," I said and applied more pressure.

"Morton," he screamed. "Morton took your pin-up."

"Where is it?"

"Under his mattress."

I let the boy up and made him show me where the photograph was hidden.

I was stripping the bunk when Morton came out of the bathroom.

"Just what do you think you're doin', pianer player?" he called and rushed me.

He was as tall as I, and I suppose he had the usual country boy's confidence that he was tougher than anyone who had ever lived in town. I punched once with my left fist—into his stomach—and then landed a solid right on his chin as he doubled up. He sank limply to the floor and stared at me out of his dull, almost colorless eyes.

"I just borrered yer pitcher," he whined. "You kin borrer some of mine whenever you want to."

"I'll never want to," I said. "And I'll break your neck if you ever lay your filthy hands on Mama's picture again."

"Mama's picture?" the ex-smart aleck said, but there was no insolence in his voice. "What a mama!"

I let his remark pass and the barracks quieted down as I put the photograph back into its frame.

The first fight, I discovered, always brought the superintendent into the barracks to make things clear for the rest of the term. It was a matter of minutes before we had our official call. We all stood at what we considered attention when Major Swann entered. He kept his cap on as he walked around the room and looked each of us in the eye.

"Now, men," he said, "we have come to the first test of our

esprit de corps. If we are to train the cadets at Highcastle to become true military men, we must first instill in them the basic truth that no military force can be effective in battle—and that is the primary purpose of military training—if there is fighting within the ranks."

He paused to let that bit of wisdom sink into our minds.

"We have just had our first fight of the year in the freshman barracks. It must be the last. Cadets Meaghan and Morton will please to step forward two paces."

I stepped forward two paces. Cadet Morton slouched forward two lunges. We faced Major Swann.

"Which of you started the fight?" the major asked.

"He did," Morton said.

"Did you start the fight, Cadet Meaghan?"

"I hit him first, sir," I admitted.

"Why?"

"For stealing a picture off my table."

"Are you sure he stole it?"

"Yes, sir. I found it under his mattress."

"Where is the picture now?"

"Back on my table, sir." I broke attention and pointed.

Major Swann glanced quickly at the picture and back at me. Then he did a double-take and let his eyes linger.

"Oh," he said, and twisted his thin lips into a sneer. "So that's the kind of picture it is. You know very well that we don't allow pin-up pictures in the barracks; that is, you should know, if you have read your handbook, Cadet Meaghan. Where did you get such a disgusting photograph?"

"It's a picture of my mother," I said.

"Your mother!" He was prepared to doubt me, but some memory stopped him. He walked over to my study table and put on his rimless glasses for a closer look.

"It's his mother, Major," Captain Hammer said from where he stood leaning against the door-facing.

99

"Ah—yes. So it is," the major said. He should have known. As I remembered, his eyes had undressed Mama more completely the first time we came to his office. "How does it happen that you chose this particular picture, Cadet Meaghan?"

"It's the way I remember my mother, sir. I spent most of my life in the circus. That's the way she dressed for her act."

"I see," he said, and somewhat reluctantly laid the picture face down on my table. He looked around at the other tables, most of which had mothers' pictures or fathers' pictures on them. "Choose a more suitable photograph for your desk in the future, Cadet Meaghan."

"Yes, sir," I said. I still believe that but for the presence of Captain Hammer the major would have confiscated Mama's photograph and delivered us a stern lecture on adolescent depravity.

"What do you have to say for yourself, Cadet Morton?" he asked as he turned to the thief.

"Nothing, sir," Morton said, blushing the color of his pimples.

The major looked at Captain Hammer before speaking again. Now, I can imagine his making a command decision in battle, if he ever got closer to a battle line than a USAFI classroom.

"Perhaps you had cause, or thought you had cause to strike a fellow cadet," he said to me at last. "In the future, report your grievances through the proper channels. Both of you will report to the commandant in the morning for punishment."

He marched out of the room with Captain Hammer, whose rubber-tipped crutches thudded softly between the clicks of the major's heels.

I have forgotten what the punishment was, but my resentment smoldered for three years before it was satisfied. My parentage is rooted equally in Ireland and Sicily, where grudges live forever and vengeance comes in time.

My fighting had just begun, of course. A mother in tights and a piano in the guardroom must be constantly defended in a

100

corps of young he-men. By common consent my later bouts went unreported, however, because I provided far too much sport for the upperclassmen to allow any official intervention in my defense of my eccentricities, both of which were further endeared to me by each successive battle.

Perhaps I practiced the piano defiantly. At least I practiced diligently and played with such force that I sometimes shocked Mr. Winship when he came to give lessons on Saturday morning.

"It may be significant, Rusty," he said more than once, "that we have shortened 'pianoforte' to 'piano,' not to 'forte.' Do you know what I mean?"

"Yes, sir," I said. "I should play softer."

"More softly," he corrected me.

"Yes, sir," I said and saved my power to punch the next philistine who did not understand the subtleties of the piano-forte.

My integration into academy life was routine, I suppose. Like all my roommates during those long weeks of homesickness, I counted the days until the Christmas recess, when I would see Mama again. I hoped to visit her in Chicago and persuade her perhaps to let me go to school there. In early December, however, she wrote that she would meet me and Ella in Indianapolis, where we would be among friends during the holidays.

I can remember yet how she felt in my arms when I saw her for the first time after three months away from her, how hungrily I clung to her and she to me. I could not help crushing her with all my strength.

"Ouch!" she said playfully. "You're too strong to be squeezing frail old women. You're a big boy now—and a handsome one in your uniform." Her eyes were all admiration and affection.

She was handsome, too, and far from frail or old, at least to me. I suppose she was thirty-eight then; but she looked more

101

like Ella's sister than our mother, when Ella arrived from St. Louis.

Strangely, that is about all I remember about that Christmas in Indianapolis. Mama took a suite at the Lincoln, a single for me and a room with twin beds for her and Ella. We received presents from Daddy and Gina, who were then in San Diego. Ella cried when we opened them; I remember that. But I have forgotten what friends we visited or what else we did. Maybe it was something which my memory rejected.

The reunion must not have been entirely satisfactory for Mama either.

"We'll go to Florida next Christmas," she said. "It will be good to see all the circus people again."

I wonder if she believed that any number of old friends could restore whatever it was that we had lost, that we missed in that Christmas meeting. I wonder if Ella believed it or if I did. But we were all enthusiastic about the trip to Florida, or pretended to be, when our holiday was over and we broke up again.

Back at Highcastle I had to face a reinvigorated corps of tormentors.

"Did you see your mama, Rusty?"

"Was she wearing tights?"

"Do you have a new picture?"

The war was on again. Fortunately for me, I was big for my age, and eight or ten years of acrobatics had given me exceptional muscular co-ordination. I acquitted myself well. Unfortunately for the world, I may have robbed it, unintentionally, of a half-dozen or more talented pianists. As I became more and more proficient with my fists, I discouraged more and more of my adversaries; but since the piano had become a fighting symbol they gradually turned on my less hardy colleagues, who began to drop out of Mr. Winship's class one by one.

By the end of April, I was the only pupil Mr. Winship had

left at Highcastle; and although he valued me highly (he said) he could not afford to come out on Saturday mornings for only one lesson. So we arranged for me to go to him instead. Actually I was pleased by the prospect of going up to Indianapolis once a week. Even the downtown section, especially the perfume counter at Ayres, held many happy memories for me.

I left on an early bus from Martinsville that first Saturday morning, and arrived in time to visit the department store and to have lunch at the Canary Cottage, at one of our favorite tables. I was under a bittersweet spell of nostalgia when I reached Mr. Winship's apartment in a fringe district not far from the circle. The building was quite ordinary, but my teacher's apartment, on the second floor, was indeed striking when seen for the first time.

"Come in, Rusty, come in," my teacher said when he opened his door. "You're just on time." His manner was overcordial, his eyes bright with welcome.

I stepped into a large room lavishly hung with champagne curtains. The only other wall decorations were masks—primitive, theatrical, stylized. Two large pictures of bulbous nudes were displayed on easels, and smaller ones stood on tables and commodes about the room. There were several bookcases full of bright-jacketed volumes and old copies of *Physical Culture*. A headless, footless bed with a champagne coverlet balanced a grand piano in the furniture arrangement. The chairs were all modern.

"Do you like it?" Mr. Winship asked eagerly as he watched me survey the room.

"Yes, sir," I said. I would not disappoint him. The room reminded me of the tent of a queer old fortuneteller who wintered in Sarasota when I was a child. Her place always frightened me.

"Good," he said. "I thought you would. We'll hear your les-

103

son first; then I'll show you my kitchen, maybe brew a pot of tea to go with some cakes I baked for you."

"Yes, sir," I said. I had hoped to stroll through Ayres again before my bus left.

"Very well, the Bach first."

He arranged the bench for me and drew up a chair beside it. When he sat down beside me I noticed that he used perfume instead of a deodorant. The effect was almost nauseating, but I forgot it as I began a three-part invention by Bach.

I played the Bach to his satisfaction, then a portion of a nocturne by Chopin, and a short selection by Debussy.

"You are doing well, Rusty," Mr. Winship said. "You are by far the best pupil I've ever had at Highcastle. Having a piano in your barracks certainly helps. The other cadets have always had to practice in the chapel or the parlor or the mess hall—wherever they could. You're the first to have his own instrument conveniently near."

I could have told him that I would probably be the last, too. It would be a long time before another cadet dared bring a piano into the barracks at Highcastle.

"Now, for our tea party," Mr. Winship said. "Do you like jasmine?"

"I don't know."

"Well, we'll see. I'll bet you do." He rose, stirring and scenting the air as he swept into the kitchen.

"Come along," he chirped, "and see where I pamper my appetites."

His kitchen was small but well appointed. Almost everything except perishables was exposed on open shelves.

"I like everything handy," he explained. "When I need an ingredient, I need it right then, no time to search for it. Time is just as important in cooking as in music, and we know how that is, don't we, Rusty?"

"Yes, sir," I said.

104

"Here are the cookies," he said, pointing to a plate of tea-cakes. "You may nibble on one, but just one, while the tea is brewing."

"I can wait," I said.

"That's right, Rusty. You have the makings of a real gourmet. Wait for the tea. Here, sniff the dried leaves."

He waved an open can under my nose. The jasmine tea did smell good, but I had no appetite. He put some of the leaves into a teapot and poured boiling water over them.

"We'll let it steep in the other room," he said. He put the cookies and teapot on a tray, which already had a sugar bowl and a cream pitcher on it, and carried the tray to a low coffee table by the bed.

"Just sit on the bed," he said. "I'll draw up a chair."

He sat down opposite me. After testing the tea himself he poured each of us a cup.

"Milk and sugar?" he asked.

"Yes, sir. One teaspoon."

He sweetened my tea and passed it to me.

"Help yourself to the cakes," he urged.

I took a cookie, but I had no stomach for any of it.

"What shall we talk about?" he asked brightly. "Dreams? Dreams are interesting. What do you dream about, Rusty?"

"Everything."

"Ever dream about girls—women?" He leered coyly.

"Just Mama," I said.

"That isn't what I mean," he said, rising. "You're almost fifteen, aren't you, Rusty? Do you ever dream about girls like these?"

He deftly produced an album from somewhere and spread it on the table before me. He opened it at two large pictures of showgirls wearing elaborate headdresses and little else. He sat down beside me.

"Only Mama," I said, remembering the unhappy business about her professional photograph.

"Oho, Rusty! You *are* a sly one." He nudged me in the ribs with his elbow and giggled. "Just look at these!"

The next girls had no clothes on at all.

"And these are only the beginning. Just wait until we finish the book." He squeezed my thigh and turned another page. "See what I mean? Don't you ever dream anything like that?"

I was frightened, embarrassed, sickened by his pictures. I looked away.

"Do you miss your mama?" he asked sympathetically and put his arm around my shoulders.

"Yes, sir," I said. I might have sobbed.

"Then, come here and let Mother Lonnie love you." He pulled me toward him.

I suddenly realized that he was going to kiss me. His sweat-fouled perfume drove me into panic. I shoved him aside, jumped up, and ran out of his room and down the stairs. I might have run all the way to the bus station; I cannot remember. But when I reached the station I was breathless. I looked around the depot vaguely.

"Where's your cap, Cadet Meaghan?" asked a familiar voice. Then I saw Captain Hammer seated on a bench near the magazine stand.

"Oh, hello, Captain Hammer," I said. "I didn't see you. My cap—" I reached up and felt my bare head. "I don't know. I must have left it in Mr. Winship's apartment."

"Why?"

"I must have forgotten it. I—I left in a hurry."

"Did you run away?" Captain Hammer searched my face steadily.

"Yes, sir," I said. I felt myself blush as I looked down at the floor.

106

"The question is, did you keep your pants on?" he asked slowly.

"Yes, sir," I said, still avoiding his eyes.

"Good," he said. "Where does Mother Winship live? I'll go get your cap for you."

I gave him the address.

"All right. Call me a taxi."

After I had helped Captain Hammer into the taxi and it had driven away, I noticed that I had forgotten my music too. As I collected my wits I considered calling Mr. Winship's apartment and mentioning the fact, but thought better of it.

It was just as well. In about half an hour Captain Hammer returned with both my cap and my music.

"I think we'd better find you another piano teacher," he said.

"Who?" I asked. We sat down on a bench in the waiting room.

"I know one." He smiled wryly. "He plays in a cocktail lounge that I sometimes visit, but he's as well schooled as your Mr. Winship, I assure you—and he's not so affectionate. I'll write your mother about it."

"Thank you, sir," I said. "What's the teacher's name?"

"Jarrell—Dick Jarrell. Ever heard of him?" He glanced at me out of the corner of his eye as he filled his pipe from a pouch of aromatic tobacco.

"He's made some records, hasn't he?"

"I believe so. He would be more widely known if he would travel, but he likes it here in Indianapolis."

"I've heard of him," I said. "I have some of his records." I had some of almost everybody's records—Count Basie's, Duke Ellington's, Earl Hines', Teddy Wilson's, Art Tatum's, Jess Stacy's. Indeed, I had spent most of Gina's hundred dollars on piano records, or records featuring piano stylists. I was thrilled by the thought of studying with a name performer.

"Could I start soon, next week?" I asked eagerly.

"We'll see," Captain Hammer said. "School will soon be out, but you might get in a few lessons before we go to camp for the summer."

Yes, Mama was sending Ella and me to camps instead of inviting us to Chicago to be with her. Camp was a sore spot with me just then, but Captain Hammer had no way of knowing it. Or did he? He was a wise counselor, and I was glad that he would be in camp with me if I had to go.

We rode back to Martinsville on the bus together. Captain Hammer had his car parked in town. It was the first time I had ridden with him. He was resolute in his movements, especially in the operation of the clutch and brake.

"A little awkward, but safe," he assured me. I had not intended to let him know that I was observing him. "We adapt. We learn to live with what we have, or what we have not. Talent or plastic feet can set us apart, Rusty, about equally; but we can get along with the flesh-footed and untalented if we try hard enough." His voice was bitter. I suppose he was talking over my head then. If he was complimenting me as a pianist, he made no issue of it.

"Do you drive?" he asked after we had turned off the main highway.

"A little," I said. Mama had sometimes risked my driving on quiet roads before she sold our car.

"Want to try?"

"Yes, sir."

"O.K." He stopped the car. "Come around and take my place." He slid across the seat.

With his coaching I did very well and drove us to A Barracks without mishap. After that I drove Captain Hammer nearly everywhere he went. The next Monday afternoon he asked me to drive him down to the practice field, where the football team was in spring training.

108

"We have a new coach, you know," he said. HMA had not won a game the last season. "I'd like to see what he can do. Did you ever play football, Rusty?"

"A little. Lots of passball," I said.

"Have you considered going out for the team here at Highcastle?"

"No, sir," I said. I was not at all popular with the athletes. I spent my physical-education periods on the tumbling mat and the gymnastic equipment—rings, parallel bars, gym horses —not in games.

"Why don't you try out?"

"I had never thought about it. Would you like for me to, sir?" I did not sense then that he was trying to get me to make a bid for my schoolmates' respect, but I wanted to please him.

"It doesn't matter what I want. You might enjoy it." He pointed to a parking place near the reserve bench. I pulled up and we both got out.

Pop Horner was sitting on the bench with a few scrubs. Coach Wijiecski was out on the field, observing two squads in scrimmage.

"Hello, Captain Hammer," Pop said. "Rusty."

"Hello, Pop," I said.

"How's he doing, Pop?" Captain Hammer asked, pointing a thumb toward the new coach.

"O.K.," Pop said. "He's beefing up the line. The backfield hasn't shown much yet. He was a lineman, you know."

"All-American mention for tackle, I believe, a few years back."

"Yeah, that's right," Pop said. "He was doing pretty good in some college as a line coach, but decided to come here. Shooting for head coach somewhere, I guess."

"I suppose so," the captain said. "We're lucky to get him." He watched the teams with a near-professional eye, and exchanged comments with Pop Horner for about half an hour.

Then the coach sent the squads into position for a kick-off and strode back to the bench.

He was a swarthy, chunky man with a heavy black beard and hairy arms. He was scowling.

"Coach, you've met Captain Hammer, haven't you?" Pop asked.

"Yes, once, I believe. How are you, Captain?" He did not offer to shake hands.

"This is Cadet Meaghan," Pop said.

"Cadet Meaghan—oh, yeah, the kid with the piano. I've heard him. His barracks is next to the gym. Hello, Meaghan." His scowl deepened and he turned his attention back to the field. His sweat shirt was wet with perspiration.

"I was trying to recruit Rusty for your squad," Captain Hammer said.

"A piano player?" The coach showed no interest whatever.

"It takes pretty smart hands to play the piano, Coach," the captain said. He had risen and hobbled over to stand beside Coach Wijiecski. "Did you notice his fingers? They'd almost wrap around a football."

The coach glanced at my hands. I flexed them self-consciously.

"Rusty's licked every sophomore on your club and some of the juniors," Pop said. I wondered how he knew, and why he said anything in front of Captain Hammer.

"Rusty might have what it takes," the captain said, ignoring the report of my fighting record. "I just thought you might give him a chance."

The coach grunted.

"Well, I've got to get back to the barracks," Captain Hammer said. "Rusty, why don't you stay awhile and watch them scrimmage? See you, Coach."

"See you." Coach Wijiecski never took his eyes off the playing field.

110

Pop Horner sidled up to him.

"Say, Coach, did you ever hear of Bob 'Sledge' Hammer?" he asked.

"Sure. All-American fullback from OU before the war? Yes, sir, he was a killer." The coach's voice was genuinely complimentary.

"Well, Coach, you've just been talking to him."

"You mean him? Captain Hammer?" The coach looked at Pop in surprise, amazement. "That crip—?"

"Yes, sir. There he goes, hobbling into that old Chevrolet over there."

The coach hastily looked at the parked car.

"So that's Sledge Hammer. Why didn't he—why didn't somebody tell me?" The coach spoke in awe.

"You didn't ask, Coach." Pop could not hide the note of satisfaction in his voice.

"I wondered what ever happened to him—expected him to turn up somewhere in a good coaching job."

"He got his feet frozen in northern Europe somewhere. That's what happened to him."

"Too bad," the coach said as the Chevrolet backed up and turned around. "He'd a made a good coach."

"He sure would," Pop agreed. "And if he told *me* a boy looked good, I'd try him out."

Coach Wijiecski turned to me and looked me over for the first time. I was taller than he was, but of course still gangling and awkward-looking under his scrutiny.

"O.K., Meaghan," he said. "Let's see you throw a few. You, there—Wilson, Higgins—shag 'em."

Two of the scrubs jumped up from the bench eagerly.

"Yes, sir!" they said and scrambled for one of the spare balls under the bench.

We went to a vacant practice area and I started throwing passes. I was no sensation, just a fourteen-year-old with a little

111

more than average distance and a little better than average accuracy; but I could see the coach watching us when I looked his way. It might have been interest in me or it might have been respect for Captain Hammer's judgment. At any rate he told me to suit out and report for practice the next day.

Spring training was rough on me. At last everybody had a crack at the boy with the piano. I stood the punishment, however, principally for Captain Hammer's sake. I could handle my body well. My timing was exceptionally good, probably as a result of the rigorous acrobatic training the Bercellis had put me through most of my life. So I came out a little tougher, a little warier, a little better able to take care of myself.

I started piano lessons with Dick Jarrell about the middle of May. A wiry, strong-fingered little man, balding, and puffing somewhat around the middle, he was an alert, conscientious teacher. I went to his house for lessons, met his wife and twelve-year-old daughter, and thoroughly enjoyed my lessons.

He was a well-schooled musician, as Captain Hammer had said, as well as a distinctive stylist in his own right. I usually spent most of Saturday afternoon at his house. After a careful session devoted to traditional piano literature, he would play for me, listen to records with me and explain what other performers were doing. Then I would play some of my own arrangements, which would have held no interest whatever for Mr. Winship.

"Man, your left hand is heavier than Francis Craig's," he said after my first improvisation for him.

I went into "Near You," as I had taken it off one of Craig's records.

"O.K., Rusty," he said with a chuckle. "You've convinced me you can do anything you want to on a keyboard. Now, we'll teach you what to do, what's cool, and what's right off the cob. You'll get hep, man, hep."

I hated to interrupt my study with him when school closed,

but I had no choice. I drove Captain Hammer to Camp Mile Away the first week in June. I remember it, but I remember that summer with the two other summers I spent there in the Ozarks. They merge. I cannot remember what happened when. I swam; I hiked; I played games; I paddled a canoe on the lake; I engaged in all kinds of handicraft activities; and I listened to records and played the piano in the clubhouse hours on end.

In August, Mama and Ella picked me up in a year-old Plymouth, and took me for a two weeks' vacation at Excelsior Springs. We had fun, a desperate sort of fun, during that holiday together. We swam together, went horseback riding together, tumbled together, though Mama and Ella were somewhat out of practice. It did not matter, since the act was dead; and it was still thrilling to do the simpler routines. Mama was as lovely as ever in a bathing suit, and Ella was beginning to fill out into something resembling a woman's shape.

It was that summer that Mama told us she had divorced Daddy. I was glad, and in a way I think Ella was glad too. I felt that it was now incumbent upon me to hurry into manhood so I could take care of Mama. I saw myself back with her again, her protector and her intimate for life. Ella would have been welcome, but I believe she had other ideas. She was unnaturally shy and reserved that summer, as I remember. She was inclined to appear wise beyond her years, too, to hint at mysteries she had learned in her convent.

"Good-by, wombmate," she whispered in my ear when she kissed me the last day and boarded a bus for St. Louis.

Mama took me back to Highcastle. She let me drive the Plymouth some. She was as sweet as ever to me the whole time, loving and kind, though she was not happy—as I thought she should be now that she was free of Daddy for good.

"We'll drive down to Sarasota Christmas," she said in parting. "It will be like old times." Still believing, still hoping that we could recapture the past. I hoped, too. Perhaps I believed.

I tried to believe. I wanted to believe. That was the way she left me when she drove away from Highcastle at the beginning of my second year at the academy.

What do I remember about that second year? It was like the first. My piano and I moved into B Barracks, indistinguishable from A Barracks. The faces were the same, the uniforms the same. My grudge battles were now fought on the football field. I was blocked harder, tackled harder, roughed up more than anyone else on the club. I played a few minutes in three of our regular games, but I was always in the second team line-up to scrimmage the first team in practice. It was there that I took my punishment, learned my lessons, hardened my body.

I was glad when the season was over. In my mind there always lurked the fear that I might hurt my hands. Perhaps it was a healthful thing. I learned to keep my hands out of danger, and consequently became a better ball handler. That was not my primary aim, of course. My hands were dedicated to the piano, so that I might one day play as well as Dick Jarrell and have a quiet home life like his, with Mama as head of the house, and Ella perhaps in the comfortable role of Dick's daughter, Linda. I somehow did not expect Ella ever to grow up.

At Christmas, however, I found her growing up, and growing a little brash and flippant, returning perhaps to her moods during those last few months in Indianapolis.

"Hi, wombmate," she called gaily when we met her at the gate of the convent.

"Ella!" Mama exclaimed in shock.

"It's all right, Mama," Ella said. "I know where we came from. We *are* twins, aren't we?" She smiled disarmingly and hugged Mama.

"Well, don't say it again."

"O.K." Ella piled into the front seat with us after I had stowed her luggage. "Off to Sarasota, the city of itching palms and blooming idiots."

We had a fine trip down. I drove most of the way—down the river to Memphis, across to Birmingham and Montgomery, then down through Tallahassee and Tampa to Sarasota. It was good to leave winter behind. We made side trips to the circus lots we had played in the cities along the way. Without the circus they were just lots. Nevertheless our spirits rose as the countryside grew greener and greener. Sarasota was exactly as I remembered it, except for its postwar expansion.

Our house, the little Spanish stucco in which we were born, was still there and in fairly good repair, though it needed painting and the grounds had been neglected for years. It was tenanted by Mexicans, as were all the houses in the neighborhood. A tiny half-naked *muchacha* trying to hide behind a small palm tree reminded me of Ella as a baby.

Mama drove by the house twice and looked at it wistfully.

"We sold it when we were divorced," she said, half to herself. Then she stiffened her shoulders and speeded up the car.

As a surprise, Uncle Tony and Uncle Mario and their families met us in Sarasota. They had children now and had also given up the circus for good. They had jobs of some kind in Jersey City but had come down for Christmas just as we had done.

I was much taller than either of my uncles.

"He'sa justa like Al," Uncle Tony said. He obviously was living in an Italian community. His English was deteriorating. "Same built. Same big fellow."

I was neither pleased nor flattered.

"Where is Al?" Uncle Mario asked.

"In San Francisco the last time I heard from him," Mama said. She bit her words off and changed the subject.

Later I heard enough of a conversation between her and Uncle Tony to know that they were discussing Daddy.

"I'll kill him if I ever see him," Uncle Tony said in the Sicilian vernacular.

"No," Mama said. "I'll take care of him."

That was all I heard. Generally we had good times together. We visited scores of circus people. Mama borrowed a charcoal furnace and cooked a fine Sicilian meal for all of us at the motel where we were staying. One day she packed a lunch basket.

"Let's have a picnic," she said, "just the three of us."

"Where?" Ella asked.

Mama thought for a moment.

"I know a place," she said. "I think I can find it."

We drove south of Sarasota a few miles and then turned off toward the Gulf. At the end of an unpaved road I stopped the car.

"I think this is it," Mama said. "At least it will do."

We collected our lunch, our swimsuits, and a pair of blankets and headed toward the beach. We found a small inlet with a sandy beach bounded by a palm brake.

"Yes, this is it," Mama said. "We can undress in the palms. We're hidden from everything here."

She and Ella spread the blankets and went back into the palm brake to put on their swimsuits. I found similar shelter nearby. I changed first and returned to the beach to wait for them. It was not until I had lain down on the blanket that I recognized the place.

"I'll race you," Mama called to Ella. The two of them ran by the blanket and plunged into the surf.

I saw only Mama, and I saw her naked, the first image in my memory, as clear as it had ever been in my dreams. I brushed my hand over my eyes and shook my head. The vision hung on. I sat up and waited for Mama to rise out of the sea. I was sure that she would not be wearing a swimsuit. My heart pounded. Was I back in my infancy again?

116

But she *was* wearing her swimsuit, a trim one-piece suit of black Lastex, when she stood up again. It was Ella, in a bikini, who appeared almost naked from where I sat.

I ran across the beach and dived into the water to clear my head. I swam underwater until my breath gave out. Then I swam still farther out to sea.

"Come back, Rusty," Mama called. "The undertow is treacherous out there."

I could barely hear her but I turned around and swam back. Mama and Ella met me and then turned and swam with me toward the beach. When our feet touched bottom we stood up and began to play. We ducked one another, wrestled, played tag underwater, and swam short races.

Ella tired first. She returned to the blankets and lay down in the sun. I ducked Mama and tickled her at the same time. She strangled and stood up. I beat her on the back until she regained her breath.

"Enough, enough," she said, laughing. "I'll race you to the blankets."

I easily outdistanced her. Ella had been watching us, but when we reached the blankets she turned her face away. She was crying.

"What's the matter, honey?" Mama asked.

"I miss Daddy," Ella said. She glanced at me but averted her eyes hastily. I could not tell whether or not she shared my memory.

"I do too," Mama said softly. "Al and I often came here. We were happy then."

So she remembered going there often. Somehow I hoped that she did not remember the one time that stuck in my memory. I was jealous of Daddy for their happiness then.

We lay in the sun for an hour or so. Mama reminded us of things we had forgotten. As we talked of the circus days Ella was quiet, but she listened all the time.

117

"How about lunch?" Mama asked at last.

"I'd like another dip," Ella said.

"All right, you swim while I spread our lunch," Mama said.

Ella stood up and stretched.

"Come with me, Rusty," she said. "I—I'm afraid of the undertow."

"O.K.," I said.

We waded out into the water up to our waists and then swam with matching strokes for a hundred yards or more. Ella stopped and began treading water.

"Did you take lifesaving at camp, Rusty?" she asked.

"Yes."

"Demonstrate. Save me!" She allowed herself to sink.

I dived under her, lifted her to the surface, and hooked my left arm under her chin. Then I began swimming toward the shore, towing her along with me.

Halfway back she started struggling. She turned in my lock and clung to me pinning my arms and pulling me under with her. I recognized her maneuver, which had been part of our training, and brought her back to the surface.

A little nearer the shore she tapped on my arm, signaling me to let go. I released her. She rolled over on her stomach and matched my strokes again.

"Thanks, Rusty, for saving me," she said and smiled.

A few seconds later we touched bottom. When I stood up, Ella clung to my arm.

"You're good, Rusty," she said. "Always save me. Don't leave us the way Daddy did."

"I won't." I said. "I'll always look after you and Mama."

"Do, Rusty. Please do. I'm so lonely without Daddy or you or anybody."

"Dinner's ready," Mama called as we came out of the water. She handed each of us a towel. Our lunch was a quiet one. I do not know what any of us really expected of the picnic.

118

The next day we started north again. Somewhere along the way Ella asked, "May I spend a vacation with Daddy some-time?"

"Sure," Mama said, "if you can find him."

"Gina will let me know where they are," Ella said. "She's good."

"Yes," Mama said, "Gina's good, too good for her own good." Her voice was bitter. No one pressed the conversation further.

It had been a fairly enjoyable Christmas. I hated to return to Highcastle. I accepted my lot, though, and doubled my practice on the piano now that the football season was over. Dick Jarrell devoted far more time to me than Mr. Winship had done, and according to him I made remarkable progress. He prepared me to give a recital a week before the team went into spring training.

He arranged for me to play my concert in the parlor of the superintendent's house. Mrs. Swann became interested and had the grand piano tuned especially for the event. She even invited me to practice on the instrument two or three hours a day for a week before my recital.

"I've heard a lot about you, Rusty," she said when I came for my first practice period. "I've been wanting to hear you play."

She was dressed as though I were a special guest. She was a pretty woman in her middle thirties with a figure just verging on plumpness—her bosom and hips and upper arms just beginning to strain at her smooth white skin. Her coloring was the same as mine—red hair, blue eyes. Her face was broad oval, almost round, with a small nose inclined to tilt up childishly. Her mouth was small, too, but her lips were full and red, a little pouty in repose, with a bee-stung quality that disappeared when she smiled.

"May I listen while you practice?" she asked. She stood beside me while I raised the lid of the piano. She came almost to my shoulders. Her hair was perfumed, faintly, pleasantly.

"Yes," I said. "I'm afraid you'll get tired of my practicing though."

"We'll see." She smiled and sat down where she could watch my fingers. I found her a much more attractive person than her husband.

I played some scales and arpeggios first, to warm up and to feel out the action of the piano. It was a good instrument. I played through Bach's French Suite in G Major (No. 5) and followed it with five or six pieces from Grieg's Norwegian Notebook. I could not forget the presence of Mrs. Swann; I was not used to playing for an audience other than the Jarrells. I suppose I wanted to show off a bit, for I tried the highly orchestral D-Major Sonata by Mozart next, and finished up with Bartók's Roumanian Dances. I did not take time to smooth out rough passages during that rehearsal—still trying to impress Mrs. Swann, I suppose. She was good for me. I resolved to perfect the weak spots in private before I played for her again.

"You play beautifully," she said. She had been dutifully silent throughout the practice period.

"Thank you," I said.

"Do you play popular music?"

"Sometimes. At least, I try."

"Play something for me."

"All right," I said. "What would you like?"

"Oh, let me see—'Tea for Two'?"

"Very well," I said.

"Tea for Two" was one of my favorites also, one I had worked hard on. I played a chorus through straight, as I thought she would like it. Then I played my own arrangement; or a mixture of several borrowed improvisations might better describe it. I glanced at Mrs. Swann. She was enjoying my second chorus; so I played a third and really let myself go, ending with a little more flourish than was in good taste at the moment.

120

"O-o-oh, Rusty, that sends me," she said, her voice quivering. "It gives me goose pimples."

I was surprised at her expression, but I was also emboldened to try "The Very Thought of You" with similar treatment.

When I finished, Mrs. Swann was standing behind me. Her hands rested lightly on my shoulders.

"I'm so proud of you, Rusty," she said. "Of your being a Highcastle boy." Her voice lowered in pitch. "If I had a son I'm sure he would be like you. He'd have my coloring—your coloring. I would wish he could play piano as well as you do. I'd be so proud of him."

She patted my shoulder and walked around in front of the piano. She watched me gather up my music and rise from the bench. Then she showed me out.

"May I listen again tomorrow?" she asked me at the door.

"Sure," I said. "It'll be the same music, only maybe worse. I'll be playing from memory."

"I can listen to that music for a long, long time," she said. "And I'll have some requests—they'll be different."

She laughed, a pretty, musical laugh, and closed the door behind me.

Mrs. Swann and I became good friends during that week. She always sat patiently through my practice and then requested two or three songs of her own. As the time for my recital approached, she invited a number of her friends, as well as the Jarrells and their friends. She poured coffee at the reception afterwards, and in general made quite an affair of my debut. I regretted not having asked Mama down to hear me play. I felt somewhat guilty in allowing Mrs. Swann to assume so prominent a role. I knew how much she wanted a son like me. It was as though I had betrayed Mama in some way.

Then spring training began. Approaching sixteen, I stood a little over six feet tall and was pushing one hundred and sixty pounds. Coach Wijiecski, who had had a fair season his first year at Highcastle—principally because of an almost impregnable line—started concentrating on his backfield. He almost idolized Captain Hammer, who came regularly to the practice field and criticized and advised when asked to do so, though he seldom volunteered any suggestions directly to the coach. The captain became my chief mentor, however, when Coach Wijiecski started grooming me for his starting fullback. It was he who watched me on every play and made mental notes on everything I did. Then he rehashed each scrimmage with me and coached me on how to improve myself. We went on long, probably unnecessary, drives together and we talked a lot about football at camp that summer.

I forgot to tell Mama about early fall practice that year and so missed my vacation with her and Ella in August. I was disappointed, since two weeks with her was more important to me than an entire football season; but she made it up to me, partially at least, by coming to three of our home games, after I sent her some newspaper clippings extolling me as an athlete.

After our Thanksgiving game, she took me to Indianapolis for three whole days and nights. She was dressed more expensively than she ever had been and attracted more attention and envy than ever when we went to dinner in what seemed to me the most expensive restaurants in town. I was proud of being allowed to squire her about.

One evening we went to the lounge where Dick Jarrell was playing, and he invited us out to his house for Sunday dinner.

"Oh, Rusty, she's beautiful," Linda Jarrell whispered to me when she was hanging up our coats.

"Are you sure this is your mother?" Mrs. Jarrell teased. "I believe she's your girl and you're just fooling us."

I blushed happily. A compliment on Mama meant far more than a compliment on me. I was pleased, of course, when Dick

Jarrell asked me to play for Mama and earnestly conversed with her after I had finished.

"He's good, Mrs. Meaghan," Dick said, "especially as a popular stylist. He can be one of the best—that is, if you don't object."

"I don't object," Mama said. "I want Rusty to do whatever he wants to do. Of course, I want him to be the best." She smiled at me when she spoke.

"We'll keep him on standard literature," Dick went on. "That's still the only way to build a solid foundation, but he'll make a lot more money as a recording artist in the popular field than he would on the concert stage, I believe."

"Whatever he likes," Mama said.

She seemed well pleased with Dick Jarrell, as she had with Captain Hammer, who had sat with her at the football games. She considered that I was in good hands. When she told me so and complimented me on how well I was doing, I swelled with pride. I felt grown up already.

"It won't be long," I said. "I'll be able to take care of you as soon as I'm out of school. I'll work twice as hard on the piano. I'll be as good as Dick Jarrell. Then we can have a house like his. Ella can live with us. I can support both of you."

"Don't push yourself." She laughed, at my enthusiasm I suppose. "I'm getting along all right, and Ella—Ella will be able to take care of herself, I'm sure."

There was no laughter in her voice when she mentioned Ella. I wondered how they had got along during their last vacation together, the one I had missed.

Whatever their relations had been, our Christmas, again spent in Indianapolis, was anything but sparkling. Now I cannot distinguish it from the earlier ones. Ella was, of course, still maturing, and looking more like Mama every time I saw her. At sixteen she was almost an exact image of the first pictures

123

of Mama in my scrapbook. When I returned to school I found myself looking up those old photographs to see if my eyes were deceiving me. They were not. The similarity was disturbing; and for some reason I resented Ella's likeness to Mama, who should have had a monopoly on her own beauty. It was as though Ella were replacing her in some way, usurping her position along with her unique good looks. It all added to the urgency of my development as a pianist.

So I practiced longer hours than ever. Mrs. Swann encouraged me to start practicing on the superintendent's piano several weeks before my second recital. She was with me constantly during those rehearsals, quiet, unobtrusive, helpful. She was especially attentive when I played my own popular arrangements. She seemed to understand what I was doing, as no one else except Dick Jarrell understood. The two of them worked out my recital program, which was divided into two sections—one traditional, the other popular and modern. I was delighted with their plans.

That spring Mama came down for my concert. She was strikingly dressed as usual, and she sat with Mrs. Swann and the Jarrells, all of whom showed a proprietary interest in my performance. I played two Scarlatti sonatas and Beethoven's Opus 14, Sonata in G Major, as the first half of my program.

After an intermission, during which Mama, Mrs. Swann, and Dick Jarrell all retired with me for my rest and complimented and encouraged me, I returned to play Dello Joio's Suite for Piano, which completed my selections from the standard piano literature. I followed that with my own arrangement of "Body and Soul," and a medley made up of "Honeysuckle Rose," "Sweet Sue," and "Dinah." "Laura" and "I Cover the Waterfront" finished my announced program.

The guests, twice as many as had attended the year before, called for more encores than I had time to give. My partisans were aglow all during the reception which followed. Even

124

Coach Wijiecski complimented me, mostly to Mama, to whom he attached himself as soon as my performance was over.

"The boy's got a great future," he said, awkwardly balancing a coffee cup as he stood with Mama and me in the superintendent's dining room. "He'll be just as good on the football field next fall, too, if I'm not mistaken."

"I just hope he doesn't get hurt," Mama said somewhat anxiously.

"Rusty?" The coach snorted. "He's tough as a boot. You can't hurt that boy. If he develops the way I think he will between now and September, nobody'll be able to lay a hand on him."

"I hope not."

"No sir—I mean, no ma'am. If I don't miss my guess, he'll be a great ballplayer—good college material—maybe several years in pro ball."

"Pro ball?" Mama asked.

"Professional football," the coach explained, warming to the subject. "Rusty can make a pot of money in pro ball before he's thirty—if he'll quit fiddling around with that piano."

"Fiddling with a piano, Coach?" Mrs. Swann asked. She had left her station at the coffee urn and joined us. "Aren't you mixing your figures?"

"Mixing my figures?" Coach Wijiecski stared at her blankly. "I figure he's gonna be my number-one ball carrier this season."

"Forget it," Ruby Swann said with a laugh. She touched my arm. "Rusty, I want you to meet more of these people. Won't you come with us, Mrs. Meaghan?"

I was not sure that her words really carried an invitation. Neither was Mama, presumably. She met Mrs. Swann's eyes for a moment before she spoke.

"The room is rather crowded," she said, scanning the mob of guests. "Anyway they're interested in Rusty, not in me."

The coach was interested in her. His eyes were devouring her as I moved off in response to Mrs. Swann's tug on my arm.

I was pleased, however, to see Mama walking toward the chair where Captain Hammer was sitting in the parlor. I doubted that he would recommend a career in pro ball.

Ruby Swann was having her moment. She held onto me and guided me proudly from group to group and basked in the compliments paid me. In all fairness I had to admit that she could justly claim me as her protégé. Recently she had done more to encourage me in my practice than Mama had done; of course for the past three years she had been in a better position to help than Mama had been. And I showed my gratitude as generously as I could. So did Mrs. Swann, as I remember now. She was gracious to Mama after the crowd had left. Perhaps she felt, as I did, that we had cheated Mama of some of her glory. Perhaps Mama felt so, too; and perhaps she understood, for she returned Ruby Swann's cordiality in full measure, if somewhat obviously.

As Mama was leaving, she said, "Rusty, your father has married again. I am taking back my maiden name."

"Then I'll change mine, too," I said. She knew where my loyalties lay.

"No. Meaghan is a better name for you," she said.

"Why?" I asked.

"It just is. You'll see. In time you'll understand. Bercelli is not for you—not with that hair." She laughed, courageously but unconvincingly.

In a moment she had kissed me and was gone. I had not even asked whom Daddy had married. I did not really care. Now Mama was completely free from him—fully released. She was all mine. I was elated by the prospect. The reception given my recital further lifted my spirits. It would not be long until I could take over as the man of the family.

Ella gave me a fuller account of Daddy's marriage as related to her by Gina.

126

So at last we have a Texas millionaire for a father [Ella wrote]. He has married a burlesque queen he knew in the old days. She is the recent widow of a big trucker down in Dallas—the Petroleum Rapid Transit Company or something like that, whatever it means.

Anyway, Daddy met her in Las Vegas, where he and Gina were playing, and swept her off her feet as only Daddy can sweep. He's quitting show business. He will manage Cassie's (that's her name) business for her. He ought to make a wonderful manager—you know how well he gets along with people, how everybody loves him.

But, Rusty, Cassie is a blonde—phony, I'll bet—and I can't see Daddy in love with a blonde, can you? He loved Mama. You know that. And she's as brunette as they come, just like me. I'm sure he married Cassie for her money, aren't you? He couldn't possibly be interested in her for herself. Opposites attract, you know.

Gina is finishing her engagement in Vegas. I suppose she'll go to Daddy afterwards, now that he has a home—a palace, according to Gina, according to Cassie—in Dallas. I think I will, too, next year, or at least the next, as soon as I finish school here.

How about you? Daddy can give us all the things he ever promised us, not that I care. We can all be together again—all except Mama. Maybe Cassie will adopt Mama, too. Hah!

Bye-bye, you lucky old rich man's son.

Love,
ELLA

Ella should have known better. The last thing I ever intended to do was to live with Daddy, no matter how rich he was. I agreed that his marrying a washed-out blonde burlesque stripper was the ultimate insult to Mama, but it was just like him—typical of his clownish stupidity. Of course he had mar-

127

ried the woman for her money. I hoped she had enough to
keep him forever.

I dismissed my millionaire father and settled down to spring
training for my last season of academy football. We lost our
best quarterback. We still had a smart field general but a rela-
tively weak ball handler; so, probably at Captain Hammer's
suggestion, the coach switched to the single wing that spring
and shifted me to left halfback in the tailback slot. His new
backfield began clicking at once.

Sports fans will remember Highcastle's 1949 season. Others
will not be interested in the details. We defeated Staunton,
Culver, Kemper, Wentworth, Gulf Coast, and our other oppo-
nents by heavily one-sided scores. The big-time sports writers
began taking notice of us early in the season and were soon
giving us more space than they gave minor college teams. I
was repeatedly referred to as a junior Choo Choo Justice. I
could run, I could pass, and I could kick. Coach Wijiecski all
but fawned on me, and he very nearly worked me to death.
Captain Hammer sat on the bench beside him all that season.
I am sure that but for the captain's presence there the coach
would have given me the ball on every play.

Fortunately I could take it. At seventeen I had reached my
full height and weighed a hundred and eighty pounds. But all
I remember is four months of cold ground and sweaty dressing
rooms. I became something of a killer—that was the way the
coach had referred to Captain Hammer—and I think my sole
drive was the determination to vindicate the captain's estimate
of me and to make him proud of me.

I had not included Daddy in my reckoning, though I should
have. Our last game, the Thanksgiving game with Salisbury,
attracted the largest crowd ever to assemble at Highcastle.
Temporary stands had to be erected to accommodate the spec-

128

tators. Daddy, of course, reserved a box. He and Cassie drove up from Texas and stopped by St. Louis to pick up Ella. They stayed in Indianapolis but drove down to Highcastle the Wednesday afternoon before Thanksgiving.

We were having our last light scrimmage before the final game, and Salisbury was strong enough to keep us from becoming overconfident and to warrant the coach's keeping our scrimmage secret. So, although we were concentrating on our practice, we could not help noticing the big yellow Cadillac drive up to the end of the playing field and wondering what big shot had been able to break through Coach Wijiecski's security lines. Nor could we make out any of the features of the four people who got out of the automobile and climbed up into the stands. Two were women bundled up in furs. Two were men in heavy overcoats and white stockman's hats.

Pop Horner came up to the team when we knocked off practice and gathered around the coach for a few final criticisms before we headed for the showers.

"Someone to see you, Rusty," Pop said. "You, too, Coach, if you can spare a minute or two."

"O.K.," the coach said. He could not help being impressed by our visitors.

Of course, I had guessed who it was by that time and I had hoped the coach would say no. But we started toward the stands when he dismissed the team.

Ella clambered down the bleachers and ran to me. She kissed me and hung onto my neck.

"Hi, Rusty," she said softly. "Ain't we the rich bitches? Cassie and I? Just feel this coat Daddy brought me. It's from Neiman's."

By that time the others had reached us.

"My sister, Ella," I said to the coach. "And my—my father. Coach Wijiecski."

"Pleased to meet you both," Coach Wijiecski said, extending a hand to Daddy.

"Mrs. Meaghan," Daddy said, indicating Cassie, "and Jack Hilliard, a scout for Southern Methodist University. Coach Wijiecski. We've come to claim our boy."

They all shook hands and mumbled greetings.

Then Daddy turned to me.

"Hello, Rusty. Long time, no see. How are yuh, son?" He was probably oblivious to the limpness of my handshake. I was surprised at his manner of speech. It was more drawly than that of the toughest hombre ever to shoot up the town of Muleshoe. I had forgotten that he was a first-rate mimic—Irish, Dutch, Yiddish, Swedish, and now Texan. I thought he was kidding.

"All right, I guess." I laughed, out of courtesy. He always worked for laughs.

"Wal, yuh shore look it, boy." He continued to pump my arm. "How much do yuh weigh?"

"A hundred and seventy-six, this morning," I said. That was about seventy pounds less than he weighed, if his bulk had any muscle at all in it. I was as tall as he was even in the fancy high-heeled boots he wore.

"Meet yore new mama," he said and turned me over to Cassie.

"So you're Rusty," she trilled. "My, you are a big boy, aren't you?" She was exactly what I had expected.

"How do you do, Mrs. Meaghan," I said.

"And this is Jack Hilliard," Daddy boomed. "My son, Rusty."

"Hello, Rusty." Jack Hilliard was dressed like Daddy but he sounded less Texan.

"Hello," I said. I tensed my muscles when I shook his hand. He sized me up shrewdly.

"We're expectin' great things from yuh tomorrow, Rusty," Daddy said. "And then a lot more down at SMU, eh, Jack?" He pronounced it *smu,* like a word.

130

Daddy tried to wink me into his conspiracy. I evaded his puffy eyes. I looked down at Ella instead. She had edged back to me and was hanging onto my arm. I was grateful for her reassuring smile.

"We'll walk up to the gym with yuh, Coach," Daddy said. "We'll have a lot to say to yuh and Rusty after tomorrow's game."

He dropped into step beside the coach. Jack Hilliard and Cassie walked with them. Ella and I lagged a few steps behind.

"Isn't Daddy realer than the real thing, Rusty?" she said admiringly. "Ol' Tex Meaghan they called him in them days."

"Yeah," I said. Daddy had not dropped his new dialect for one second.

"He'll own Dallas by the time we get to SMU," Ella said.

"He'll own all of Texas by the time I get to SMU." I must have sounded disgusted.

"Don't be like that, Rusty." Ella squeezed my arm. "Of course we're going to SMU. I'm going into pre-law, and you'll be the sensation of the Southwest Conference. I've heard them talking all the way from St. Louis."

"Them?"

"Daddy and Jack Hilliard. We all know that you can pick your college, but wait until you hear Daddy's offer. Everything you want. Your own car, all the money you can spend. Everything. And it will all be legal. After all, Ol' Tex is your father. Nobody can object to his spoiling his own son."

"I can," I said.

"You should hear him talk about you. You've no idea how proud he is of you. Oh, Rusty, it would mean a lot to Daddy to have you running wild in the Southwest Conference."

"Yeah, I'll bet."

"Really. You're all-American material. Jack Hilliard says so, and Daddy agrees with him. They're serious. Please, Rusty, do it for Daddy." Ella caught on fast.

131

By that time we had reached the gymnasium. We stopped in an awkward sort of huddle.

"Well, Mr. Meaghan, Rusty is my boy until game time," the coach said genially. "See you tomorrow."

"Shore thing," Daddy said and slapped the coach jovially on the back. He had probably promised Wijiecski the head coach's job at SMU if we would come down together. And the coach probably believed him. Daddy could be persuasive.

Ella hugged me again and all my guests were noisy in their good-bys.

"Have you got a professional picture of your sister, Rusty?" one of the die-hards asked as I entered the locker room.

I swung on him, but two of my friends grabbed my arm before I connected.

"None of that," one of them said. "We can't be efficient in battle if there is fighting within the ranks."

We laughed at his impersonation of Major Swann and began to strip down for our showers.

I lay awake for a long time that night, tossing and seething with resentment at the way Daddy had moved in on me at Highcastle. He had obviously impressed everyone with his show of affluence and his big talk about SMU. But it had been Mama who had sent me to Highcastle and kept me there. I hated to see Daddy and his entourage outshine her the next day. I considered telephoning her and warning her of what to expect when she came down, but it was so late that I hated to disturb her.

I had underestimated Mama, however. She came down to have Thanksgiving dinner at the academy, and she came in style—in a black Cadillac limousine driven by a wiry little uniformed chauffeur named Rocco, who opened doors for her and saluted her as though she were queen of something. She looked the part, too, as smartly groomed as the Duchess of Windsor and swathed in a sable coat that made Cassie and Ella look

132

positively dowdy. At the game she sat with Major and Mrs. Swann, in the superintendent's box. That left no doubt as to whose son I was. I was proud of her, so proud that tears came into my eyes when I vowed to myself that I would find out how much it had cost her to rent her coat and rig, and repay the sum a hundred times over.

It was for her that I played that Thursday afternoon. The game was a classic which Highcastle alumni will be recounting until the last one of them is blasted into eternity by an ICBM. Salisbury was the strongest team we met that season, but their strength served merely to make us look good; and Coach Wijiecski, probably striking for the job at SMU, had the quarterback feed the ball to me every time there was a possibility of a spectacular play. It was almost as though the entire game had been rigged to make me a hero. Certainly it gave Daddy something to brag about until spring. I think by May he was telling his Dallas friends that I had been born in Texas.

He was really high that week end. He threw a big party at the Lincoln for me and Coach Wijiecski. He invited Mama, of course, and Major and Mrs. Swann. I insisted on the Jarrells; so there were a dozen people at his table Friday evening. We had a long, champagne-drenched dinner, followed by dancing and then a determined effort to close up all of the night spots in Indianapolis.

Throughout it all Daddy kept up his pose. He let nothing drop that would indicate that he had ever been anything except a big truck operator from Texas. There was no hint of his circus-burlesque background. When he learned that Coach Wijiecski and Major Swann were planning to go up to Fort Wayne and Toledo to do some recruiting over Saturday and Sunday, he pointed out the futility of their returning to Highcastle and called back to the hotel to reserve another suite for them.

133

"The best yuh've got," he said magnanimously through the telephone which the waiter plugged in at our table.

"We really should go home," Major Swann objected. "I should drive Ruby—Mrs. Swann—home. We'll be driving the coach's car upstate."

"We'll run Ruby down there in the morning," Daddy said.

"Rusty can drive me home tomorrow," Mrs. Swann suggested. "We have two cars here."

"Shore," Daddy agreed. "Rusty can drive Ruby home. Now y'all jest relax and we'll all have beds awaitin' fer us when they run us outa this joint. It's all settled." He waved his hand, dismissing any further objection.

I could not be sure whether Ella's admiration was genuine or not. There was no doubt about Cassie's. She adored Daddy. Her first, or immediately preceding, husband had not known what to do with his money. Daddy did know, and she heartily approved.

Mama was positively regal. Impotent rage, inexpressible disgust, or perhaps native reserve kept her serene and aloof from all that was going on around her. From a great height she smiled at us and at the waiters. As Cassie, Ruby Swann to a lesser degree, and even Ella began coming apart sometime before dawn, Mama still looked as fresh and well-groomed as she had when she sat down to dinner. I kept my composure, too, as befitted her escort, and I was glad when we closed the last night club and got back into the Cadillacs—Daddy, of course, having commandeered Mama's limousine and chauffeur to help keep his party mobile.

"I'm not going to SMU," I assured Mama when I sat back beside her in her car. We were driving the Jarrells home.

"Go anywhere you like, Rusty," she said. "I can send you. I, too, can afford the best now." Her voice was soft—either tired or restrained.

"Rusty can go just about anywhere he wants to on his own,

134

if those athletes know what they're talking about," Dick Jarrell said.

"How many athletic scholarships does Juilliard offer?" I asked. Dick Jarrell laughed.

"You can get in there O.K.," he said. "Or if you want to play football at SMU, Van Katwijk is still there, and some good stylists play the clubs in Dallas. Red Camp lives somewhere down in Texas. He's worth listening to."

"Where do you think he should go, Mr. Jarrell?" Mama asked.

"Anywhere, so long as there is a piano on the campus. Ask Captain Hammer. He seems to be a wise Joe."

"That is a good idea," Mama said. "But, make up your own mind, Rusty. I'll see you through." She patted my hand reassuringly.

"I'll think about it," I said.

We let the Jarrells out, and Rocco drove us back to the hotel. He too was still calm and courteous at five o'clock in the morning. He was worth whatever he was costing Mama.

"I'll want the car about noon," Mama said to him when he let us out at the hotel.

"*Si, signora*," he said. "*Buona notte*."

"Good night, Rocco."

I hoped Mama would let me stay with her, but at her door she kissed me good night and said, "Breakfast about eleven?"

"All right," I said. "Good night."

I was tired. An evening with Daddy was more strenuous than the Thanksgiving game had been. I had only time enough to leave a call for ten-thirty before falling asleep.

Mama called me about the time I closed my eyes, or so it seemed.

"Time to get up, Rusty," she said.

"It can't be," I said.

"Oh, but it is. Breakfast in half an hour."

The operator called again as soon as I hung up. It really was ten-thirty. I dressed hurriedly and went by to pick up Mama. She was already dressed and packed for her trip back to Chicago.

"Let me go with you," I urged.

"You have to drive Mrs. Swann back to Highcastle. Remember?"

"That's right. I had forgotten. But, sometime, can't I come to visit you? I'd like to see where you live and how you live." She had never told Ella and me very much about Chicago.

"It doesn't matter where I live or how I live, Rusty," she said as we walked toward the elevator. "It's why I live—I live for you. Remember that."

"I will," I said. "Can you really afford to keep me in school?"

"Certainly. I have my own cosmetic shop now and I've added a model agency. I learned a lot at Ayres."

I wanted to cry. The closeness of Mama in the elevator, her perfume, brought back those good days when she and Ella and I lived together, played together, tumbled together. I ached to go through the old routines, with Mama and Ella in leotards, lithe and graceful and firm to hold. I was big enough and strong enough now to be understander on a four-high stand. Why had we ever left the circus?

The coffee shop was almost deserted at eleven. Mama and I had a table to ourselves, off in a corner. Our breakfast was over entirely too soon. We met Daddy and his Texans in the lobby. All except Ella looked horrible in daylight, and I was glad that we did not have to eat with them.

"When are you leaving, Nestra?" Daddy asked. His voice was subdued.

"As soon as I get my bags and Rocco brings the car around. When are you leaving?"

"About the same time. Well, it was nice seeing you." He lost some of his Texas accent.

Mama said good-by to the others and we turned to leave.

"You'll be hearing from us, Rusty," Daddy said. He must have sensed that I would not see him again if I could help it. "It'll be official, too, with the SMU seal on it."

"O.K.," I said.

Ella hugged me impulsively and whispered in my ear, "Do what Daddy wants. It will mean so much to him—to all of us. Take care of us, Rusty. Please."

She kissed me on my mouth and hurried after Daddy into the coffee shop.

I saw Mama off and then called Mrs. Swann on a house telephone.

"Hello, Rusty," she said brightly. "I've had breakfast in my room. I'll be down in a minute. Have my car sent around."

I ordered the car and practically hid from Daddy's crowd until I saw Mrs. Swann come out of the elevator. She was dressed in a green wool suit and a green hat. She carried her coat. A bellboy followed with her bag.

"I hope I got everything out of your mother's room," she said. "I changed there last night, you know, before your father rented the bridal suite for us."

She laughed. She too sensed my lack of regard for Daddy.

"Did the major get off all right?" I asked.

"I suppose so, at some ungodly hour. I didn't wake up. I doubt that he and Coach Wijiecski slept two hours. How did you sleep?"

"I died."

"So did I. Well, I'm glad I'm alive again. Isn't this a lovely day?"

It was indeed, crisp and clear, with almost no wind. The porter stowed our bags, and I helped Mrs. Swann into the car. It was a Buick belonging to the academy but it did not have

137

the Highcastle crest emblazoned on its doors, as did the station wagon which the coach usually drove.

I started the engine and pulled out into traffic. Mrs. Swann sighed as she sank back into the seat beside me.

"Highcastle will be deserted," she said. "I don't think there's a soul on the place."

"I guess not," I said.

"Let's not go there," she said abruptly. "I have an aunt in Cincinnati. It's such a beautiful day to drive, let's go visit her."

"Sure, Mrs. Swann. Anything you say."

"Take Highway 52. There's a sign."

I followed the signs out of town and then picked up cruising speed. I liked driving the Buick. And I liked talking to Mrs. Swann. She talked about my music—I had heard enough football to last me until spring.

"Will you go to SMU, Rusty?" she asked after a lull.

"No."

"You sound rather positive. I gather that your father will make it quite attractive." She looked at me sidewise.

"He couldn't make it attractive enough."

"Well, I'm glad. I hope you stay nearer here—go to Indiana or Illinois. I'd like to see you play—and to hear you play occasionally. You know we become quite attached to Highcastle boys in four years. We hate to lose them—especially outstanding ones like you."

I suppose I blushed. Anyway she laughed at something.

We reached the outskirts of Cincinnati in an hour and a half.

"Pull over to that drugstore," she said. "I'll call my aunt from here."

I stopped and let her out.

"I'll be right back," she said.

She disappeared into the drugstore and was gone five minutes or so.

She was frowning when she returned.

138

"There's nobody home," she said when I got out to open the car door for her.

"Well, it was a nice drive anyway," I said.

"Yes, wasn't it? I suppose we can start back."

I made a U-turn and started back out Highway 52.

"Rusty, let's rest a while before we drive back. I had a hard night."

"Didn't we all?" I laughed. "Where shall we go?"

"There—that looks like a nice place."

She pointed to a luxurious new motel on the north side of the highway. I drove up to the office and started to get out.

"I'll register," Mrs. Swann said. "This is my party."

I felt something less than manly, but I let her go into the office and register. She returned in a few minutes with a key in her hand.

"Number twenty-two," she said. "It's this way. The help is off right now."

I drove to number twenty-two and parked the Buick in a carport.

"I'll need a bag," Mrs. Swann said.

She unlocked the door while I got her bag for her. The apartment was bright and new, with wall-to-wall carpets and indirect lighting.

"Thanks," she said when I put the bag on a rack. "Your room is through the bathroom. I hope you don't mind."

"Not at all," I said. Actually I felt that I could use an hour or two of sleep.

I went through the bathroom and closed the door behind me. I took off my coat and tie and shoes and dropped onto the bed. It felt good. I dozed off immediately; but I could not have slept very long before I was awakened by a knock on the bathroom door.

"Rusty," Mrs. Swann called. "Rusty, you aren't asleep already, are you?"

139

"Just dozing," I said.

"May I come in?"

"Sure." I sat up on the bed and then stood up when she came into the room.

She had changed into house slippers and a brown silk robe. She still wore make-up, or she had put on fresh lipstick. Her bee-stung lips looked redder than ever.

"Do you sleep with your clothes on?" she asked, a little nervously.

"In the daytime."

"Well, sit back down." She sat in a chair by the bed. I sat down on the bed.

"Rusty, your mother is delightful," she said.

"Thank you."

"And I envy her so much—I mean having a son like you—looking after you as a little boy, and nursing you when you were ill, and bathing you and putting you to bed." She smiled and then her lips pouted thoughtfully as she looked at me.

"My most cherished memories go back to my own childhood," she continued, "when Daddy would take me on his lap and undress me for bed."

She was getting close to home. I had such memories, too—dear, precious ones.

"We'd sit before the fire and make a ritual of it." Her voice was low, her eyes almost closed but focused on my face and neck and open collar. "I've missed it. I miss it now—there's no intimacy, no real family ritual in my home." Her words were suddenly rapid, urgent, tinged with bitterness. Her eyes opened wide, too, and met mine boldly as though they had just discovered something.

"Rusty—" She hesitated and then went on. "Rusty, may I undress you and put you to bed? I've never had a son of my own."

140

"Uh—uh, sure," I said, and I know that I blushed that time. "But I'm kind of ticklish." I laughed, or tried to.

My consent brought her to my side immediately. She unbuttoned my shirt, slowly, carefully, and took it off and hung it in the closet.

Next she pulled my T shirt off over my head, caressing my back and shoulders as she eased the sleeves down off my arms.

"Stand up, baby," she said gravely.

I stood up. In her slippers she barely came to my shoulders, her red hair just high enough to perfume my nostrils.

Still taking her time, she unbuckled my belt and unzipped my fly. I sat down, in embarrassment, so she could draw my trousers off over my feet. Again she folded the garments meticulously and hung them in my closet.

"Up," she said and looked into my eyes as she returned to the bed.

Hypnotized, I obeyed her. She ran her hands around my waist and pressed her body against mine before she fingered the grippers on my shorts. By that time it had become apparent that she was not going to put me to bed.

Someone was going to *take* someone to bed in a matter of seconds. As my shorts dropped to the floor Mrs. Swann gasped and slid her own robe off her shoulders and dropped it beside them.

She wore nothing under the robe. I looked down for one quick glimpse of her straining breasts and erect pink nipples before they began boring into my chest as she eased her arms under mine and hugged me to her.

"Oh, Rusty," she said, drawing the *s* out into a long sigh. "Rusty, baby."

She relaxed her grip and struggled to get her arms around my neck. I lifted her clear of the floor as my mouth found hers. At first her lips were open, her tongue sweet and busy. Then she drew back.

141

"Bite me, Rusty, bite me!" she said and forced her closed lips between my teeth. I needed no urging.

"Hm-m-m," she moaned and pulled away again slowly after long contact.

"Now, Rusty, now!" she said.

I swiveled around and laid her on the bed. I was awkward, I suppose.

"I'll help you Rusty, I'll show you how," she said eagerly.

And she did help, beautifully, wonderfully.

"Quick, Rusty. Quick this time. You're young. We'll have it lots of times, but quick this time. Quick! Now! Now!" Her voice was hoarse, still a mere whisper, but an urgent, vibrant whisper.

I was quick, too quick it seemed from all I had heard; but I was gloriously satisfied, and satisfying, if I could judge by her sob of release. I had heard such a sob only once before in my life. It all came back to me in an instant. Now I knew what it meant.

We were both reluctant to break our embrace, but as our brief violent passion subsided we gradually relaxed and lay back side by side.

"Rusty," she said softly. "It was just right, just perfect. You've given me something you can never give another woman. At least I think you have. Do you know what I mean?"

"I guess so."

"I mean I'm so glad that I was your first. I wish you had been my first—or someone very much like you, when I was your age. Maybe I've robbed you."

"You haven't robbed me," I said. I was beginning to feel guilty, but I could not have wished that she had been a virgin my age. "You've—you've—"

"Don't even try to say it. Whatever it is, you can't say it. I understand."

Her voice was soft and low, but there was no huskiness in it.

142

It had a lyrical, flutelike quality in all registers, from its present tone of intimacy to its trilling soprano laugh. I have detected the same timbre in the voices of other women like Ruby Swann. It always excites me, promises me quick ecstasy if I dare follow it.

"People—your mother—might say I have wronged you, Rusty; but I haven't," she went on. "Believe me, I haven't. If I had a son I think I would want some mature woman to do for him just what I've done for you—what I couldn't do for my own son —not let him spoil his—his debut, shall we say?—by fumbling with some awkward, frightened little girl. Say you believe me, Rusty."

"I believe you," I said. I did believe her. I saw that people might very well be mistaken in their mores.

"We're properly matched, baby, according to the physiologists. A woman is at her best at my age and a little older, and a man from eighteen to twenty—a biological throwback to some primitive time, socially different from ours, when mothers did initiate their sons and so bring renewed vigor into the tribe. Does that sound offensive to you, Rusty?"

"No," I said. The talk was strange but not offensive. It was all new, as new as my experience with Ruby Swann. I had never discussed such things with adults, certainly not with a woman who was so learned in such matters as she seemed to be.

"I'm glad," she said. "I hope I never offend you, Rusty. You're so sweet to let me do as I wish—silly things, like undressing you and—and counting your freckles. May I count your freckles, baby?" She had raised up on one elbow and laid her bosom across my chest. She stared at the bridge of my nose.

"I guess so," I said. "Remember, I'm ticklish."

"Not on your nose."

"No."

"Then I'll count."

She pecked at me with the tip of a bright lacquered fingernail as she counted.

"One, two, three, four, five, six, seven, eight, nine, ten—I must kiss you on every tenth freckle."

She kissed the side of my nose, then my cheek, all around my chin—birdlike kisses—and finally smothered my lips with her moist open mouth.

"Hm-m-m, I hope you have a million freckles." She chuckled contentedly and continued, "Eleven, twelve, thirteen—"

I wished for a million freckles, too, but not at one uninterrupted tabulation. At fifty, she whispered, "Bite me, baby," and forced her pouting lips between my teeth again.

"Be quick this time, too, Rusty," she urged.

I was quick again—and again—and again, until we finally dozed off in sheer exhaustion. When we awoke it was dark.

"Hungry, baby?" she asked.

"Yes, I guess so."

"Then let's get dressed and find a place to eat."

"O.K."

She petted me languidly for a few minutes and then went into the bathroom, dragging her robe behind her. I heard her singing in her shower. She sang well. I thought how nice it would be if she became a singer and we toured together. But that did not fit into my plans for Mama; so I dismissed the idea at once. My guilty feeling returned as I bathed and dressed. It all but rooted out my regret at seeing our excursion come to an end.

We ate at the restaurant in the motel.

"No one would ever guess that you are not my son, Rusty," Mrs. Swann said after we had ordered. "I was so proud to have you escort me through the dining room. You know I was right jealous of your mother last night when you were squiring her about. How I envied her!"

144

I made no comment.

"But not any more. You're more like me—like my family. I was a Murphy. I too had a big redheaded Irishman for a father."

I frowned at that.

"Oh, Rusty, you don't have to be loyal to your father on my account. I understand. Broken homes leave their scars.

"Don't let him lure you down to SMU. Go to Indiana. Bloomington is less than twenty miles from Highcastle. You could visit us. We—I could come down there to see you—to the football games. You'll get an offer from Indiana. I'm sure of it. The major—and Captain Hammer—will see to it if you want to. Won't you consider it?"

"I'll think about it," I said.

Our food arrived then. I did not have to pursue the conversation further. But Ruby Swann did.

"Indiana has a fine music school. And you could keep on with Mr. Jarrell."

My mouth was full. It would have been impolite to talk.

I assumed that we would return to Highcastle after dinner. I was wrong.

Back in our apartment Mrs. Swann stopped me in her room.

"Let's play in here this time," she said, "and let's change the game. You be Daddy and I'll be little Ruby. You undress me." She kicked off her shoes and spread her arms for me to take off her suit.

Standing in her stocking feet before me she did look like a little girl, a very fetching one, with her pouty little mouth puckered up in anticipation of our game. It is amazing how fleeting guilt can be in such circumstances.

Somewhat clumsily, I am afraid, I unbuttoned her coat and blouse and unzipped the placket in her skirt. I helped her off with the garments and, taking my cue from her, I hung them

145

neatly in her closet. She was standing in the center of the room, in her slip, when I returned. I paused before attempting to remove it.

"You take little girls on your lap to undress them," she said teasingly. "Didn't you know that?"

"No." I said.

"No, what?"

"No what?" I repeated, puzzled.

"No, Ruby."

"No, Ruby." I liked the game. I would play it her way.

I sank into an easy chair and drew her down on my knees. She put her arms around my neck and kissed me, tight-lipped, as Mama or Ella or Gina might have done.

"My stockings first," Ruby said, sticking her legs out stiff and wiggling her toes.

I raised her slip until the tops of her stockings and the clasps on her garter belt showed. I fumbled with the clasps, my fingers big and awkward. Ruby offered no help, just smiled in amusement at my inexperience. The task was not impossible, of course. I undid the clasps in time.

"Roll them," she commanded when I started on her stockings. "Slowly, carefully. They're quite sheer."

I could feel the satin-smooth flesh of her thighs rise into goose pimples under my palms as I rolled the stocking into a soft ring around her leg. I took my time, slowly, carefully, as she had instructed me. I did an even slower, more careful job on the second stocking.

Then I lifted her slip off over her head and, again with vocal instructions but no help, I unfastened her garter belt and slipped it out through the waistband of her panties. Her breathing became heavy and irregular as I caressed her bare body and removed her brassière, for which she really had no need, because her breasts supported themselves proudly and firmly. It was the first opportunity I had had to explore those beauties

146

under optimum conditions. I made the most of it, though I found myself rushing to finish my fatherly task of undressing Ruby.

"Quick, again, just this once," she said, breaking the rules of our game in her impatience, "and then we'll play any way you want to after this."

I was always quick to learn—at tumbling, at football, at anything physical. I gained experience rapidly that night. After a time I was even able to take a somewhat detached view of what I was doing. I remembered Major Swann, the way he had looked at Mama and at her picture.

"This one is for you, Major," I said to myself sometime after midnight, and proceeded to avenge myself upon him with all the force I could muster. I think I succeeded in full measure.

"Thank you, Rusty," Ruby said and relaxed with a long contented sigh. "Now I can sleep forever."

We slept, not forever, but until mid-morning and then drove back to Highcastle. The place was still deserted. I delivered Ruby Swann to the superintendent's house and carried her bag inside for her quite decorously. Again I was the courteous cadet and she the major's wife. We behaved exactly as if I had merely driven her home from Indianapolis.

After I parked her car in the garage I returned to my barracks, to my piano. I could not concentrate. I noodled around for a while and then started practicing exercises from Hanon's *Virtuoso Pianist*. Once I set the pattern of an exercise, I could trust muscle memory to see that my fingers repeated it endlessly, running up the keyboard until they touched wood and then down through the bass to wood again. My mind was free to wander, to roam, to speculate, to remember, while my hands perfected the dexterity which would one day enable me to claim Mama again and find the peace Daddy had blasted when he stole Gina from us.

There was an unprecedented round of banquets and honors

147

functions after the football season ended. I made every sports writer's all-American academy team. The festivities lasted through the Christmas holidays, depriving me of another vacation with Mama. She, of course, was invited to some of the dinners and attended two, but I had little time with her. Fortunately Daddy was unable to attend any, but he never relaxed the pressure on me to attend SMU, nor did Ella.

Even Gina wrote me one of her rare letters. Before opening it I assumed that she would be putting in a word on Daddy's behalf. She did not even mention football, however. Instead she wrote that she was getting married.

> He's a pianist, Rusty [her letter said], not a very good one—no better than you were when I last heard you play, not nearly so good as you must be now. But he's kind and unselfish, and he adores me. The important thing is that I love him. I'm sure that I always will.

That was important. Gina could love wholeheartedly. Maybe she was the only one of us kids who could. She went on to exhort me to keyboard excellence and to make my success as a pianist seem like the most important thing in the world. But hers was about the only nonathletic correspondence I received during my months of indecision.

I had offers of scholarships from almost everywhere, including Indiana. I suppose I appeared to be a very stubborn holdout. Actually I could not make up my mind. I was able to do good work on my piano during the second semester. I did not play a recital that spring, however. Since it might be my last time to study with Dick Jarrell, I urged him to teach me all he could about modern styling, to help me analyze the work of such newcomers as Erroll Garner and Dave Brubeck, to coach me on improvisation rather than prepare me for a concert.

I never mentioned a recital to Mrs. Swann, and she did not press me. I seldom saw her, and when I did I was afraid to look at her very closely for fear I might betray us by some gesture or expression. Perhaps that was why I did not want to give a concert. I doubt that I could have practiced on her piano very many days without precipitating some sort of crisis. Anyway I dared not risk it.

When spring training began, I was back in the news again. Some writers were positive that I would go to SMU. Others saw me staying in the Midwest. A few showed signs of impatience with my behavior and wrote somewhat acidly about my high opinion of myself.

"God, Mother, and Football, Rusty," Captain Hammer said to me. "You can't trifle with that holy trinity and be an all-American. You'll be branded a subversive if you don't make up your mind pretty soon."

But he smiled indulgently behind his stubby pipe and never once tried to sway me. I think he wanted me to go to OU, and he held my first loyalty as far as football was concerned. I suppose I had leaned toward his school all along.

I still had reached no decision when I was invited to appear on Johnny Fox's television program, "Youth Parade," in Chicago. I accepted the invitation—otherwise I would certainly have been dubbed un-American. Daddy, of course, heard about it and he and Cassie and Ella and an influential SMU alumnus picked me up and drove me to Chicago. We took a suite at the Ambassador, though I would have much preferred to stay with Mama.

As it was, I got off Daddy's rowdy merry-go-round only long enough to have lunch with her.

"If you think he can do more for you than I can, go with

him," Mama said. It took an effort for her to say that. Her voice was strained, her face tense, as she spoke.

"That's the last thing I'll do," I assured her.

"But if he ruins you as he has ruined Gina—it will break my heart. And—and I'll break him." She had never spoken so viciously before.

"Ruined Gina?" I asked.

"Ruined her career. She's married, as you know, to a musician. She may be happy—but she'll never amount to anything professionally. And she had such talent, she could have been our diva."

That was Avolo speaking. Mama felt that she had let him— all the Bercellis—down. Hers was the unforgivable sin, by Sicilian family standards. She was quiet after that, for the few more minutes we had together. She gripped my hand tightly under the table.

I did not see her again until I appeared before the television camera with Johnny Fox.

"Folks, now is the time you should wish for color TV," Johnny Fox said as the camera moved in on us. "You ought to see this guy's hair! I give you Rusty Meaghan, all-American halfback from Highcastle!"

The brass sounded an impressive fanfare, and the orchestra played one chorus of "Highcastle to the Fore."

Johnny's enthusiasm was matched by the applause of the studio audience, a roomful of teen-agers, adults with teen-age mentalities—and Mama. Daddy's gang was prominently seated down front, as was to be expected, but it was several seconds before I located Mama, a few rows back on the right aisle. She was dressed in black and wore a smart little black hat. She stood out incongruously among the others. I thought she looked small, alone—and aloof even in the crowded theater.

"If you could see the color of this hair you'd call him Rusty, too, on first sight," Johnny Fox said. He reached up and play-

150

fully tried to rumple my hair. Although I had had my crew-cut modified somewhat after the close of the football season, my hair was still rumple-proof.

"Well, Rusty, how does it feel to be an all-American?" he asked.

"All right, I guess." I suppose I was the perfect picture of a mute football hero as I stood before the camera, awkward, embarrassed, ill at ease. It was no pose with me. Maybe such characters are real, after all.

"Do you like football, Rusty?" he asked and then mugged idiotically at the camera as though he had asked the most inane question ever heard on television.

"I guess so."

"He guesses so, folks!" Johnny exaggerated his reaction to what he considered my understatement of the year. "He guesses so! Well, Rusty, we guess so, too—those of us who have seen you run wild on the old gridiron. Now, Rusty, what do you consider your greatest thrill in football?"

"I don't know," I said. "I hadn't thought about it."

"He hasn't thought about it! Isn't this guy a character, folks?"

I followed his eyes to the monitor and saw that one of the cameras was panning the audience. They thought I was a character. I glimpsed Mama briefly before the camera swung back and focused on the Texas delegation.

Johnny Fox nudged me just before the red light on the nearest camera came on again.

"Or maybe it's all thrilling to you, Rusty. Is that it?"

"I guess so, sir."

"Sir?" He looked into the camera. "There's a cadet for you, folks. Just call me Johnny." He mugged again and the audience howled at "Just call me Johnny," which was his nationally famous tag line.

"How about that eighty-yard run against Staunton, Rusty? Or the twenty-two-yard field goal against Kemper?"

151

As he rattled off the high points in my career, I followed his eyes again. He was reading the statistics from an idiot board. I took time to pan the audience myself. Daddy was beaming. He looked significantly at his partners in the SMU conspiracy every time Johnny read one of my feats of last season. Cassie and Ella were eating up everything the announcer said. They looked at me each time and continually tried to catch my eye. I could see them all in the stands in the Cotton Bowl or Longhorn Stadium, with dozens more like them. Even if I went to OU, we would play Texas in the Cotton Bowl. Daddy would pop with pride every time I gained a yard.

Mama seemed to shrink smaller than ever, lonelier than ever. I ached as I thought of four years in college, and two more in military service, probably—six long years before I could return to her, comfort her, care for her, love her, prove to her that she was not alone.

"And his parents are right here in the studio audience," Johnny was saying. "Let's have a look at them. Right down here in front—Mr. and Mrs. Al Meaghan, from Texas!"

I glanced at the monitor. It showed a close-up of Daddy and Cassie. Cassie wore her professional smile and Daddy clasped his hands above his head in congratulation to somebody. He grinned broadly above the cowboy shirt and string tie he was affecting at the moment. He stood up and faced the audience. They roared and clapped their hands.

When the studio quieted down, Johnny Fox faced me again. He spoke to me confidentially—in front of the cameras.

"Rusty," he said, "this is our chance to scoop everybody. You say you haven't thought about your thrills last season. Have you thought about where you're going to play this fall?"

"Yes, Johnny," I said.

"Have you made up your mind?"

"Yes." My reply startled him momentarily.

152

"You have? Well, how would you like to tell our studio audience—all the world—what you've decided?"

"I'd be glad to," I said. Again I threw him off balance. I guess I was playing him the same way Captain Hammer had taught me to play football.

Gravely he faced the camera and held up his hands to quiet the studio audience.

"Quiet, everybody. Rusty Meaghan is going to tell us what college will have him in the backfield next season. O.K., Rusty, out with it!"

He smiled expectantly, half at me and half at the camera.

I looked first at Mama and then directly into the lens.

"I am not going to play college football," I said.

"You're not going to play college football?" That was Johnny's worst jolt of the evening. "What's the matter? Are you afraid you might get hurt or something?" He did have the presence of mind to kid me about my statement.

"Yes, sir."

He let the *sir* pass that time.

"He's afraid, folks. Big Rusty Meaghan is afraid he might get hurt. Isn't this guy a character?"

The audience joined him in laughing at his joke.

"Just what are you afraid of, Rusty?" he asked good-humoredly.

"I might hurt my hands."

"He might hurt his hands, folks!" The crowd roared. "Why does that bother you?"

"It might affect my piano playing."

"It might affect Rusty's piano playing, folks. Isn't he a character? I'd like to keep you on my program regularly, Rusty. You're quite a comedian. Now, seriously, what do you plan to do?"

"I am serious," I said. "I've told you what I intend to do and why."

"You mean you'd rather play piano than play college football?" His eyes were hard when they were on me instead of the camera.

"Yes, sir."

"And you—Big Rusty Meaghan, all-American halfback, the best academy man of the year. How good are you on piano?" His sarcasm bit me where it hurt.

"Pretty good," I answered belligerently. There is some of Daddy in me at times, I have to admit.

"Pretty good, huh. Well, let's see how good you are. Will you play for us?" His tone was vicious now.

"I'll be glad to."

"Move over, Arthur," he called to the pianist as he led me toward the orchestra. "What are you going to play, Rusty?"

" 'Reflets dans l'Eau,' by Debussy," I said. I sat down at the piano and kneaded my fingers.

"Rusty Meaghan, all-American halfback, will now play 'Reflets dans l'Eau,' by Debussy," he announced with a maddening mixture of sarcasm and condescension.

I played the Debussy number as well as I had ever played in my life. My anger had shot enough adrenalin into my system to carry me through. The stunned audience applauded politely, probably unintentionally. The orchestra was more cordial. Johnny Fox was in the curve of the piano, with a microphone boom hanging over him, when the applause died down.

"Very nice, Rusty." He all but sneered at me. "Anything else?"

"Yes, if you like."

He did not like, but he had no choice. After all, he had invited me to play. It was his program—or had been, up to a point.

I leaned forward and played a chorus of "Sophisticated Lady," then modulated into another key, picked up the tempo, and played a chorus of "Honeysuckle Rose." Charlie Baxter, the leader of the "Youth Parade" orchestra, caught my eye and pointed toward the orchestra and waved his baton. Would it be all right if they joined me? I nodded.

On the second chorus of "Honeysuckle Rose" the band began to come in, softly at first, just noodling around in the background. They played a strong second ending, leading into the third chorus. On that one I played block chords and sustained figures and let the other instruments improvise fill-ins ad lib. Charlie took us through in grand style and polished it all off with a solid, full-band ending.

The audience—part of it, at least—came through with enough decibels to give me some confidence in my performance.

Charlie Baxter came over to shake my hand. "Great, real great," he said.

"Cool, man, cool," the pianist said when he reclaimed his bench.

The entire band was chanting, "Crazy, crazy," in soft voices as I rejoined Johnny Fox at his microphone. Johnny was angry. I have no idea what part of his program I had replaced, but time was running out. His script had gone to hell.

"Since you're not going to play college football, Rusty," he said, "for fear you might hurt your hands, will you tell our TV audience what campus will be graced by your musical genius, this fall?"

"None," I said. "I am joining the Marine Corps in July."

"The Marine Corps? Aren't you afraid of getting hurt in our peacetime Marine Corps, Rusty?" That remark, incidentally, was what sent Johnny Fox's rating down seven points the next week, or so the TV columnists wrote. In some quarters, United States Marines rank with and above football heroes.

"No, sir," I said.

"Well, time's running out. Be seeing you around, Rusty." With that he dismissed me and I *never* saw him again.

155

The effect of my decision on Daddy was about the same. He did not even offer to drive me back to Highcastle.

"How could you do this to Daddy?" Ella asked. She was crying when she kissed me good-by.

"I haven't done anything to him," I said. "I am simply through with football."

Mama was equally inquisitive, but not at all displeased.

"Why did you do it, Rusty?" she asked after Daddy's party had left the studio and she and I were alone for a few minutes.

"It's what I want to do," I said.

"Are you sure your father didn't make you do it, trying to push you into SMU the way he did? He can be very annoying."

"No," I said. "I don't want to go to college. I can do just as well on piano with private teachers—better. I can concentrate on piano alone."

"But we—Avolo—wanted you to be a good American, an educated one."

"I'm an all-American halfback—junior grade, anyway," I said with a laugh. "I'm doing what I want to do. Believe me. By the time I serve my hitch in the Marines I'll be able to make a good living for both of us. You'll see."

"You don't need to worry about me, Rusty. I'll get by. I'll never be a burden on you."

I suppose I was on the verge of tears. Mama saw it.

"*Va bene, bambino mio,*" she said soothingly as she petted me in the empty studio. "Do whatever you want to. And you played beautifully tonight. You'll be a fine pianist—you are already. I'm proud of you."

The way she hugged and kissed me was ample reward for my behavior on "Youth Parade."

I was glad then that she had not figured in the program, that Johnny Fox had not known about her and sent one of his cameras to transmit her loveliness onto a million tawdry TV

156

screens across the country. So far she had not had to share in my shame.

"Now, since your father has run out on you—as he has done before—I'll have Rocco drive you home," she said. "I can't go with you, but I'll send him—tonight, if you want to go."

"I want to go," I said. I was disappointed that she could not come with me, more disappointed that she had not asked me to spend the night at her place; so the sooner I got out of Chicago the happier I would be.

Rocco was waiting outside the studio, in the same limousine Mama had brought to Highcastle on Thanksgiving. She told him to drive me home and gave him some expense money. It was obvious that he was a more permanent employee than I had supposed. After I hailed a taxi for Mama and told her good-by again, Rocco drove me to the Ambassador, picked up my bags, and headed out toward Indianapolis.

It was a long, lonely ride home. Rocco said very little, and almost always spoke in Italian. He was respectful and courteous in answering the few questions I asked him. I did not quiz him about Mama, any more than I had ever tried to pry into her affairs.

Ella and I could never ask questions, except of each other, and we had not been able to discuss Mama and Daddy very calmly between ourselves. Perhaps each of us feared that the thing that had split our parents might come between us; and ours had always been a loyalty too intimate, too precious, to risk sacrificing to curiosity, however troubled either of us might have been at times. I saw Daddy's weaknesses quite clearly, though Ella seemed blind to them. It followed that Ella might have sensed Mama's shortcomings, the existence of which I would have denied forever with complete conviction.

So, although I rode up front with Rocco, I was alone in the world. I felt the freedom of loneliness, the unwanted freedom to let my mind wander through its maze of memory, to seek all the causes of my sudden decision to join the Marine Corps, to speculate upon the implications of my choice. As the limousine sped through the night under the expert control of Rocco, I was hardly aware of the towns we passed through. Once beyond Hammond, Rocco got me home in something less than four hours.

At that time of the morning Highcastle was asleep. I tiptoed into my barracks and went to bed without turning on a light. Reveille sounded before any of my schoolmates knew that I was back. Then I learned how the telecast had been received at Highcastle.

No one said good morning.

"How are your hands, Meaghan?" one or two asked sarcastically as I passed them in the bathroom.

That set the tone for the rest of my year at Highcastle. Overnight I had become a pariah, despised not only on my own campus but on nearly every sports page in the country. The most impersonal of the sports writers regretted my defection because of the demoralizing effect it would have on the next crop of high-school hopefuls. I had struck a blow at the sense of responsibility all able-bodied young men owed to athletics. Some columnists editorialized on the possibility of the United States' losing out in world leadership if the younger generation refused to flex its muscles. At least one international-minded journalist wondered sneeringly if the U.S. expected to impress Russia with the quality of its pianists or the strength of its Olympic Team.

A few music critics who had been caught before their television sets when "Youth Parade" came on the air applauded me, but practically no one—certainly no one at Highcastle, except perhaps Ruby Swann—read those notices. I received three or four clippings of that nature among the hundreds of diatribes sent me by irate sports fans from all over the country.

158

I was placed in Coventry by the cadet corps. No one spoke to me if he could avoid it. I was addressed as Meaghan. The great Rusty was dead. Coach Wijiecski never spoke to me again.

Captain Hammer was some comfort, but only for a few days. He had to leave his job because the stumps of his legs were bothering him again.

"I wouldn't worry too much if I were you, Rusty," he said the day he left. "They're chipping away at me again, too. I'm going to the Fort Logan VA Hospital in Denver, where I'm sure they'll take off a few more inches of me and add more plastic above the ankles of these scientific marvels." He tapped one of his feet with a crutch. His bitterness was not particularly reassuring.

"I can't help worrying," I said miserably.

"Neither can I," he said with a grin. "I was putting up a false front. Not to worry in this day and time is to be an idiot."

After he left, I spent my time tying up loose ends in my schoolwork before graduation. Ruby Swann was more on my mind than she had been. I thought of calling on her under some pretext but kept putting it off. There must have been some degree of telepathy operative between us, for I did receive a note from her in the campus mail the last week of school.

DEAR RUSTY,

You know how much I would like to see you before you go, but don't try to see me. I don't dare risk it. Best of luck in the Marine Corps.

Love,
R.S.

I was not eligible for the Marine Corps until my eighteenth birthday, in July. By that time it was a wartime corps, or officially a peacetime corps engaged in the most violent and most extended police action in its history, the Korean mess.

159

CHORUS

THE GREAT Rusty Meaghan was beginning to shape up for us. Excitement ran high in the colony after the séance in Teresina's pad. Word from cats in the East and in Denver laid it that Rusty Meaghan had indeed dropped out of sight; not that any of them had ever seen him, but by sounding a few jazzmen in the know they had it that, whatever his kick, he was on it somewhere. Maybe he was in a laughing academy, maybe in a sanatorium, maybe on a binge. Nobody knew. Rusty was just out of circulation.

Now, we respect those things. Like it's a cat's privacy. If he's in Bellevue or Camarillo or Seeley, down in Galveston, we respect it. If the monkey gets too heavy and a junkie is slammed for a stretch, all the cats dig that. So our sounding aroused no suspicion at first. The answers we got merely fanned our frenzy, strengthened our hopes that Barbarossa was the real gasser.

You can imagine our ecstasy on hearing Barbarossa search how he kicked college football. Up to that point, he might have been just another square trying to make the scene, but that story was a clincher.

"Like I remember Highcastle's 1949 season," Clara Bergson said, misty-eyed. "Rusty was the coolest halfback in academy football. All the girls in my set were drooling over him."

We knew that she was lying. The girls in her set, wherever they were in 1949, were laying the most easily accessible athlete, star or scrub, with no thought of his all-American po-

161

tential. They were not about to drool over a Highcastle cadet tucked away in D Barracks six nights a week. Still we accepted the tribute in the spirit Clara intended it. It was her way of saying that Barbarossa's story sounded solid. This man had kicked squareville's richest rewards—one of which, however, was still on ice for him whenever he cared to avail himself of it. Our way of life had its compensatory delights.

Kurt did not care to claim that he had ever seen the Johnny Fox television show, but he could not let himself be outdone by Clara, not where Barbarossa was concerned.

"It's the symbolism," he said fervently. "Like it's positively poetic, Rusty Meaghan looking into the lens of that TV camera and hurling defiance at the gods. That lens is the eye of god, the Eye of Evil, Evil Eye, omniscient, omnipotent, malevolent—" He paused and beat out a rhythm figure on a board fence.

We were walking home from Teresina's pad. Neither Kurt nor Clara openly expressed very deep feelings about Barbarossa in Teresina's presence.

"It's Homeric in stature," Kurt went on, "pre-Hellenic, heroic, titanic in its majesty. I must do a poem, 'rusty spits in the evil eye.' I must do it now!" He removed his loose-fitting sandals and ran away barefoot into the night.

"Mad!" Kay Ferguson exclaimed. "Mad!"

"Sad," Clara corrected her. "There's no place for Rusty Meaghan in fairyland. Kurt is wasting his emotions."

Kurt wasn't the only one. We could feel the tension in the air. Dick was welding away like crazy on his piece of junk sculpture. Foulard was painting Brittany skies on every flat surface in the district. The monkeys were clawing and pot-heads were burning roaches so short that they singed their beards. A climax was approaching. We could hardly wait to hear Barbarossa search the Marine Corps.

Military service is harder to kick than college football. Like you don't have to play football. You may be considered sub-

162

versive if you kick it; but you don't get *greetings* from the President, followed by a call from the fuzz when you're late for spring training. Like, now, we're all brothers. We're as much opposed to killing as we are to betting our bread on the race between horsepower and obsolescence. We're conscientious objectors; so each of us, at one time or another, has to deal with the military shuck.

Kurt comes with a built-in rejection. Foulard has a diploma from Bellevue. Paul was a four-week section-eighter. There is a goodly sprinkling of these types in our neighborhood, but not all of us are so fortunate. Consequently the prospect of having a cat as far out as Rusty Meaghan search the military for us was a tantalizing one.

We were about equally divided in our prophecies. Roughly half of us felt certain that Rusty had kicked military service altogether, and we were eager to dig his dodge. Others were equally sure that he had served a hitch in the Marines Corps and wanted his formula for beating the rap from the inside— just in case. A few of the chicks, most of whom were beginning to form four-square sentimental attachments for the shaman, toyed with the idea that he had served, shot, killed, suffered, and emerged with his miraculous radiance undimmed. Their musings were sickening, of course, unworthy of our search, a downright drag to those of us still eligible for greetings from Mount Olympus.

Teresina's pad was the only one large enough to hold the crowd when word spread that Barbarossa might get high enough to tell how he won the battle of—

QUANTICO, 1950

How MANY men have fretted about the time wasted in military service? How many boast of heroic careers in the Korean action? How many angrily lay bare the scars inflicted on their psyches by the brutality of war in general and the Marine Corps in particular? How many shrug off failure with *"C'est la guerre"*?

Waste? I was marking time anyway, still fulfilling those obligations to state and society required of a boy before he can become a man. Heroic career—at the chapel organ and the officers' club piano? Scars on my psyche? *E pluribus unum*. Failure? How could the Battle of Quantico-on-the-Potomac account for congenital weakness?

To many a fighting marine, Quantico is Mecca, the pine-scented shrine of *Semper Fidelis*. To me it was a half-hour drive to Washington, an hour and a half to Baltimore and Olga Vladishenka, a long way to Chicago. The Marine Barracks was simply D Barracks with the cadets a year older, trying out their dirty new mantalk.

After boot camp—not a whit more strenuous than a football season—I was ordered to Quantico for specialized training. Upon my arrival I found Ruby Swann's second, and last, note waiting for me. It ran:

DEAR RUSTY:

I found out where you are from a questionnaire sent to the superintendent. (I am quite close to him, you know.)

I have a surprise for you. At least I think I have—I tried

165

to hide it from you until you left the academy. I have the dearest little baby boy in the world. He has my red hair and blue eyes, and I have every reason to believe that he will grow up to be just like you.

I hope he does. You know how much I have wanted a son like you. Since I can't claim you, he will be a wonderful substitute. I'll adore him forever. You won't mind too much if he replaces you in my affection, will you?

Don't write me and don't ever try to see me (us) again. Believe me when I say that I am happy and grateful. May you find happiness too.

As always,
R.S.

Admittedly I was stunned. I sat on my bunk and stared at the letter. How did I feel about Ruby Swann and her baby? It may be to my discredit to say that I could find no place for her in my heart or in my life. After all, I hardly knew her—a few weeks of companionship and one ecstatic afternoon and night. I, too, was grateful, for her appreciation of my music, for her quick-rising passion, for her gift to me, for the flattery implied by her sex-hunger. But I had no love for her.

I am sure that she never expected me to love her—considering the disparity in our ages. And yet that disparity was not the cause of my lack of feeling. Perhaps I was incapable of the kind of affection that went with wives and babies. Certainly it did not figure in the family life I had cut out for myself. I *was* glad that she was happy, and I believed that she was. But happiness for myself? I hoped to find it elsewhere. Ruby Swann was not part of it.

While I was still holding the letter in my hand I received a summons to the chaplain's office. Immediately I connected the call with Ruby's letter, and I reported with strong misgivings.

"Private Meaghan?" the chaplain asked when I entered his office and stood at attention.

166

"Yes, sir," I said apprehensively.

"I am Lieutenant Sullivan, another good Irishman," he said with a smile and extended his hand. He was dark Irish, dressed in a Navy work uniform.

"Glad to know you, sir," I said.

"Sit down. I have a very interesting report on you from Highcastle Military Academy."

I sat down and he settled back in his chair informally.

"Seems you were quite a football player there, quite a man." Neither his tone nor his manner suggested sarcasm, but I was still troubled.

"Well, that's a fine thing for a big strapping youth like you," he went on, "but I'm more interested in some of your other accomplishments."

He paused and I waited for the worst. His face went serious.

"How well do you play piano, Private Meaghan?"

"Better than I play football." I think my boasting was prompted by the relief I felt.

"Then you must be pretty good." He chuckled. "Have you ever played organ?"

"No, sir," I said.

"Do you think you could?"

"With practice, I think so," I said. "It might take me some time to learn the pedals."

"I can arrange practice time for you—have you relieved of some other duties. Our organist has just shipped out. If you will, I would like you to take over his job."

"I'd be glad to, sir," I said. I am not sure that I had a choice. One seldom has in the Marine Corps, but he left the impression that I had.

He dismissed me and I returned to my barracks to find a similar summons from the mess officer. Upon reporting to him I learned that the pianist who had been playing in the officers' club had just shipped out—the same musician, I was sure.

Could I take his place—at once, that very afternoon, beginning at the cocktail hour in the bar?

I could and did. So began my career as a fighting marine. There seemed to be an abundance of expert riflemen in the corps but only one keyboard specialist. As a result I was given probably the strangest duty ever assigned a United States marine. I was librarian, chapel organist, chaplain's orderly, and permanent entertainer at the bar and dining room of the officers' club. I rapidly became indispensable—to Quantico, if not to the units in the field. Detachments came and detachments went, but I stayed on forever.

It is true that I had to play a lot of Liberace piano in those days, especially for Mrs. Bragg, the wife of an old supply officer who seemed to be a permanent fixture on the base. Wives being what they are and supply officers being what they are, there was sufficient power in the combination to have swayed the Pentagon, had that been necessary to assure my being on hand for the regular Wednesday afternoon party for officers' wives. I was on hand—for three long years—the darling of the senior officer set.

I had ample opportunity to play my own selections, however; and many of the younger officers and wives who passed through Quantico had heard of other pianists besides Liberace; so the corps contributed much to my preparation for life, as promised on the recruiting posters. In time I was granted liberal privileges, largely through the good offices of the various chaplains and Mrs. Bragg.

On Mondays and Tuesdays, I was free to go into Washington or Baltimore, sometimes to Philadelphia, whenever a fine pianist was appearing at the Click or one of the other clubs. The trips were easy after Mama bought me a Jaguar and had it delivered by a dealer in Washington. I protested in a letter, but Mama assured me that the Jaguar had not strained her finances. So I conscientiously put the little sports car to good use by arranging to study with Olga Vladishenka, a seventy-year-old pianist who had a studio near Johns Hopkins University in Baltimore.

She was the most thorough and the most demanding teacher I ever had. She had known Auer and Rachmaninoff well, and she had kept up; so she could drill me understandingly on Bartók and Copland as well as the traditionalists. All in all, I owe her a lot, including my brush with the security officer at Quantico.

It was reasonable to suppose that my Jaguar and my liberties would arouse envy, if not downright suspicion. It did come as a surprise, however, that I was picked up at the gate one Tuesday afternoon and escorted to the security office.

"Private Meaghan," the security officer began, "we have been investigating you, and we've caught you red-handed. What do you have to say for yourself?" He was a stubby, red-faced captain whose neck was all leather.

"Nothing, sir," I said, "until I know what I'm charged with."

"Who do you visit in Baltimore every Monday?"

"Madame Olga Vladishenka."

He seemed surprised.

"You admit it?" he asked.

"Yes, sir."

"Is that the name you have, Sergeant?" he asked my escort.

"Yes, sir, Captain Morgan, but I didn't know she was no madam. We just looked up the address in the city directory after we tailed him there. It don't look like no cat house. *Olga Vladishenka* it said, like I wrote on that report."

"Did you know this woman was a Russian?" Captain Morgan asked me.

"Yes, sir."

"And you go to see her, openly, in the daylight?"

"Yes, sir."

169

"She must be some babe. Is she your girl? Or is she a professional?"

"She's my piano teacher, sir," I said.

"That's a good one. How old is she?"

"About seventy, I think."

"Seventy?" The captain was dubious. "We can check on her, you know."

"Yes, sir. I know."

"Don't think we won't." He turned to another paper in the file. "Now who is this Nestra Bercelli in Chicago?"

"My mother, sir." The Kefauver Crime Committee was in session then and the papers were full of Italian and Sicilian names, but for the first time I felt their impact on me.

"But your name is Meaghan. Did you change it?" the captain asked. I suppose he was as leery of the *Mafiosi* as he was of the Communists.

"No, sir. That's her professional name," I said.

"Professional name? Is she a madam too?"

At my reaction, Captain Morgan eased off the pressure.

"O.K., Meaghan. Don't get sore. Madame Vladishenka, Madame Bercelli—they could both be musicians. But the names are funny-sounding. Don't think we won't follow up."

There was a disturbance in the outer office, and Mrs. Bragg barged in on us.

"What's going on here, Captain Morgan?" she demanded. She was pink-haired and, at the moment, pink-faced from the exertion required to rush her considerable bulk to the security office.

"We are questioning Private Meaghan," the captain said.

"So I heard." Security was not airtight at Quantico. "What about?"

"About his trips to Baltimore to see Olga Vladishenka."

"What about his visits to Madame Vladishenka?"

"She's Russian, ain't she?" the captain asked defensively.

170

"White Russian!" Mrs. Bragg exploded. "Her people were fighting the Bolsheviks before you were born, Captain Morgan. She hates them, and she's a fine pianist. We know all about Rusty studying with her, and we approve."

"Just checking up, Mrs. Bragg. That's our job."

"Well, our Rusty is doing his, too. We haven't a finer boy on the base."

"I'm sure we haven't, Mrs. Bragg," Captain Morgan agreed. I doubt that he meant what he said, but he dismissed me when it became evident that Mrs. Bragg was not going to leave the security office without me.

Captain Morgan shipped out a few weeks later, and his successors never bothered to pull me in again for offering comfort to the enemy.

I did pay closer attention to the Kefauver hearings, though, especially when they were televised; and I began to understand why Mama had insisted that I keep my Irish name. After Mayor O'Dwyer's testimony before the Crime Committee, however, I wondered whether or not Meaghan was to be preferred to Bercelli. Presumably it was, for Costello drew a jail sentence and O'Dwyer an appointment as ambassador to Mexico.

All of this made me impatient for the Korean war to end and my hitch in the Marines to be over. Mama had to bear the Sicilian name and more than ever I felt the urgency of her need for me, for someone to provide the comfort and security which were her due. Her letters were cheerful and optimistic but often vague. I could sometimes read unhappiness between the lines.

Gina seldom wrote, and then only short notes. Ella was more voluble, even fulsome, in her glowing reports of life with Daddy.

He is well liked [she wrote], all over Dallas and especially at SMU. The athletes love him, he's so generous

171

with them. I do wish you had come to the university with me. We could have such fun together.

Daddy is accepted everywhere as a native Texan, and loves it. He's like a Catholic convert—more convincing than the natural born. And I say this fondly, Rusty. On Daddy it looks good. He's such a dear. If only he could have Cassie's money without Cassie. I do believe she's becoming a mite jealous of me, but I do love him so.

And he's paying our way. He handles the trucking firm marvelously. Right now the union is trying to organize his drivers but he's standing up to them like a champion. They're making a test of his firm. Other oil carriers are backing him to the limit. He's their hero, just as he is mine —and Cassie's, though I hate to admit it. He'll win. He'll show everyone that Ol' Tex can't be pushed around.

Rusty, why don't you come to SMU after your hitch in the Marines? You can still play football, probably better than ever. Daddy'll forgive you, I'm sure. He'll take you into the firm after you graduate, too. By that time I'll be his lawyer and we'll all have it made. Think about it, 'cause

We love you,
ELLA

Ella was having exactly the opposite effect on me from the one she intended. I boiled as I thought of Daddy clowning his way to success among Texas oilmen while Mama spent her beauty selling cosmetics to envious old women. I certainly had no intention of helping him run his truck line and letting Mama live alone until her chance at happiness had passed.

My restlessness was reflected mostly in my music, since there was little I could do about being in the Marine Corps, which held me like a bear in a trap. I continued to practice until my wrists ached, then to read everything in the library I was supposed to tend, and finally to wear myself out in the gymnasium so that I could sleep at night.

172

Madame Vladishenka was most sensitive to my condition.

"Forte means not that loud," she said with a laugh. "My poor piano cannot stand it. Now, again."

My technique was satisfactory, but my dynamics were exaggerated beyond the intentions of the most violent composers. I played again for Madame, but still not quite to her liking.

"What you do now, Rusty?" she asked when I had finished my lesson. "You still got all night."

"Go to a club or two," I said.

"With a girl?"

"No," I said.

"You need a girl." She sighed, nostalgically. "How I would like to be your girl for a while! I would not fear your forte." She cackled suggestively. "But you need a girl. Find one."

She preceded me to the door of her musty Victorian studio and stood aside as I opened it.

"Find a girl," she advised again when I left her. It was not the first time she had made the suggestion, not by any means.

I was not looking for a girl. I had met several in my rounds. I was well enough acquainted to sit in with a combo or man the piano for a few minutes in several of the clubs I frequented; so I knew a number of the entertainers as well as the regular customers. But no girl was worrying me. It was time, slow dragging time, and duty to my country.

That night I went to the Blue Point, where a new show was opening, and ordered dinner at a ringside table. When the orchestra came out I knew most of them. Only the leader and the book were new; the side men were the same. I nodded, and the pianist came by and said hello before they started playing.

The book was good, written as it was to feature the name leader, who played trumpet. The selections played during dinner were soft society arrangements for tenors and muted horn, nothing flashy, but solid and rhythmical, with a lot of inconspicuous piano fill-in.

173

At showtime, the new emcee was so-so—reasonably fresh material but a far from fresh style. He still asked us to give the little girl a big hand—the first little girl being a hundred-and-sixty-pound torch singer who belted out her numbers like Ethel Merman. Indeed she included several Merman songs in her repertoire and did all right by them.

The next performer qualified. About a hundred pounds of Latin beauty dedicated to satire in the modern dance, she caricatured sex with just enough wit to make the final stripper acceptable to the somewhat sophisticated clientele of the Blue Point. I even remembered her name, Linda Lassieur; so I could call it when the pianist brought her to my table between shows and introduced her.

"Nick says you play piano, too," she said as she sat down in the chair I held for her. She looked as attractive in her black sheath as she had in almost nothing.

"A little," I said.

"A lot," Nick corrected me. "Maybe he'll stick around until the crowd thins out and show us a thing or two."

"Would you?" Linda asked with professional eagerness.

"Maybe," I said. "What are you drinking?"

"Very little. Rosolio?" She looked questioningly at the waiter.

"Rosolio, *sì*," he said, and waited for me and Nick to order.

We ordered something a little stronger than rosolio and lit cigarettes.

"So you are a marine," Linda remarked after the waiter had left us.

"Yes."

"You sort of remind me of a marine I met in Boston."

"And you sort of remind me of my mother," I said, studying the regular features of her oval face.

Linda laughed.

"Well, that's a new approach," she said. "I'm not sure whether I like it or not."

174

"If you knew my mother you would like it," I assured her. "She's the best."

"I'm sure of that. It's just that I never thought of myself as the motherly type. I don't think I am."

"Neither is Mama. At least I have never considered her a type. She's something special."

"I could twist that into a compliment, I suppose." Her eyes teased me.

"No twisting needed," I said. "It would be a compliment if you were not really something special yourself."

"Nick, that sounds like blarney to me," she said, turning to our companion. "Meaghan, did you say?"

"Meaghan," Nick said. "Just like in Boston."

The waiter brought our drinks.

"Where are you from, Rusty?" Linda sipped her rosolio.

"Quantico."

"I mean where is your home?"

"Quantico," I repeated, somewhat bitterly I suppose.

"Sorry, Rusty. I wasn't probing." She seemed genuinely sorry. Her face was as expressive as her body had been during her dance.

"It's O.K.," I said. "My father lives in Dallas, my mother in Chicago."

"So Chicago is your home." She was perceptive, too.

"Not yet."

"But after the war?"

"I guess so. I hope so. Where are you from?"

"Boston, of course. I knew Nick there."

There was no point in mentioning my Boston ancestry; so I skipped it. Nick returned to the bandstand. Linda and I listened for a while, then talked music, then war; then it was time for her to change for the second show. I paid more attention to the way the band cut the show than I did to the show itself, until Linda came on again. She was a lot like Mama, or more like Ella of recent years, both in appearance and in manner-isms. She would have fit into the Bounding Bercellis' act. It would have been a pleasure to serve as her understander. I imagined myself handling her near-nude body in close-in routines. It was an appealing idea.

Sensing my appreciation of her performance, she played to me during the second show and returned to my table for the short period of dance music before closing time. Neither of us drank any more. We danced most of the time. As I held her close, the easy grace of her movements verified my judgment. She belonged among the Bercelli women.

"Stick around, you two," Nick said when the last dance was over and the musicians started packing their instruments. "We eat here."

"I've eaten," Linda said.

"I have to stay and play for Nick while he has supper," I said. "Turn about, you know."

"*Ha detto ciò per persuadervi,*" Linda said to Nick.

"*Su ciò non v'è alcun dubbio,*" I said with as natural a flow of Italian as hers.

Dick laughed as Linda turned on me in surprise.

"Rusty, you sneak!" she said. "You were eavesdropping."

"I told you that you were a lot like my mother. Her name was Bercelli."

"And mine is Rosa Lazari, but I don't hide my lineage under a red fright wig."

"Only behind that phony French Linda Lassieur," I said. "Are you going to sit at the table with those bums or at the piano with me?"

"At the piano, of course. I told you I had already eaten."

"Well, come on." I offered a hand and helped her up onto the bandstand.

She sat on the bench beside me.

"This one is for you, mother mine," I said and began playing

"Liebestraum" in an inept but flamboyant style. I threw in just enough clinkers to make it convincing.

"Oh, brother!" Linda said. She was not sure whether I was serious or not, but she did risk getting a candle off one of the tables and placing it on the piano. I saw the new bandleader look up at me in disgust and then at Nick for confirmation. Nick kept a straight face.

I played "Liebestraum" through and smiled at the musicians' table, showing all the teeth I could. The band applauded soberly.

Next I played the new leader's arrangement of "Melancholy Baby," which had proved quite popular earlier in the evening. I played the trumpet part with my right hand and used my left hand and the sustaining pedal to approximate the full-band background.

"Whose foot are you using, Rusty?" Nick asked from the table. "Sounds like Father Hines' to me."

With that suggestion, I played the entire second chorus in the Earl Hines style. I felt Linda put her arm around my shoulders and squeeze.

"I'm so glad, Rusty," she said in my ear. "I thought at first that you were as square as a kitchen table. I'm glad you're not, really glad."

After that we got on well. She requested numbers, sang a little, even did an impromptu dance routine to one show tune to complete our floor show for the help. By the time the band had finished eating I had begun to think that Madame Vladishenka knew what she was talking about. I needed a girl. In Linda I was finding at least part of what I hungered for every day of my life.

That was in 1952. "La Vie en Rose," "Mona Lisa," and "Good Night, Irene" had given way to "Because of You," "Too Young," and "My Heart Cries Out for You," which in turn were being replaced by "Moulin Rouge," "Blue Tango," and "Wish You

177

Were Here." I was twenty that summer, but I looked much older because I was so big. Linda, in daylight, turned out to be twenty-six; but for over a month we were the same age.

It hardly seems possible that I saw her only eight or ten times, on my weekly trips to Baltimore. I went early on Mondays and stayed late on Tuesdays. We ate together, raced the Jaguar together, played together, danced together and, yes, slept together —once.

We were sad the week she closed at the Blue Point and prepared to move on to Denver and then to Las Vegas.

"That's too far away even for the Jag," she lamented. "Can't you get a transfer? Don't they have marines in the West?" We were parked on a side road near Owings Mills. It was almost sundown.

"I don't know," I said. "But I can't get a transfer to anywhere. I'm as permanently fixed in Quantico as the flagpole."

"What'll we do?"

"After I am discharged maybe we can team up in a double."

"I mean what can we do now? Not after the war, if it ever ends." The note of urgency in her voice was no new thing in my experience. "I don't want to leave you, not for years, or months, or even a moment."

"Could we try it? I mean should we see if we want to wait? I mean—" I floundered. I could not tell exactly what it was that held me back.

"I know what you mean," Linda said. She sat quietly beside me for a minute or two. "I'm not a virgin, you know. I've been married. Yes, we could try it. Maybe we should. We ought to know before we make any plans—any promises."

"Tonight," I said. "I can't get away again before next Monday."

"And I close Saturday night. Yes, tonight, if ever."

"After the show—I'll get another room." It sounded rather

178

cold-blooded, all these arrangements. It lacked the spontaneity of my affair with Ruby Swann.

"Hell, we can go to my room," Linda said. "I've been a good girl ever since I've been in Baltimore, and I'll be gone in a week. What do I care?"

"All right, whatever you say."

She kissed me then, lingeringly—thoughtfully, I think. We certainly were not being stampeded into our tryst, now that we had made our decision.

"I have a show to do," she said. It was beginning to get dark.

We drove back into town. I dropped her off at her hotel and went back to my room for a few minutes. I had dinner at my usual table. I knew all the routines by now, but I never tired of watching Linda. That night there was, of course, a new immediacy in my pleasure. I probably could have taken her to bed the night I met her, or the first week—casually—but we had gone beyond that. Now it was serious. She had become a person, a very dear person, to be cherished, not a near-naked dancer to be appraised as a toy for an evening.

I was jealous of her that night. She was lovelier, more animated, more desirable than ever before. I resented the fact that I had to share her performance with a hundred other men. I remembered how Bert Marks and Major Swann and Coach Wijiecski had looked at Mama. My resentment then was the same. I was glad when Linda completed her last number, and not only in anticipation of things to come either.

Linda feigned a headache as an excuse for skipping our usual supper show for the band, and we left immediately. We walked to her hotel, where we made our way to her room unnoticed.

Her undressing was no revelation, as Ruby Swann's had been, nor was the feel of her body entirely new to me.

"This is how I look, Rusty," she said after she had removed her clothes. "As if you didn't know already."

"You look good indeed," I said. "As if you didn't know."

179

We both laughed, a little nervously. Modesty is a mystic thing. It can appear in the most unlikely places at the most unexpected times. Despite our weeks of intimacy we approached each other modestly that night. Linda was strange, and yet familiar to my touch—as though I had known her forever. I fondled her almost reverently for a long time and felt her lithe, resilient body respond in kind, until our union could be put off no longer.

She was different from Ruby Swann, my only basis for comparison. Hers was no swift, demanding fever, but the gentle bestowal of a favor, fully as rich in fulfillment as all the major's wife had had to offer.

"It was—" I began.

"Don't talk, Rusty," she interrupted me. "Not now. Just hold me."

She shivered slightly and clung to me in silence. I think she cried a little. I was in no condition to be objective at first. But as she lay locked in my arms, I did begin to think, to wonder, and finally to explore again, to assure myself of the miracle that had happened. I could not believe it all; so I thought, and reasoned, and remembered, and tried again.

The second time convinced me. I had never known such ecstasy. But Linda reacted differently. She did not cling to me. Indeed she edged over to her side of the bed and, after a few minutes, got up and went into her bathroom and put on a robe. When she returned she sat down in a chair and lit a cigarette.

"Now, we can talk, Rusty," she said.

"All right," I said eagerly. "Let's talk." I too got up and put on my shorts.

She offered me a cigarette. When I accepted it she looked me in the eyes for the first time. Hers were troubled, her face a puzzle. I lit our cigarettes and sat down facing her.

"No," she said, and shook her head slowly. "Rusty, you're

180

sweet. You loved me as no one ever loved me before or ever will again."

"Then, why no?" I am sure that my expression was as puzzled as hers.

"That was the first time. But—Rusty—the second time. I don't understand you. You're a weirdie of some kind."

"How? What did I do wrong?" I should have known all along that Linda was too good to be true. Yet she must have understood me, if any woman did. For a month she had been closer to me than anyone else had ever been.

"I don't know how or why," she said, almost in anger. "How old are you, Rusty?"

"Twenty. Am I too young? Is that it? Too young to play with the big girls?" I was angry then. Time—time was all I needed, ever. Time to grow up.

"No." She waved her hand vaguely. "I don't know. I thought you were older. Maybe I should have known better."

"So that is it."

"No—I can't put my finger on the trouble, but it won't work." She wrinkled her brow and paused for a moment. "Oh, Rusty, I love you. I'm sure I do, but—but don't ever tell another girl that she reminds you of your mother. Don't! For your own sake, don't."

I felt my body flush and burn red all over, but Linda did not see me. She had dropped her head and covered her face with her hands. I know she was crying then. I could not comfort her. I did not try. I could not force myself.

She hid her face until I finished dressing. Neither of us spoke until I was ready to leave.

"I'm going," I said then.

She rose and came to me at the door. She held up her face and closed her eyes. I leaned over and kissed her without touching more than her lips. She opened her eyes after that. They were wet.

"I love you, Rusty, but it won't work. I couldn't stand it—not again."

"But what—what if—" I remembered Ruby Swann's last letter.

"Don't worry, Rusty. I know how to take care of myself." She smiled even as a rigor shook her body. "Good night."

"Good night," I said.

The second miracle that night was how I got back to Quantico without being picked up by the police or running into something. I kept the accelerator of the Jaguar on the floorboard every mile of the way. Neither I nor any other man could ever have done that again.

I brooded all the next morning and was still surly when I went to the club to play for the Wednesday party for officers' wives. My mood showed in my music as well as in my face.

"Our Rusty is unhappy today, I think," Mrs. Bragg said to two or three other women who came to the piano with her to make requests. Her hair was newly pinked, her perfume saccharine sweet when I could distinguish it from its sister scents fogging the air around me.

"What's the matter, Rusty?" she asked me.

"Nothing."

"There is, too," a slender little mother said. "I can tell. I have boys of my own. Your heart is breaking."

"What would you like me to play?" I asked.

" 'Chant d'Amour.' "

"Brahm's Lullaby."

" 'Tenderly.' "

Requests came at me in a torrent. The women were trying to help. I hated them. I hated the way they looked at my freckles, the way their faces tried to register sorrow, the way Mrs. Bragg stroked my hair.

"You just go ahead and break your heart on this little old piano," Mrs. Bragg said. "It'll do you good. And we'll listen while we play bridge. We'll all grieve with you. It'll be like praying together. Then if you want to tell me about it after the party—" She left her invitation open, and the women returned to their tables.

I broke my heart—and theirs, deliberately. For the next hour I creamed and sugared every nostalgic tune that Liberace ever slithered over the keys of his Baldwin. The party broke up in a sob-happy stupor. It had been a huge success.

"Now, do you want to tell me about it, Rusty?" Mrs. Bragg asked.

"I've told it all," I said dramatically. "My music spoke for me."

"Yes, and I understood." She was quick to match my mood. "Don't you feel better?"

"Much better," I said and went into the bar to play while the war-weary officers cried into their beer until dinnertime.

I did not touch the piano, but spent the entire cocktail hour at the godbox recently installed in the bar. It was the ultimate in self-torture. I loathe electronic organs—all registrations on them sound like modulated belly-rumblings to me. So I experienced another satisfactory, if not enjoyable, hour of music, an orgy of wonderfully poignant masochism.

My despondency was lessened somewhat the next day by a letter from Ella. She wrote, toward the end,

Daddy's enemies are playing dirty pool. They are being horribly mean to him. The engines in half a dozen of his tractors have been syruped—completely ruined. Two of his tankers have been rammed by driverless jalopies. They exploded, not only killing his drivers but some other people, too. Now he's being sued. Imagine suing Daddy because somebody ran into his trucks!

They have thrown acid in some of the drivers' faces too. His men love him—as who wouldn't—but some of them are quitting. They're afraid to drive for him. But he's not

183

afraid. He's so brave—like always. He's mad now, though. He says that he'll fight those bastards to his last breath and last penny. He will, too.

They're hard to fight, though. Nobody knows who they are. None of them ever shows in a line-up here. I'll be glad when I get my law degree. I'll bet I can find out who they are and send them up for life, or get death sentences for them—only killing is too good for them.

Rusty, please come and help us out when this pesky war is over. You wouldn't be afraid to drive for Daddy. You're so much like him. You wouldn't be afraid of anything. I know you wouldn't and

I love you,
ELLA

I felt better only by comparison. It was good to know that Daddy was having troubles, too. He deserved them. I was more eager than ever for the pesky war to be over. I was confident that I could work out my problems satisfactorily as soon as I was free of my leather collar. I asked no help; and neither Ella nor Daddy had any right to ask help of me.

After Linda, I restricted my Baltimore trips to Mondays only —just my lesson with Madame Vladishenka, one club, and back to Quantico. I never heard from Linda. She had left no doubt as to the firmness of her decision; so I wrote her off as a diversion, a dangerous diversion which would serve as a warning in the future. I could not afford to swerve one degree from my course until I was a recognized pianist securely established in Chicago.

I held rigidly to that course all winter and spring, until the cease-fire order in Korea on July 27, 1953. In August, I left Quantico, a man—free, white, and twenty-one, as my Southern comrades were wont to say.

CHORUS

BARBAROSSA WAS qualifying fast. He was making the scene. He was one of ours—a passive marine, father of a bastard, suspected fellow traveler. (We are strong believers in innocence by association.) Even though he still spoke that quaint classroom dialect of his, we dug him completely. We could attribute his nonuse of cool cat language to the insistence of an immigrant family that he "speak like a native." Whatever square corners there were left were rapidly rounding off. He was our shaman-elect.

He had neither kicked the military hitch nor done harm to his brothers. All you had to do to shuck the Marine Corps was play piano like Rusty Meaghan. That was what was in store for us next. We had gradually picked up Teresina's analysis of her guest. He was living his life as he searched it. Now he was ready to start his career as a jazz pianist. His talents there we already knew, unless the whole Barbarossa scene was one big shuck.

For fear of bugging his search, we had obediently kept our Rusty Meaghan records off the air—Teresina again. Now we began taking them out and looking at them longingly, even playing some of them secretly with the volume turned low. Of course there's no kick in hi-fi if it isn't splitting your eardrums, but we were willing to forego that ecstatic deafness for a whisper of Meaghan's music, a stolen nibble of the feast to come.

185

The thought was sobering. Within a matter of days now we might know for sure that Rusty Meaghan had come to us. As soon as he played for us we would know. The world would know. Then would come responsibility, that ogre which had ravaged our other worlds. But other colonies had their Corsos, Kerouacs, Ginsbergs, Patchens, Rexroths, Perkoffs, and Ferlinghettis. Our Rusty would top them all. Could we accept the burden?

"I've about decided that Brittany skies are a shade darker," Foulard said critically one bright morning. "I wonder if I have time to run over to France for a few days."

We couldn't advise him. We sorrowed over his wavering confidence as he sucked the end of a paint brush and scratched uneasily.

Dick Ferguson was calmer. His scrap-iron statue had grown to such proportions that he had had to cut it into sections and move it out of his pad. Now he worked in the alley from a tall stepladder. He was using both the Eye of Fate and the Disc of Destiny; and although he had not yet attached the phallic worm gear he knew where it was going. He had not forsaken his aesthetic principle.

Kurt was obviously under great strain.

"As soon as he plays I must have a jazz canto ready to perform with him," he said. "We shall both be immortalized. God, how I wish I believed in immortality!"

Clara was more subtle. She lured a piano tuner to her pad and kept him there until he overhauled the action and put her instrument into perfect playing condition. Then she suggested to Teresina that perhaps the next séance should be held where Rusty would have access to an in-tune piano if he felt inclined to play. The offer bugged Teresina for several days. No one will ever know how much torture she went through before she agreed. But in time she did agree.

Clara tried to be selective in her guest list; that is, she in-

186

vited a roomful of cats to come in at dusk and bring food, drink, and marijuana with them. These few pre-empted the floor space and formed the principal circle at teatime. They raised a sort of barrier between Barbarossa and the world outside. We all felt that if this was the night we might be safer trying a dry run before blowing our good fortune and holding open house.

When Barbarossa fell in, Clara very deftly seated him near the piano with her on one side and Teresina on the other. The two of them shared his reefers and led him into his truth-talk. As we had hoped, he told us about his career as a jazz pianist. What is more, as he talked, he turned to the piano and played a tune now and then by way of illustration. But best we start from in front, as he did, in—

DETROIT, 1954

MY ROUTE to Chicago required some tacking. I worked a month in Baltimore, where I was already known, another in Philadelphia, and two, including the Christmas holidays, in Jersey City. I could not play in New York because I could not afford to wait out the time required for a card in Local 802. I was attracting some notice but I was still playing for scale, and I could not support Mama on that pay. I was not ready for Chicago.

I did acquire a Chicago agent, however—Paul Ade, who booked me into the Free Border Lounge in Detroit at slightly above union scale, just about enough to pay his commission.

The Free Border was a small, intimate club which did not employ a band and had no dance floor. The policy was to use a pianist or an organist and one big-name act at a time. I was booked in with Lola Rivers and her accompanist, Pokey Brown. I knew their records well and looked forward to studying Pokey's solo style.

I played for an hour before they came on. The club had a stand only slightly larger than the piano and the organ console. The bar was in an alcove off to one side, and the customers sat in low easy chairs arranged in a semicircle facing the stand. Drinks were served on cocktail tables and side tables. I felt as though I was playing a concert, as indeed I was, to a friendly, appreciative audience. They applauded softly and called their requests from where they sat. The tips were good. My opinion of Paul Ade rose as I played.

At showtime I found a chair close up, but a little to one side, where I could watch Pokey's fingers and pedal work. I never saw either. Early I sensed that Pokey had no style other than an attempt to keep Jelly Roll Morton up to date; but Lola Rivers was a revelation. When she came on she completely dominated the place. She was a big, handsome, healthy woman, with the warm dark earth of the levee in her body. She wore a skin-tight dress of white satin, as dazzling as her teeth when she smiled and eased into "Some of These Days" with only a whisper of pitch sounded by Pokey.

Her voice was much too big for the Free Border, but you knew that intuitively. She held it just right to fill the room. And fill the room she did, with blues and torch songs and ballads and work songs, for three-quarters of an hour—and then for another fifteen minutes, with requests called from a dozen chairs at once.

"I'll be back," she said as the spot followed her off stage. "I'll be back. Jest y'all wait."

I had to be reminded that I was supposed to go back to the piano myself. After Lola Rivers, anything would have been anti-climactical. She had left her listeners entirely too well pleased for them to be very critical for the next few minutes, however; so I had time to work myself out of her spell, relying on muscle memory and subliminal suggestion until consciousness of my own work returned. I suppose I started echoing Lola's numbers, or pieces brought to mind by them, and gradually drifted into my personal repertoire. Perhaps the audience and I recovered together. At any rate, by the time they began thinking of requests again I was able to fulfill them.

Lola and Pokey returned while I was playing. I did not know when; but before the end of my hour they were making requests themselves and I spotted them at a table off in a corner. Lola smiled broadly when I played a song for her. She came by the piano on her way back to her dressing room.

190

She patted my shoulder and said, "You're with it, boy. You're really with it."

I attributed the compliment to her native generosity, but I silently thanked Paul Ade for booking me into the club with her. For a month at least I would be in the best of company— "in high cotton," as Lola was to express it many times thereafter.

My chair out front was still empty when time for the second show approached. I hurried to it and settled down with a drink for my second treat of the evening. I resolved to watch Pokey that time, to make the most of the month I had ahead of me.

Lola came on to a roar of applause. The audience was becoming more sincere than polite in their response.

Lola shushed the house long enough to whisper, or almost whisper, "Easy Ridah."

The house stormed their approval but quieted immediately when Pokey began his introduction to "No Easy Rider Blues." Then Lola cast her spell again. Her numbers were all different. She probably could have sung forever—and I cannot imagine anyone who would not sit and listen to her forever. I sat and listened. For a time I tried to study Pokey; but I soon learned that there was no Pokey Brown—merely an extension of Lola herself. He felt her moods, sensed her nuances, heard her phrasing before she phrased, and merely stayed with her. He was nothing—nothing but wonderful as he became her own two hands on the keyboard. So I relaxed and stayed with Lola, felt my way along as Pokey was doing.

Other nights were the same. I would have worked for nothing just to have been able to stay in the Free Border and absorb what Lola had to offer. The nights were long. January was cold. So I got to know Lola and Pokey very well indeed. Sometimes we stayed at the club all night, rehearsing, swapping ideas, playing for one another, waiting for the snow to stop.

Then the worst snowfall of the year set in, about the middle of January. I hardly made it to the club; but I had to go. Lola would draw a crowd, whatever the weather. She arrived soon after I did, while I was noodling around on the piano to an empty house.

"It's really snowing out there, isn't it?" I said when she came up to the stand. She was bundled up like a washerwoman.

"Snowin'?" She sounded disgusted. "You ain't seen no snowin' till you see that Pokey Brown."

"Pokey?"

"Yeah. You know he's been snowin', don't you?" she asked.

"I suspected it."

"Well, he's gone this time. They done picked him up an' took him to a sanitarium. He's gone." She shook her head and clucked her tongue.

"What are you going to do?" I asked. "Without Pokey, I mean."

"I got you, ain't I, Rusty, boy?" She began shucking her heavy coats as she warmed to the temperature of the lounge.

"You mean I should play your show?"

"Sho' do. You kin do it, jest like we been doin' around heah aftah houahs."

"But I was just noodling around, following along."

"That's all it takes. Le's run through a few." She was down to her street clothes now—a comfortable house dress. Off stage Lola was everybody's mammy, homey but beautiful.

"O.K.," I said.

"Gimme 'Beale Street Blues.' I really got them blues tonight. Wisht I was back in Memphis."

I played an introduction, and Lola sat down beside me and sang the blues just loud enough for me to hear. She was a hypnotist, a Svengali; and like Trilby I went along without knowing how or why.

"That's jest right, Rusty, boy. Now, 'Alabama Bound.' "

We ran through several more tunes. By showtime Lola had

given me enough confidence to carry me through. There was a small crowd, but a crowd, in the Free Border that night. They seemed satisfied. Lola could have sung unaccompanied and satisfied them. I kept reminding myself of that, lest I claim some of the credit.

Pokey really was gone. The Free Border hired a local pianist to take my place and I became Lola's regular accompanist, not only at the lounge but also on an LP album which she had promised to make for Pan-Orpheus in January. We went to a local radio-TV station and taped her numbers. She insisted that I tape two sides for a forty-five at the same time. So I recorded "April in Portugal" with "Avalon" for the flip and shipped them along with her tapes to Los Angeles.

"I'll jest call that Mistuh Meyuh and tell him to press 'em when he makes mine," Lola promised.

Evidently that was all it took. Within a few weeks my first disc bearing the P-O label was on the stands. My name and picture appeared on Lola's *All Tired Out* album, too. I was really in high cotton, all because of Lola.

We were held over for another month at the Free Border, and then Paul Ade wired Lola that she was booked into the Marble Hall in Chicago, beginning March 2. He asked about Pokey.

"Pokey ain't gona git outa that sanitarium fo' a long time," Lola said to me. "When he does, he's goin' to jail. I'll jest call that Mistuh Ade and tell him you comin' with me. O.K.?"

"O.K.," I said.

"How much you makin', Rusty?" She looked at me quizzically.

"Scale plus twenty-five."

" 'T ain't 'nough. I'll tell that Mistuh Ade to git five hund'ed a week fo' you."

She headed for a telephone booth, counting her change as she went. She closed the door and dialed.

Chicago and five hundred a week! I could hardly believe it.

That sounded like enough. I hoped I could persuade Lola to settle in Chicago permanently. She could certainly work there the year around for the rest of her life. She was my short cut to Chicago. I wondered how I would fare there if she left and I stayed on my own.

Lola was back in a few minutes.

"What did he say?" I asked.

"He say, 'Kin the boy cut it?' An' I say, 'Sho' he kin.' An' he say, 'O.K. bring him on.' That's what he say."

"And the pay?"

"Five hund'ed. Mistuh Ade, he don't argue."

Not with Lola Rivers. She was his hottest property at the moment. I had no idea how much she drew, but I was sure that it was plenty. I did know that she was paying for Pokey's keep at the sanitarium.

February dragged on. With Chicago in sight, time hung heavier than ever. I did not tell Mama that I was coming. I preferred to surprise her. I wrote Ella of my good fortune. She acknowledged my letter but devoted most of her reply to Daddy's troubles.

> Things are really bad. Daddy is down to six tankers and six drivers. There is no letup. Bombs, collisions, acid, syrup, everything that can happen to a truck. But Daddy is still standing firm, bless his heart. We've given up the house in Preston Hollow. Daddy and Cassie have moved into an apartment and I'm living in a dormitory at SMU.
>
> It won't be long, though. Daddy will lick 'em. You'll see. I wish I could help. I wish you were here. We need you and love you,
>
> ELLA

Daddy and I were opposite stars. It was symbolic that his nadir promised to coincide with my zenith. I would not have had it otherwise. I did feel sorry for Ella. Perhaps she would

194

come into my household after all—as soon as Mama and I set up one. The thought reminded me of Dick Jarrell and I wrote him of our opening in the Marble Hall. He answered my letter promptly, wishing me luck but regretting that he had work to do at home and so could not attend. He had heard my P-O recordings. He complimented me on them. His letter arrived on my last day in Detroit.

The Marble Hall is a huge place on St. Clair Street. It seats several hundred, with a large dance floor and complete dinner service. It has an elegance that strictly contemporary décor can never quite achieve. Nowhere is the cotton higher—and the floor show was in proportion.

We opened with a complete new bill backed by Rex Fenton's fine eighteen-piece band. Fritz Manning, the emcee, sparkled as he brought on a chorus of twelve frisky ponies, then a vocal quintet, and a dance team from Jamaica.

"And now," he said, "the star of our show. Lola Rivers—everybody's sweet, sweet mama—with Rusty Meaghan at the piano."

The applause was that of the Free Border amplified ten times. The band brought us on with eight bars of "Beale Street Blues" and then faded as the lights dimmed and a pair of stagehands wheeled my piano into the spotlight. I followed Lola's scintillating white satin into the glare.

One of Fenton's violinists plucked the pitch very softly, and Lola began "Some of These Days" before I even sat down at the piano. From that moment, the Marble Hall belonged to her. At last she was in a room big enough to hold her, as she held everything else in it. She crooned. She shouted. She sobbed. She joked. Then she rested for a minute.

"Y'all gotta let me git my breath," she said, "while Rusty, heah, plays the pieces on his new P-O disc. Rusty!"

She eased into the curve of the piano and watched with rapt adoration while I played "April in Portugal" and "Avalon."

195

"Ain't that great!" she shouted and clapped her big hands for all they were worth.

The audience joined in. They would have agreed with her if I had played "Chopsticks" with two fingers.

"Stand up, Rusty," Lola commanded.

I stood up.

"That's my boy, Rusty," she said proudly.

I sounded her pitch as I sat back down, and she was singing "Mississippi Mud" by the time the applause died out. After two more numbers and two encores, we bowed and left together. We returned for a second bow as the house lights came up.

Then I saw Mama, seated at a choice table with an immaculately dressed Italian, whose mustache and temples were just beginning to turn gray. They were both applauding, but neither appeared to be particularly happy as I left Lola to take her last bow alone.

A stripper came on next and then the chorus line for the finale. As soon as the show was over, I hurried to Mama's table. Mama was expecting me. She offered her cheek as I bent over her, but I kissed her lips instead. It was good to be returning to her triumphant and claiming her again.

"This is Mr. Ricardo, Rusty," she said. "My son, Rusty." It was good to hear her low voice, with its ever-so-faint foreign inflection.

"How do you do," I said.

"Hello, Rusty," Mr. Ricardo said. "Your mother has told me a lot about you, but we wasn't expecting you here tonight." His diction held much stronger traces of Sicilian accent, and his face was right off the TV screen—one of Kefauver's culprits.

"It was a surprise," I said. Instinctively I hated the man.

"It sure was," Mama said with a laugh.

"Pokey Brown, Lola's regular pianist, couldn't make it. So I'm filling in."

"You did very well," Mama said. "We've heard your records."

196

"Good," I said. There was no other chair at the table, and the waiter brought none. Obviously I could not invite Lola out to the table.

"Won't you come back and meet Lola?" I asked.

"Why, yes—yes, of course," Mama said.

I held her chair and she stood up.

"I gotta make a phone call," Mr. Ricardo said. "You go on, Nestra. Glad to have met you, son."

"Glad to have met you, sir."

I escorted Mama to Lola's dressing room and knocked on the door.

"Are you decent?" I asked.

"Sho', Rusty, come on in," Lola called.

I opened the door. Lola was in a bathrobe, sitting before her dressing table drying her feet on a towel. She bathed after each performance. She worked so hard that she had to—like an athlete after a strenuous drill.

"Lola, this is my mother," I said, "Mrs. Bercelli."

"Sho' 'nough. My, she's pretty." Lola rose and extended her hand. "Howdy, Mrs. Bercelli."

"How do you do?" Mama shook hands with Lola.

"You sho' got a fine boy, Mrs. Bercelli."

"Thank you. I think so," Mama said.

"And he was really with it on that piano tonight."

"He was with *you*. You're a real artist, Lola."

"Thank you, ma'am. I jest sing like I was born to sing. That's all, Mrs. Bercelli."

"Well, it's wonderful. Where are you staying, Rusty?"

"At the Drake," I said. "Shall I take you back to your table?"

"Yes, please."

The two women said good-by and I escorted Mama back to Mr. Ricardo, who was waiting for her. I immediately excused myself and returned to Lola's dressing room. A colored bus boy met me at the door.

197

"Can I come in, Miss Rivers?" he asked.

"Sho'. You, too, Rusty. What you want?"

"Miss Rivers, we kinda gotta look out for our friends—like your boy, here."

"Yes. What about him?" Lola asked.

"I seen him kiss Mr. Justice's girl and then I seen her come back here with him. I thought I ought to warn him. Don't nobody lay a hand on that woman and live."

Lola looked at me but did not give me away.

"Why?" she asked the bus boy.

"She's special. I been in this town all my life and I know who's who. Mr. Justice Ricardo owns this town. His girls come and go; but this one, she's been here six-seven years. Don't nobody mess with her but the boss.

"You don't want your boy to get hurt. So I'm telling you and him, he done tore his pants. He better look out. Now, I gotta go before somebody sees me."

"Thank you," Lola said as the bus boy darted out of the door.

I sat down heavily on Lola's bench. My whole body slumped.

"It don't mean nothin', Rusty, boy," Lola said soothingly. "Yo' mammy is a good-lookin' woman. A big man like Mistuh Ricardo is proud of a good-lookin' woman. He's jest lookin' out fo' yo' mammy, keepin' the wolves away. You oughta be happy about it. If they was anything wrong she wouldn't be 'round no six-seven yeahs. He'd git tired of a woman befo' six-seven yeahs. I know all 'bout that."

"I guess you're right," I said. I suspected that she was lying. But she was good. I wanted to believe her.

"Sho' I'm right. Yo' mammy's a good woman. I kin tell. Now, let's eat somp'n befo' the last show."

"O.K.," I said.

We ordered dinner sent to Lola's dressing room. We each had a Martini and then ate slowly. Lola did not let me out of

198

her sight until time for her to dress for the second show. Even then she kept me with her while she dressed behind a screen.

"Zip me up," she said, backing out into the room.

I zipped the fresh white satin gown. It was no easy task. There was no fat on Lola. Her body was as firm as mine, and her clothes were made to fit. One ounce more or one ounce less would have spoiled the whole effect.

"There you are," I said at last.

"Thank you, Rusty. Now, le's go watch them monkey dancahs from Jamaica."

She put on her jewelry as we made our way to the entrance from which we could watch the dancers. I strained my eyes to peer into the darkened room. Justice Ricardo's table was vacant. Mama had gone.

After the second show we found Paul Ade waiting for us in the hall.

"Why, howdy, Mistuh Ade," Lola said. "This is Rusty. He was great, wasn't he?"

"Great, real great. Hello, Rusty," Paul Ade said nervously. "We've gotta go somewhere and talk." He was a short, balding little man in his middle forties. Energy or nerves kept him busy all the time.

"O.K.," Lola said. "I'll jest throw on a wrap. We kin go to my room. Git yo' ovahcoat, Rusty."

Paul Ade had a taxi waiting. We went directly to Lola's room. Whatever her taste in street clothes, Lola lived in style. Her room was a big one, well furnished, with a fully stocked bar just inside the door. She mixed Martinis and served us. Paul Ade would not sit down.

"What we gona talk about, Mistuh Ade?" Lola asked.

"About Rusty."

"What about Rusty?"

"Well, seems he's poison in this town right now."

"What do you mean?" I asked.

"I don't know exactly, but you can't work here. The word is out."

"What word?"

"Justice Ricardo's word. Ever hear of him?"

"I've met him," I said.

"You have? Well, he's the don, the boss of just about everything—all the clubs. I don't know what he's got against you. He don't tell much.

"He controls the juke boxes. Your records are on every one of them and the disc jockeys are plugging you. So you're a right guy there. But you can't play in Chicago. You gotta go."

"When?" I asked.

"Now. You're through. You can work anywhere else—at your present pay or better, but not here. We've gotta get Lola another accompanist."

"Oh, no, Mistuh Ade. Rusty come heah with me. I leave heah with Rusty. Ain't nobody else gona play fo' me. Not even ol' Pokey when he gits outa jail."

"Now, Lola," Paul argued, "we'll take care of Rusty. He ain't gona lose."

"No, suh. And I ain't gona lose him neithah."

"Be reasonable, Lola. Are you doing this because the boy's good or because of that big soft heart of yours?"

"Both. Rusty's good. He's better'n Pokey evah was. And right now my heart is softah fo' Rusty than anybody. Book us in. Book us out. But book us double. You heah me?"

Paul Ade shook his head in resignation and paced the floor.

"O.K., if that's the way you want it. I can send you back to Detroit and bring Flo and Larry in here. The Marble Hall customers won't be happy, but the Free Border ones will. So will Flo and Larry."

"So will me and Rusty," Lola added.

"Tomorrow morning," Paul said.

"Tomorrow mo'nin'," Lola echoed.

He drained his glass and left.

"I gotta take my bath," Lola said, "befo' I cool off. You kin have one mo' drink, Rusty."

She went into her dressing room and then into the bathroom. I could hear her shower running.

I poured another Martini and sat down to brood. Perhaps I had been hating the wrong man for the last seven years. I was beginning to suspect that it was not Daddy at all but Justice Ricardo who was standing between me and Mama. Once Mama had told him how much I meant to her, and she to me, I could see why he would not want me around—whatever their relations.

All my plans had to be revised. I had wanted to get to Chicago; now I was there, at five hundred a week—but for one night only. Still, my star was rising, I argued. Mama would get away somehow. After all, I *had* surprised her. That was my fault. As soon as I was established somewhere she would come to me. She had to. That was how we had planned it. In the meantime—

Lola came out of her bath. She wore a white silk dressing gown, quite different from her backstage wrapper, and was toweling her short hair.

"You all right, Rusty?" she asked.

"I guess so. I hate to leave Chicago. I've planned on coming here for so long."

"You hate to leave yo' mammy, you mean."

"Yes."

"She sho' is a pretty woman. I don't blame you fo' hatin' to leave, but the man say we gotta go."

"You don't have to go," I said. "You can stay. There are lots of good pianists around."

"Ol' Lola ain't gona leave you, Rusty, boy." She sat down on the bed. "Not evah, unless you walk out on her."

"Like Mama walked out on me. She didn't even stay for the second show."

My earlier logic crumpled under that fact, as I was crumpling under Lola's kindness.

"Maybe she had to go. She's in business, ain't she?"

"Yes—cosmetics and a model agency."

"See? She's gotta work tomorrow."

"And we have to leave tomorrow."

I stood up and walked toward the door. I stopped at the bar and idly handled the gin bottle. Lola was watching me.

"Don't you leave heah, Rusty," she said sternly. "Don't you go to bed with no bottle tonight. You come ovah heah and go to bed with me."

I looked around at her. She was serious.

I protested weakly. I wanted to stay.

She rose and turned down the covers. Then she turned out the ceiling light, slipped out of her robe and lay down—the black beauty of her body striking, contrasting, inviting on the fresh white sheets. She looked like everything she sounded like when she sang.

I undressed and lay down beside her. It was like going home again.

"Now, you jest fo'git yo' troubles, Rusty. Lola ain't gona let nothin' hurt you."

Her caresses soothed whatever was tearing me apart. She was the World Mother—safe, abiding, comforting. I sought the balm she offered—a little too eagerly for Lola. She held me back.

"Don't shove, Rusty. We got all night. You gotta learn to be a easy ridah if you want me fo' company."

She showed me what she meant. She set the mood and the rhythm, just as she did when I played her accompaniments. And an easy rider she made me as we shared her wise, abundant passion. Her love was vast, gently ebbing and flowing for a long time, then rising steadily into a storm and subsiding into calm again, ending as quietly as it had begun.

"Rusty, boy," she said at last. "You sho' are all man—easy, easy ridah. I ain't gona leave you nowheah to fret all by yo'-self. An' I don't hafta sing 'No Easy Ridah Blues' no mo'. We gona ride double till evahthing works out yo' way. Go to sleep, baby."

She drew my cheek against her bosom and crooned softly until I fell asleep. If I dreamed at all I dreamed of cribs and cradles and Pullman cars clacking over rail joints in the night.

When I returned to my room I found that I had had several telephone calls during the night, and one that morning. I asked for the last number.

"Priscilla Smart Agency," a woman's voice answered brightly.

"Mrs. Bercelli, please," I said.

"Madame Bercelli, just a moment."

Captain Morgan had been right. It was Madame Bercelli now. I supposed it added tone to her establishment.

"Hello," Mama said.

"Hello, Mama."

"Where have you been all night?"

"Oh, just walking. I couldn't sleep."

"Why?"

"I learned that your *Signor Ricardo* doesn't want me around." I am sure I sounded bitter. Again I had a vision of Justice Ricardo staring insolently at me from Senator Kefauver's TV screen.

"Oh?" Mama said.

"The word is out. I'm going back to Detroit today. Could we have lunch?"

"Rusty—if you had only let me know you were coming, I could have planned for you—but I've made other arrangements. I really can't. I'd love to."

"Why don't you come to Detroit with me? I'm making five

hundred a week now. I can support you on that. You can quit work."

"Oh, no, Rusty. I have a big investment here. I've worked hard. I can't quit now. Later—"

"*Signor Ricardo* would buy you out," I said sarcastically. "He owns everything else in town."

"Now, Rusty, you're just angry and disappointed. I know how you must feel, but be patient. It has taken me a long time to get where I am—it will take some time for me to get out.

"What Mr. Ricardo is doing—if he's doing what you say he is—must be for your own good. There may be things you don't understand. If you stay you may be hurt by something that doesn't concern you. I'll write you."

There was some hope in that. I realized that Mama could not talk very freely through a switchboard or whatever telephone arrangement she had in her office.

"O.K.," I said. "Maybe I don't understand, but I don't like it, either."

"Well, be good. Don't do anything rash."

"I won't. Must I say good-by without even seeing you?"

"Yes. It's better that way. I'll write. Good-by."

After I hung up, I bathed and dressed and packed for my return trip to Detroit.

I considered looking up the Priscilla Smart Agency and checking on Mama's activities, but I could not bring myself to do it. It would be breaking a trust. It would be—I was afraid to follow up my suspicions. Drearily, I ate lunch by myself, stopped by a record shop and bought a new George Shearing album, and then picked Lola up in a taxi and drove to the airport, where we took a plane to Detroit.

The Free Border gang welcomed us back. The manager, Tony Bufano, asked no questions. He seemed to know more about our business than we did and made no objection to my pay raise. In fact, he treated me with more respect than he had before. A little affluence works wonders even among those who provide it.

Mama wrote, as she had promised. After her usual paragraph of personal advice and queries she added,

Remember that your name is Meaghan, not Bercelli, or Ricardo, or Costello, or Genovese, or Profaci. You are doing well. You have a great future, but it is yours from here on. You have the best chance of any of us of fulfilling Avolo's dream.

You look like what you are—a fine, wholesome all-American. Never forget that. Stay away from Chicago, from Ricardo, from me, until I can be your mother, Mrs. Meaghan, again sometime, somewhere—a little old lady no one will notice. That will be best for you, believe me. You'll be doing it for yourself and Avolo, all of us. You are all we have, now that Gina is lost and Ella is with your father.

Can't you see why Chicago is off limits? Don't think that I don't love you. I do, very, very much.

MAMA

I could guess why Chicago was off limits, as Mama explained it. The Sicilian names she had chosen were not those of our most illustrious countrymen. I had no doubt now that Justice Ricardo belonged among those mentioned. If he ran Chicago and Mama did business there, she probably had to pay tribute to him. It was possible that he had forced her to write the letter. Senator Kefauver had left no doubt about how powerful such men were in a good many cities.

Mama might even be held captive in some way, forced to go out with Ricardo to protect her business enterprises. A wave of love for her engulfed me. I felt sorry for her, trapped as she was, as I had been at Highcastle and Quantico. The pitiable attempts at reassurance contained in her letter almost brought tears to my eyes. Now I could not tell whether the letter expressed her own true exhortations to excellence or Ricardo's veiled threats intended to frighten me by reference to the big bad *Mafiosi* featured on TV's Kefauver Hour.

I was still wallowing in frustration when I arrived at the club. I carried my torment to the piano with me. There I seethed as I plotted ways to free Mama from Ricardo and all his kind. I knew the true state of affairs. Every trouble I had was the result of Ricardo's jealousy. It was as simple as that, and I understood it. He was as frustrated as I was. He could get nowhere with Mama because of me; so he had run me out of Chicago. He had that kind of power. But there must be some other kind of power that could break him. I had to find it and exert it. Yet I knew that I could not. It was not the sort of thing I understood.

My mind settled on the piano. I was playing "Jalousie" and having some trouble with the exact figures I wanted in the bass. I repeated one phrase several times, experimenting with rhythm and a countermelody line as I went.

Lola entered and stood behind me while I practiced. There was no one else around except the bartender. I tried and tried, varying my left hand and pedal foot every way I could think of in my frustration.

Lola put her hands on my shoulders and kneaded gently.

"What you diggin' fo' ain't in that li'l ol' piano, Rusty," she said. "It ain't in nobody's music box nowheah. You gona hafta dig somewheah else befo' you find it." She gave my shoulders a final affectionate squeeze and went on toward her dressing room.

Lola was probably right. She knew all there was to know about music and emotions. She sustained me during my time of torment. Her generous body provided the dark Elysium where I found such moments of peace as I knew in those restless days. Her heart held mine together. Her musicianship deepened, broadened, polished mine. She was all I had.

We played another month in Detroit, a month in Milwaukee, in St. Louis, in Kansas City, and then booked into the Ten-to-Three Club in Denver.

After I had been in town awhile I called up the VA Hospital and learned that Captain Hammer was still there. When I went to see him I found him in a wheel chair on the sun deck.

"Hi, Rusty," he said cordially. He had lost weight. The thinness of his face was emphasized by the fat stubby pipe he was puffing on.

"Hi," I said. I shook his hand. It was as strong as ever.

"How are you getting along?" I asked.

"They're still chipping on me. They're above my knees now. Downright indecent, I think. I'm ticklish above the knees." He laughed unconvincingly. "How are you doing?"

"Fine. I have several records out now, and I'm working with Lola Rivers."

"Yes, I know. I've been keeping up with you. I read the announcement of your opening at the Ten-to-Three. Sorry I couldn't be there." He chuckled again. "How was the Marine Corps?"

"So-so," I said. "I was the hero of Quantico for three years—but I'm afraid I lost the Battle of the Potomac."

"We all do. We can't throw enough dollars across it to win."

"I guess not. I still haven't figured out why I'm here." I laughed self-consciously.

"Where are you, Rusty?" His eyes quit trying to be funny.

"I don't know—Denver—Detroit—everywhere but Chicago."

"Why not Chicago?"

I told him. I had to tell someone, and he was the wisest man I knew.

"And you consider Chicago your world—the one you prepared for?"

207

"I suppose so."

"Well, it isn't your world, or your mother's, not all of it. It's only one part of a gigantic complex. The world I prepared for no longer exists, either, and I don't fit into this one any better than you do."

"What is our world?"

"Well, it isn't the world of the artist or the scholar or the philosopher."

He relit his pipe and sucked on it slowly. "It's the world of Ricardo and Luciano, and Dale Carnegie and Norman Vincent Peale and the Overstreets, and James Hoffa and Dave Beck and Harry Bridges, and Einstein and Von Braun, and Billy Graham and Bishop Sheen, and the Atomic Energy Commission and Congress and a packed, capricious Supreme Court. They created it, and like the gods of old they call the turns, by decree or by suggestion.

"Until we understand them and know their will we are no better off than the aborigines trying to read their destiny in the gizzard of a goose—not half so well off as the Greeks. At least they expected their oracles to speak in riddles."

His pipe had gone out again. Neither of us spoke while he knocked the dottle out of it, refilled it, and relighted it. He puffed until the fresh tobacco was burning evenly. I lit a cigarette.

"If I sound bitter," he said, "it's because I am. I can't think and hold onto my integrity. I can't teach any more. If I were able to coach football somewhere, each Saturday's game would be more important to me than the world itself—as it is for millions and millions of idiots from Labor Day to New Year's.

"You ducked college football, Rusty. Power to you. You can duck the rest, too. Just hide behind your piano, the way I do behind my plastic feet, and say, 'To hell with it.' These modern prosthetic devices provide an excuse for everything.

"Just whine, 'I'm sick.' We all are."

208

Captain Hammer was no help. He was anything but a cheerful invalid just then. Still there was enough sardonic banter in his conversation to make me think that he might be goading me on to snap out of my own despondency. Physically I was exactly what he had been and wanted to be again. But my return was not blocked by any physical disability other than the weakness of one man against a system.

I went to see him once more—after Ella came to Denver. She dropped in at the Ten-to-Three unexpectedly. I was playing requests between shows—I did double duty there, but it was a rather informal arrangement. Ella was beside my bench before I even knew that she was in town.

"Hi, wombmate," she said.

I looked up in surprise. She was beautiful, in a trim summer dress and a perky little hat.

"Hi," I said.

"If you can tear yourself away from that ill-tempered clavichord I'll buy you a drink."

"I can buy drinks cheaper," I said. "I work here."

"So I see. You've worked long enough. Knock it off and join me."

I finished the chorus I was playing and rose from the piano. Ella was full grown now and well filled out. She could have worn Mama's clothes without raising a hem or taking in a seam.

"I have a table," she said. "Right over there." She pointed at a table for two.

"How did you get in here?" I asked. "Didn't you see the sign about unescorted ladies?"

"I'm no lady. I told them I was your sister. They didn't believe me, of course, but they evidently thought you might like me. So here I am."

"I do like you." I held her chair for her.

"Good. Who's your girl in Denver?"

"I don't have one." I sat down facing Ella.

"And you've been here three weeks?" She arched her eyebrows in mock disbelief. "What's the matter? Don't you like girls?"

"Sure. Girls like you. There aren't any in Denver."

A waiter came and took our order. Ella took rye on the rocks.

"I'm surprised you didn't order the same," she said. "That's what Daddy drinks. You're just like him every other way."

"I wouldn't say that. How is he?" I could at least be polite.

"Gone to hell. They finally ruined him, put him out of business. He lost everything he had."

"And it got him, huh?" I could find no sympathy for Daddy.

"Yes. You know how it is with people like Daddy. Once they've had it and lost it, they've *had* it. He went to pieces. I couldn't bring myself to write you about him; so I came to tell you."

"Where is he now? Still in Dallas?"

"No. Cassie finally pulled him together and patched up the Bozo in him. Gina got a job for both of them in burlesque. They're back in Boston. Danny Meaghan rides again!"

Ella took a substantial drink of rye.

"I tried to keep Daddy in Dallas. I had a good job offered me in the D.A.'s office—well, a job anyway. I could have kept the apartment until Daddy made a comeback. He was well liked. You know that. He knew all the big oilmen.

"But, oh, no. He had to listen to that blonde bitch he married. She told him he belonged in burlesque, with her. Cassandra, the Exotic—Reveals All, Knows Nothing. Did you know she was a tassel dancer, Rusty?"

"No," I said with a chuckle. "I knew she was equipped for it."

"Well, she was—is. I can just see her—and Daddy, at the Howard. And he was so wonderful as Big Tex. He's too good for Cassie. He should never have left Mama or me—us."

210

"But he did," I reminded her.

"It wasn't his fault. He always did what he thought was right. I think I know who ruined him—at least I'm on the trail. Did you ever hear of Justice Ricardo?" Her eyes hardened and focused on mine.

"I've met him," I said guardedly. Ella could read me. "He's a big man in Chicago." My heart was pounding.

"He's a big man all over, Rusty. He's at the top of the syndicate. His word is law. He metes out justice—he can make or break anybody."

"Justice is his name." I could hide behind inanities until I found out how much Ella knew, and maybe keep her from knowing what I knew—or suspected.

"Or nickname—I don't know which," Ella said. "*Giustizia*— that means justice. It also means gallows, too. Remember? And *giustiziare* means to execute, to ruin—and *giustiziere* means executioner as well as justiciary. Wonderful language, the Italian—so clear and straightforward. Justice Ricardo is all those things." Her tongue was loosening up.

"How do you know all this?" I asked.

"Oh, you know. In law school we got to know people around the courthouse. When things got rough with Daddy I began snooping, had a few dates with one of the D.A.'s investigators. Nobody could really help Daddy, but a lot of people learned a lot of things they couldn't quite prove."

"But you can, I suppose."

"I might." She tried to impress me by fixing her gaze—it wavered. "Look, Rusty, I'm the smartest one of the family. I never could sing or dance like Gina. I couldn't play piano like you, handle my body like Mama, or win friends and influence people like Daddy—but I'm smart. I proved that at SMU. Want to see my transcript?"

"Do you happen to have it with you?"

"No. But I can get it." She was beginning to sound belligerent. "I didn't finish; that is, I haven't got my law degree yet, but I led my classes, and I can prove it."

"I believe you." I looked at my watch. "I have a show to do. Can you spare me?"

"I'll trade you for another rye on the rocks."

"You won't need that. Just wait until you hear Lola Rivers. She'll be good for what ails you. Sit right here. I'll be back."

I checked in with Lola a few minutes before showtime and we came on together. As always, she was wonderful. The crowd —flat-country *bourgeoisie*, mountain climbing for the summer— had never heard anyone quite like her in person. They warmed gradually and were hers, enthusiastically hers, before we finished the show. I waited for her to take her ritual shower, and took her out to meet Ella.

"So this is yo' twin sistuh," she said as she sat down at our table. "She sho' is pretty. She don't look much like yo' sistuh, but she sho' do look like yo' mama's daughtuh. What you doin' in Denvuh, honey?"

"I came to see Rusty."

"Ain't he lookin' good?"

"Wonderful."

"And ain't he great on that piano?"

"Real great," Ella said. She had not had another drink. She studied Lola shrewdly. "You're great, too, Lola."

"Shucks, honey, I jest sing natural like. I can't even read— music, I mean. Rusty's the boy that knows what he's doin'. He knows what evahbody's doin', like that blind English boy. What's his name, Rusty?"

"George Shearing," I said.

"Yeah. He's great, too. Rusty says he is. Le's drink somp'n."

"I have to go back to work," I said.

"Awright. You run along. I'll look aftah yo' sistuh."

I left them together and returned to the stand. I played my

212

own selections for a while; then requests began coming in as the crowd mellowed. After our second show everybody was happy. Ella sang "Don't Sit Under the Apple Tree," with the personality frills she had learned back in Indianapolis. Other customers got into the act, and the evening finally degenerated into a sing-song, beginning with "Down by the Old Mill Stream" and ending with "Good Night, Ladies" at closing time.

I took Ella to the Brown Palace, where she was staying. She was gayer than she had been earlier in the evening, until we got to her room.

"Why don't you stay with me and cause a scandal?" she asked. "Nobody will believe I'm really your sister."

She hugged me and kissed me. For a moment I thought *she* had forgotten that she was my sister.

"I'm not going to pay rent on an empty room," I said.

"Well, sit down long enough for a nightcap anyway."

"O.K.," I said.

She ordered ice and poured drinks for both of us.

"We had fun tonight, didn't we?" she said.

"We sure did."

"Just like old times. Weren't we happy then, Rusty?"

"Yes."

"Will we ever be happy again?"

"Sure. It takes a little time to get adjusted. We're still trying our wings. When will you get your law degree?"

"I may not take it." Ella studied the ice in her glass. "I may not be a lawyer. I may decide to be the best legal secretary in the world—that might be better for a woman."

"Might be," I said.

"Rusty, are you sleeping with Lola?" she asked suddenly and flicked her eyes back to my face.

"Sometimes," I said after a pause. "Why?"

"I thought you were. I don't like it."

"Why?" I asked again.

"I just don't, that's why," she answered, with irrefutable woman-logic. Perhaps she was wise not to be a lawyer after all.

"I don't see how where I sleep concerns you," I said.

"Well, it does. You're my brother—my twin brother. Everything you do concerns me. I love you—better than anything." She added the last slowly. She was thinking of Daddy. "Lola loves you too—big love, generous love, unselfish love. She wouldn't care where you slept.

"I'm not like her—but I guess I wish I had someone like her. Oh, Rusty, I'm so lonely, with Daddy gone—and you and Mama and Gina and Avolo." The misery in her voice was unmistakable.

"I'll get whoever ruined us all, too," she said slowly, deliberately. "So help me God, I'll track him down and see him burn."

She was serious. It never entered her mind that Daddy was to blame, that he started it all by sacrificing Gina, the pride of the family. Ella finished her drink in one swallow.

"Sleep it off," I said lightly and rose to go.

"What are you doing, tomorrow?" she asked.

"I'm going to see Captain Hammer at the VA Hospital. Won't you come along? He likes company."

"I'd love to." She got up and followed me to her door. "What time?"

"I'll pick you up about one."

"Fine. I'll be ready."

She kissed me good night and laid her head on my chest and hung onto me desperately. She did miss Daddy.

The next day we found Captain Hammer at his usual place on the sun deck.

"I've brought a right special little package with me this time," I said as we approached his wheel chair. "My sister Ella, Captain Hammer."

214

"Ella—I'd have known you anywhere." He shifted his pipe and took her hand.

"Because I look so much like Rusty?" Ella laughed.

"No. Like your mother. We sat through some football games together. I got to know her pretty well. Beautiful woman."

"May I say thanks?" Ella asked.

"Sure. For both of you. Sit down."

I drew up chairs for us.

"You're the lawyer, aren't you?" Captain Hammer asked.

"Maybe yes, maybe no," Ella said. "Right now I'm a little disgusted with the law."

"So am I," said the captain. "Just look at this." He lifted a newspaper off his lap and pointed to two headlines.

"Hot-check artist gets ten years," he read. "Business-college executive sentenced to eighteen months for swindling VA out of a hundred thousand dollars. The hot-check artist netted five hundred from his activities. See, Rusty, I told you our world was not for artists."

"Yes," I said. "I guess I should go in for swindling."

"I can see how you might find the law puzzling at times, Ella," the captain said. "Still it is a noble profession."

"Oh, I'm not being noble," Ella said. "I'm being nasty."

"Good for you. I'm a little nasty myself. Ask Rusty."

"He hasn't shed his cocoon yet," Ella said.

"Have you?"

"I'm emerging." She lit a cigarette, inhaled deeply, and let the smoke out her nostrils. "See? I smoke. I contribute regularly to the cancer fund—and I pay taxes to subsidize the tobacco industry. I know what I'm doing. I appreciate the paradox."

"Bright girl."

"Sure. I'm so bright I sometimes hurt my eyes." Her voice was bitter.

"You're good for mine. I'm glad Rusty brought you along."

215

"I insisted on coming. Rusty says that you are wise. Are you wise, Captain Hammer?" She studied him as she was wont to study me.

"No," the captain said.

"Don't disappoint me."

"Why not? I've disappointed everyone else—including myself. Why make an exception of you?"

"Because I'm special. I'm me."

The captain laughed. He was enjoying Ella, for all their cynicism.

"What can *we* do, Captain Hammer?"

"Join up."

"Must we join up?"

"I'm afraid so—sometime. I never did, but look at me now."

"Sometime. I'm glad you said that," Ella said. She sounded grateful. They were talking way over my head, but they seemed to understand each other.

"We can fight awhile—struggle awhile before joining up, can't we?" Ella asked insistently.

"I think maybe you can, long enough to learn the rules—the requirements."

"Yes, yes. I understand that. No one knows what the law is until he breaks it."

"And is punished," Captain Hammer added.

"And is punished." Ella nodded her head vigorously as she repeated the captain's words.

"Five yards for off-side, five for illegal motion—"

"Fifteen for clipping."

"Right," the captain said.

"But we can try."

"Certainly. Everybody gets hurt for trying."

"And the rules are modified every year."

"Every year," the captain agreed.

"Send me in, Coach!" Ella's eyes were bright.

216

"I believe you're ready." He shared her excitement.

"I'll run interference for Rusty," Ella said and looked at me teasingly.

"That's what I meant," the captain said.

"I know it. Oh, Captain Hammer, you *are* wise." Ella leaned over impulsively and kissed him on the cheek. "Thank you, wise man."

"Don't mention it." He waved his hand magnanimously. The conversation seemed to have solved something.

Ella settled back into her chair and let me and Captain Hammer talk for a while. We solved nothing, but it was a good hour we spent on the sun deck.

In the taxi back to town Ella told me more of her plans.

"I'm going to Chicago," she said.

"You can't do anything in Chicago," I warned her. "I doubt that you can even stay there. It's strictly off limits for me."

"I'm different. I'm no celebrity. No one need know I'm there. Anyway I'm a girl. That's really the big difference.

"And I look like one of them," she added under her breath.

"One of what?"

"One of those damned sleazy wops who showed up every time anything bad happened to Daddy. Lloyd—he was the D.A.'s man I went with—saw a pattern in it. They never appeared in a line-up. They never were picked up, but they were always hanging around union headquarters about the time trouble broke out.

"Out-of-town hoodlums, no record in Dallas. Usually from Chicago—Ricardo's boys."

"How do you know?"

"I just know; that's how." More of Ella's irrefutable logic. "I hate him."

"So do I." I did not elaborate. "Can I help?"

Nothing would have pleased me more than to see Justice Ricardo hang.

"No, not now. Rusty, you're a good ball handler, but somebody has to call the play, and somebody has to run interference for you. Captain Hammer has given me all the help I need right now."

"He didn't even know what you were talking about," I said as we pulled up at a stop light.

"Didn't he?" Her tone was contemptuous. "He told me to go ahead. Ever hear of basic research—pure science?"

"Sounds familiar." The light changed.

"That's what we were talking about. The practical application is idiot work. I'll do that. He doesn't need details."

"Well, I do. Just what is on your mind?"

"You wouldn't understand, Rusty. You've been wrapped in cotton all your life." Ella patted my hand affectionately. "Mama, Highcastle, the Marine Corps, the piano you hide behind, and now Lola. You really haven't been anywhere and you haven't met anybody."

"I suppose you've been everywhere and met everybody." Traffic was getting heavy. The taxi moved by jerks and starts.

"I've been to college," she said, "and I've been to the courthouse, and I've met Captain Hammer."

"So have I."

"But you don't know him the way I know him." Ella had always been a little condescending toward me. Now her attitude rankled.

Perhaps she had a point, however. It was true that I knew little or nothing of the world she and Captain Hammer talked about—only a small corner of it which had been ruled off limits the moment I glimpsed it.

Ella was gayer that night, though she drank less. She left the next morning, and I did not see her again for nearly a year. She wrote several times while we were in Las Vegas, but she told me nothing. I got two letters in Reno, and one in San Francisco. The last was only a note.

218

I'm on the trail. I'm moving. Send your itinerary to my old address and don't write again.

Love,
ELLA

There was no return address. Ella had never once mentioned Mama, and Mama's letters made no reference to her. Both sent me presents at Christmas. Again Ella gave no return address, but her package was postmarked Chicago.

Lola and I spent the winter in southern California, where we made a number of records for P-O and I had an opportunity to study Andre Previn's work. In the spring we worked our way back through Phoenix, Tucson, and Albuquerque. At the Texas border we split up. Lola flew to Memphis for a vacation, and I rode a Pullman on to Baltimore.

A telegram was waiting for me there in care of the Blue Point.

MEET ME AT CIRCUS BAR PICCADILLY 7 PM MAY 27 ELLA

CHORUS

CRAZY, man, crazy!

Cats in catalepsy!

Cats in catatonia!

The joint was strewn with them, stoned out, way out, far out, fallen out, flipped, wigged, and high—gone, gone, gone! Rusty was with us. Rusty was with it.

His few piano interludes, thrown in unconsciously, had brought Lola Rivers right into the pad with us. They sounded his story for us. They sent us. We dug him. We dug Ella. We dug Captain Hammer. Blow, man, blow! We had to press, those of us who were not completely stoned into a coma. It was a real ball. We wanted to keep it swinging all night, forever.

"Play for us, now, Rusty," we cried. "Blow, man, blow!"

Rusty, however, picked himself up off the piano bench— with Teresina, that sturdy watchman at the gate, hanging on to him, limp as a Victoria vine—and smiled at us politely.

"Oh, I never play any more," he said. "I haven't touched a piano since I killed Mama. There's no reason to play now."

With that he and Teresina cut out, leaving us more thoroughly stoned than ever.

There we were, quiet quivering bodies lying around like vestal virgins, cool chicks in heat, oestrus everywhere, rut and ritual rampant—and our daddy-o cut out on us.

"He has killed his mother." Kurt was first to speak. The poet always finds a voice.

"But that's not like war." Clara was quick to come to the defense of our shaman. "He hasn't killed an enemy in hate. He only killed his mother. He did it in love, I'm sure. 'Yet each man kills the thing he loves/By each let this be heard.'"

"Oh, for Christ's sake, Clara, don't go Wilde," Kurt said. His voice was pitched higher than hers. "I'm not blaming Rusty. I love him. I, too, killed my mother. I'm closer to Rusty Meaghan than any cat here. Like I know what he's done, and why. Mama was his kick; so he kicked her. Like Mama is harder to kick than pot or horse or gin. She's the worst monkey of all when she's on your back. Mumsy was on my back until I was fifteen years old."

He was all but screaming.

"Daddums was a preacher. He died when I was five. Mumsy made me sleep with her until I was grown. She liked it. I was miserable, stiff every morning, aching and backing away. Like it was

make it with mumsy
work the wench
shag the hag
ball the bag
or
beat it boy beat it.

Oh, my God, I'm composing—rhyming and alliterating at the same time!"

He was crying now. Huge tears rolled down his cheeks, and his whole body twitched with emotion.

"So I beat it. I ran away. And it killed Mumsy. I was all she had. She was all I had. She had no daughter, no girl child. I'm all there is left of her. I have to *be* Mumsy now, because I killed her. Don't you dig that, Clara?"

Kurt hid his face in his hands and sobbed hysterically.

"I must be Rusty's mother, too," he wailed. "And wife and mistress, too. All those things he lost when he killed her. All those things I lost when I killed Mumsy. I must, I must, I must!"

"You goddamn sniveling fag," Clara sneered. "I'm what Rusty needs. He'll play for me. I have a piano."

A more sympathetic chick brought a pail of water and drenched Kurt with it. He quieted down a bit, but continued to whimper until Clara made him cut out for his own pad. That left us to search among ourselves, such of us as were at all articulate. Those with an O.D. of Rusty's music never knew what happened after the truth-talk. We kept it as quiet as we could.

If Rusty would not play, then we were right back where we started, nowhere. Like our shaman-elect would become an ex-shaman in short order. But we are wise in the ways of wig-flippers. We've seen too many of them come back after they've fallen out, seemingly forever.

We were especially careful to keep the little scene between Kurt and Clara from Teresina. So in time we arranged another séance. The cats who fell out early came to hear Rusty play. The ones hip to the whole scene came to hear how Rusty killed Mama in—

WASHINGTON, 1955

I WENT ON to Washington and registered at the Willard. Ella had given me plenty of time. The twenty-seventh was the next Friday; so I made the rounds of the bars and clubs, looking up musicians I knew who played regularly in Washington. I ran down to Quantico for a day, just to open old wounds, and then picked up my luggage and took a train to New York.

Ella was just turning off Broadway onto Forty-fifth Street when I crossed Times Square. She was wearing a warm-red Italian silk suit and a hat to match. Her jacket was fitted around the waist and flared gently at her slender hips. The seams of her stockings pointed straight down into black leather shoes. She wore short gloves and carried a black leather bag. It was a pleasure to watch the familiar grace of her movements as I followed her west on Forty-fifth until I overtook her in front of the Circus Bar.

"Hi, wombmate," I said, coming up from behind.

"Rusty!" She spun around and hugged me.

"I'll buy a drink," I said.

"It'll have to be a quick one. We're going to a show."

"We have lots of time," I said. "It's only seven."

"Oh, not one of these," she said, pointing vaguely at the Booth and the Plymouth across the street. "We're going over to Jersey—for a family reunion."

"Not me," I said, as I escorted her into the bar.

"Please, Rusty, you must. It's very important. We must do that first. Then we'll get on with our business."

225

Ella persuaded me, as she always had, while we rushed through our drinks. She chatted nervously all the time about nothing, deliberately about nothing. When we finished we took a taxi through the tunnel and to a dingy little burlesque house in Jersey City.

In the dimly-lit foyer were four lobby boards: Al "Bozo" Meaghan with the rubber nose and baggy pants; Perry Klein, a seedy-looking straight man in a Buster Keaton hat; Cassandra (Reveals All) in tassels; and Flame O'Dare, a life-sized picture of Gina blown up from a negative about ten years old.

The carrot-headed female in the box office looked at Ella and me in surprise. Our appearance must have startled her.

"You're just in time for the first show, *sir*," she said, making a quick recovery and acquiring very cultivated diction on short notice.

As we opened the door we were engulfed by a nauseating wave from unwashed bodies. The house appeared to be completely dark. I finally made out a wheel chair full of blubber which took our tickets and tore them in half. We felt our way down several rows to two vacant seats on the aisle. As our eyes became accustomed to the darkness we saw that the house was practically empty—not over fifty customers, widely dispersed.

The light came on at the piano in the pit, and a lone musician jangled a medley of old show tunes for an overture. When the floods came on, the curtains opened on Cassie and Gina, dressed in short schoolgirl frocks. They danced like third-graders as they sang,

> We are the little girls
> Living in the big house
> Up on top of the hill—
> Her name is Jenny [*Cassie, pointing at Gina*]
> Her name is Mamie [*Gina, pointing at Cassie*]
> We've a big sister, we call Jill [*Both*]

Cassie and Gina wore their strikingly dyed hair in pony tails with childish bows and revealed tight ruffled panties with every step they took. Gina was almost as plump as Cassie now; and, with identical make-up, she looked like Cassie's sister. Her voice held the same bored stridency, too.

They finished the first chorus, danced the second, showing a much broader expanse of panties. Daddy, after a prat-fall entrance, joined them in the third chorus—a parody with unprintable lyrics. Ella had not said a word since entering the theater. I could not tell whether she was crying or merely holding a handkerchief to her nose to keep out the people-stench welling up around us.

After an encore, the trio danced off stage. Daddy returned before a garden drop, mumbling a monologue which brought lewd chuckles from the few men sitting down front.

Presently Cassie, still wearing her little-girl dress, edged shyly onstage as though looking for something. Finally she summoned enough nerve to speak to Daddy in a small, lisping voice.

"Have you seen my sprinkler, sir? I have some sprinkling to do."

Daddy answered some nonsense and produced a sprinkling can.

"Thank you, sir. Now I can sprinkle." She exited down right, sprinkling imaginary flowers as she went.

Next Perry Klein, whom I now recognized as the pianist, came on stage in his Buster Keaton hat and a suit as tight as Daddy's was baggy. He also was looking for something.

"Have you seen my mower, Bozo?" he asked. "I have some mowing to do."

Repeating his former business, Daddy produced a lawn mower and Perry pushed it off stage, saying, "Now I can mow."

Out came Gina. She had let her hair down. It hung in loose red curls around her shoulders. She wore a tight sheath dress with a slitted skirt, as she prissed across the stage. She stopped down left, tossed her head, winked at Daddy, twitched her bottom saucily, and prissed on into the wings.

Daddy stared after her for a moment, leered at the audience, then assumed a fencer's *en garde* stance and shouted, "Has anybody seen my rapier?"

The stage blacked out. Audience response was negligible.

Cassie came on again—a society matron this time, in a tea gown with hat and gloves—and did a routine strip ending with mechanical bumps and grinds. After another blackout, featuring the entire cast, Gina appeared as a French cocotte and repeated Cassie's performance, movement by movement. After another bit of ensemble obscenity, Cassie returned in five tassels: one pasted on each nipple, one on her navel, and one on each of her generous buttocks. Her specialty was the art of keeping the pairs of tassels spinning, sometimes in the same direction, sometimes in opposite directions, while the odd one flapped the basic rhythm. Admittedly she demonstrated remarkable muscle control, if her assorted protuberances could be called muscles.

"And now, ladies and gentlemen, Flame O'Dare, the star of our show!" Daddy tried to make his announcement sound impressive.

After Perry's introduction to "When You and I Were Seventeen," Gina waltzed out of the wings. In a filmy pale-green party frock she looked like everybody's best girl on her way to the senior prom. She danced beautifully, and her voice was quite different from the one she had used in her first duet with Cassie. She still managed to create the illusion Bert Marks had talked about that afternoon in Indianapolis.

Gina sang two complete choruses in her sweet soprano voice before discarding as much as her scarf. After that she took her time about disrobing. She waltzed sixteen bars with each cast-off garment before laying it aside—her bodice, her skirt, her

228

slip. She danced a full chorus in stockings and conventional teen-age underwear, but in time she worked her way down to a pair of sequins and a G-string. Perry segued into a boogie rhythm, and Gina surpassed anything Cassie had been able to do in the way of bumps, grinds, and dips. The illusion was gone, however, for anyone who watched her face. It set into a dead-pan expression, broken by an occasional perfunctory leer or professional smile of invitation, as businesslike as the countenance of a tile-setter laying mosaics.

After her third bow and final fanny-flip as she disappeared into the wings, the audience began straggling out. Few stayed for the finale. It was Gina that the old lechers had come to see.

"All right, Rusty," Ella said. "Let's go backstage."

I was reluctant, but I knew better than to buck Ella. We stumbled down the dark aisle and crossed over to a door marked by a red exit sign. A dim yellow light was burning in the wings. We found our way to the half-open door of a dressing room.

Ella knocked.

"Come in," Gina said.

We pushed the door and saw Gina, still unclad as she had been on her exit, pulling her stockings on again. Perry Klein stood behind her, looking at himself in her mirror.

"Rusty! Ella!" Gina exclaimed and jumped up from her bench. "I thought it was Cassie."

Ella started to embrace her.

"Wait," Gina said. "You'll get Spanish whiting all over you."

Perry handed Gina a robe—"wrap-around" came to mind—which she slipped into hastily. Then she and Ella hugged each other crushingly. Over Ella's shoulder Gina's face, though momentarily happy, looked older than Mama's ever would.

"It's good to see you kids!" Gina said. She let go of Ella and came to me.

I kissed her and returned her hungry squeeze when she clasped me to her.

"Oh, Rusty. You look wonderful," she said. "So big and handsome—and successful."

She backed away and looked up at my face. Her eyes were wet.

"You kids have never met my husband, have you?" she asked, when she remembered.

"Rusty, Ella, this is my husband, Perry Klein." She reached for his hand and drew him toward us.

Perry was an eager little man, with a complexion the color of cigarette stain, and thinning brown hair. He greeted Ella respectfully and turned to me. His eyes were bright with excitement.

"Hey, you're really Rusty Meaghan, ain't you?" His strong fingers made for a firm handclasp.

"Yes," I said.

"Man, you're great, real great," he said rapidly. "You're with it on that piano." As if he could tell, after the way he had banged on that box in the pit!

"Thanks," I said.

"Yeah. Me and Gina got all your records. We read about you, too, in *Down Beat*—right up there with the greats. George Shearing, Erroll Garner, Hampton Hawes, Don Shirley, Father Hines, Pete Johnson—"

"Liberace," I said.

"Yeah, Liberace," he went right on. He did not know the difference, but I was sorry that I had proved it. He was a good little guy. Fortunately Ella and Gina were too deeply interested in their own conversation to pay any attention to ours.

"Where's Daddy?" Ella asked at last.

"Other side," Gina said. "Come with me."

We passed behind the movie screen through the dialogue of *Virgins in Hollywood*, or some such exposé, which was run-

230

ning between stage shows. The opposite dressing room was just like Gina's—bare brick walls, grease-paint smears, autographs and telephone numbers jotted down in lipstick. Daddy sat at his table with a tumbler of whiskey in his hand. Cassie wore a faded robe, open in front while she patched up a hefty thigh with Spanish whiting.

"Look, Al," she said, "the twins!"

Ella rushed by us all and plumped down on Daddy's lap. She bypassed his rubber nose to plant a kiss on his stubbly cheek.

"Ella, baby!" he said, sloshing his drink as he wrapped his arms clumsily around her.

"How are you, Rusty?" Cassie asked. She put aside her sponge and modestly closed her robe.

"Fine," I said. "How are you?"

"O.K., I guess." She took my hand. "Sorry you found us like this."

"We wouldn't think of missing your show," I said.

She looked at my face quickly to see if I was in earnest. I tried to conceal how I loathed the whole business.

"Where are you playing? Still with Lola Rivers?"

"Lola's in Memphis," I said. "I'm taking a couple of months off."

Ella disentangled herself from Daddy and rose to greet Cassie.

"Hello, Daddy," I said.

"Hi, Rusty, long time no see." He extended his hand but made no attempt to rise. "I laid 'em in the aisles tonight, didn't I?"

"Yeah," I said. "You really had 'em rollin'."

"Every night's the same," he said with self-conscious modesty. I dropped his hand. There was no grip in it any more.

"How about dinner, all of you?" Ella asked brightly.

"No time," Gina said. "We do three shows a night."

"Then later," Ella insisted, "after the show?"

Cassie looked uncertainly at Daddy and then answered for all of them.

"No," she said. "We'd better not—not tonight. We'll be too tired for any fun."

"Tomorrow, maybe?" Ella asked.

"We're closing here tomorrow night," Cassie said hesitantly. "We'll be busy packing all day, I'm afraid."

Cassie frowned as Daddy poured another drink from the bottle on the table. She looked pleadingly at Gina.

"I want to visit with the twins awhile," Gina said quickly. "Come by my dressing room when you're decent."

"O.K.," Cassie said.

Gina hurried us out of the dressing room. Daddy waved vaguely as we left.

"Be seein' ya," he said thickly.

Perry did not come with us. Back in the other dressing room, Gina moved the costumes piled on the only chair and made room for Ella. She sat on her bench. I stood beside her.

"Don't stay," Gina said. "By the last show Daddy won't know whether you're here or not."

"I'll stay," Ella said. "I'll help."

"There's nothing you can do," Gina said. "Cassie will take care of him. She's good to him, but nobody can help him. All we can do is humor him."

"Why don't we put him somewhere?" Ella asked. "I'm working. Rusty makes lots of money. And you can do much better than this professionally."

"This is Daddy's life—what he has left," Gina said. "We play where they'll book him. I won't take it away from him, and we don't need help. We get along all right."

"But—"

"Leave us alone, Ella." Gina's voice had an edge on it. "Don't let Daddy break your heart as he has already broken mine and Mama's."

"Mine, too." Ella sniffed. "I love him as much as you do."

"He isn't Daddy any more," Gina said. She looked me up and down. "Rusty is the Daddy we knew and loved—young, tall, handsome, clean. He is just like Daddy used to be, isn't he? You look after Rusty, Ella. Keep him that way. And both of you take care of Mama. Daddy's in good hands."

"We'll take care of Mama," Ella said in flat tones. "And don't add to your worries. I'll see that nothing happens to Rusty."

"You two talk as if I weren't here, or wasn't able to take care of myself." I was a little angry. "I can look after myself—and the whole lot of us for that matter."

"Don't get mad, Rusty," Gina said. "We love you. You *are* a lot like Daddy—and look at him now. But I know you'll be all right. We're very proud of you. Just leave us alone, you and Ella. Keep yourselves clean."

"Clean!" Ella exploded.

"Yes." Gina was gentle. "You're a fine, healthy pair. Stay that way. You're Avolo's last chance. Don't spoil it. Now, run along. You've seen enough."

She stood up, as a cue to Ella, who rose from her chair reluctantly. Gina kissed both of us.

"Out the stage door," she said, and showed us to the back of the theater. "It's just a few steps down the alley to the street. You can get a taxi there."

Ella hugged her again.

"Thanks for coming," Gina said. "But don't come back—ever. I'll call on you if we need you."

I held onto Ella firmly until we reached the street. She was crying, but she straightened up when we came to a lighted area.

"All right, Rusty," she said. "You've seen what Justice Ricardo did to Daddy."

233

"Yes," I said. I could lose nothing by humoring her just then.

"And what he could do to Mama," she added. I could never tell how much Ella knew or intended for me to know.

I hailed a taxi, one of the big, old-style ones.

"Where to?" I asked her.

"Back to Times Square, the Circus Bar."

"Forty-fifth and Broadway," I said to the driver.

We settled down in the back seat. Ella huddled against me, and I put an arm around her.

"I'm glad I didn't see Daddy without his make-up on," she said softly. A shiver ran through her body. She sniffed back her tears. I patted her but said nothing.

"Maybe we can't help Daddy, but we can avenge him," she said after she regained some of her composure. "I learned plenty in Chicago."

"Anything positive, anything that will stand up?"

"A bag full."

"How did you get it?"

"Every way." Her voice sounded strange. It took on a new timbre, a vehement quality that I had heard a few times in Mama's—and been thrilled by then. "I've been sleeping around some myself since I last saw you. A girl can pick up a lot in bed." She sounded as though she were spiting me.

"She sure can," I said, disturbed. "Like a family, for instance."

"Not me," she said in the most miserable voice I had ever heard her use. "Rusty, I'm a freemartin."

"What's that?"

"A sterile heifer calf born with a bull—an incomplete twin. The doctor tells me I have an infantile uterus. I'll never grow up inside."

"I'm sorry," I said.

"Don't feel sorry for me," she snapped. "I feel sorry enough for myself. I don't need any help of that nature. But I do need

234

help, Rusty. I have the furies all the time now. I hate me for all I am and all I'm not.

"I'm not even a woman. Add one more failure to my dismal record. I can't sing, dance, play the piano—or have babies. Nothing is for real." She squeezed my arm convulsively.

"I've tried. I'm good in bed, Rusty. Men have told me that. Because I try so hard. I am a delight to those I don't scare away. And I don't even know who they are. I don't care who they are. I'm trying to make something of myself, something I'm not—a woman, a mother. I know I can't; but I keep trying, and I drive them crazy or drive them off.

"But that's all over—I think. I got what I went after in Chicago, I put what I had to good use."

"Tell me about that," I said as gently as I could. Ella had never been in such a state before. At least I had never seen her that way.

"Well, I started on the fringes, names I had picked up in Dallas. It didn't take me long to find out who was Ricardo's lawyer."

The taxi pulled into a stream of heavy traffic on one of the approaches to the Lincoln Tunnel.

"Tommy Kaufman, you've heard of him." Ella said.

"No."

"Well, all lawyers and all law students have. He's the best criminal lawyer in Chicago. I went to him and applied for a job as a legal secretary. He knew me the minute I walked in, Rusty. It was uncanny."

"How did he know you?"

"He knew Mama. Rusty, did you know that Mama knew Ricardo?" She looked up at me shrewdly as the taxi came to a full stop.

"Yes. That's how I met him. I told you I had met him."

"Well, it turned out that Tommy had a yen for Mama. He shared Ricardo's taste in women. He's a steely-eyed, steely-haired little man with no sex appeal at all. It made him feel big to share the boss's women, I guess.

"Anyway, the story was that he made a big play for Justice Ricardo's cast-off mistresses, and usually won. I've heard that he moved in on some of them before Justice moved out. It was probably all rumor, because Tommy is still alive. But, then, he had ways of protecting himself.

"He thought Mama was just another one of Ricardo's women, and he propositioned her once. He told me that—after I had known him a long time. You know Mama. He couldn't get anywhere with her."

Ella must have felt my muscles go tense.

"Even if she had been Ricardo's mistress," she said hastily, "Tommy wouldn't have had a chance. Justice would never have cast her off—not Mama. I don't know why Daddy did—

"Daddy didn't really, Rusty. Mama cast him off when he took Gina. But he was doing it for all of us. Honest, he was, Rusty."

I suppose Ella thought she had placated me. She went on with her story.

"Tommy hired me as a legal secretary, or a substitute for Mama, or something. I was the best secretary he ever had—and the best substitute he could possibly have found. I look exactly like her—to Tommy at least—and I worked at it. Even with him, I went wild in bed—trying to prove myself or something." Another rigor shook her body. I petted her, tried to soothe her.

"I'm ashamed, Rusty," she went on. "And Gina called us clean! But I'm telling you this because you *are* my twin, the other half of me. We were conceived together, born together. We belong together. I feel so good now, so safe, close to you. I'm home again.

"But I must tell you everything. You have to know. You're my better half—literally my better half.

"I loathed Tommy Kaufman, but he never knew it. I forgot who he was when I went to bed with him. And I was too much

236

for him. He's getting old—far from impotent, but not nearly so virile as he would like to think himself.

"So whenever he felt inadequate he would drink a little, and brag a little. About how he was bigger than Justice Ricardo, how Justice was afraid of him, how Justice couldn't get along without him, and all that.

"Little by little I learned that he had a file of transcripts and tape recordings and all kinds of evidence cached away to blackmail Ricardo with if Ricardo ever thought of doing away with him.

"He in turn was afraid of Mama, of what she might do if I ever told her about us. For all he knew, I was her favorite child. Actually I saw Mama only once and I ducked out then. She never knew I was in town. Neither did Justice, I hope. All of his mob steered clear of Tommy's offices. Everybody knew he was Ricardo's mouthpiece, but the mob made sure that no firm connections were ever established. Even Justice met him in secret, alone.

"When Tommy defended one of his men, there was no traceable connection. As far as the courts knew, the defendant was just another client—independent. Only Tommy knew who was who—even more than Justice, I believe."

The driver started down into the Jersey entrance of the tunnel.

"I needn't go into detail, Rusty. It's best you don't know the rest—it might get you into trouble. Anyway, I became Tommy's confidential secretary. I found his cache; and while he was away on trips, I located what I needed. I photographed transcripts, even bought a recorder and transferred tapes.

"It's all there, Rusty. All about Daddy and the Rapid Petroleum Transit Company—the syrup and acid and bombings and collisions—with payoff arrangements and everything."

"Where?" I asked.

"In a suitcase in a locker in Penn Station. Here's the key."

She opened her purse and, after rummaging through it for several seconds, slipped two keys into my hand.

"The locker number is on one key; the little one unlocks the bag," she said. "Now the ball is yours. Run with it."

The taxi reached bottom. Its motor started laboring up the climb to Manhattan.

"Where?" I asked again.

"To Washington," Ella said. "The stuff would be no good in Chicago courts. I can't do any more. You take it to somebody in Washington—to the FBI or Senator Daniel's subcommittee on narcotics. There's narcotics evidence in it. Some of the bombers were addicts and insisted on being paid off in heroin. Their conversation is on tape.

"Or Representative Bender of the House government operations subcommittee. They're investigating labor racketeering —you know, the Presser business. There's that kind of evidence too. Surely you can make some contact in Washington, can't you? You must know someone there, or someone who knows someone? In the Marine Corps maybe?" She was breathless, anxious.

"Maybe," I said. I knew a number of musicians and bartenders. Bartenders always know someone else.

"Then you'll do it? To avenge Daddy—and to save Mama?"

"I'll try," I said. We came out of the tunnel and turned left toward Forty-second Street.

"The material is all arranged, documented, and coded, with a brief and an index. You needn't even open the bag. It's better that you don't know any more about it. It's dangerous to know too much."

"What about you?"

"I just hope I'm lucky. I left Tommy on good terms. I was too much for him. In another year I might have worked him to death. He protested when I said I was leaving—not very strongly

—but I think he was glad to see me go. I was beginning to embarrass him." She laughed bitterly.

"What are you going to do?" I asked.

"Stay here in New York, for a while at least. I'm going to work for a firm that's experimenting in motivational research."

"What's that?"

"Well, from what I learned from my contact in Chicago it's a sort of black magic. You find out what people want, whether they know it or not, and then you sell them a package that looks like it but usually contains something else. My law training tells me it's just barely legal, which probably means that it will be highly effective and quite lucrative."

It made no sense to me. Ella was hysterical, probably.

The taxi had threaded its way to the Piccadilly. We got out and I paid the driver. I took Ella's arm and started toward the bar.

"No," Ella said. "I don't want to be seen with you any more than we can help. I *might* be under suspicion. I may have been followed here."

"Then it's good night?"

"Yes. Oh, Rusty, I'd like to kiss you good night right here. I'd like to be close to you all night—forever—the way we were in the taxi. I feel so safe with you. But I'm afraid right now.

"If this business comes out all right, and we get through it safely, I'll come to you or you come to me and we'll grow old together and die together—just the way we were born. I'm not complete without you. Good night. Get out of town."

"Good night. I'll be at the Willard, for a few days at least."

"I'll send you my address, when I find a place." She squeezed my hand and walked briskly toward Broadway. I did not even know where she was staying. She had not wanted me to know. It seemed that all my family were trying to get me out of their way. When Ella disappeared into the crowd I turned and went into the Circus Bar. I had not had time to notice what kind of music they had earlier in the evening.

Back in Washington, I took a job in the Pampas Lounge to explain my extended stay in the Capital. I merely played and listened to people in the bar and in the Willard lobby. I learned when the House government operations subcommittee was re-organized, on June 10, and Congressman Hoffman was named chairman. After another week or two I met a young law graduate, legman for a lawyer employed as counsel for that committee, who was almost as enthusiastic about progressive jazz as he was about getting ahead in his profession. It was to him that I ultimately delivered the suitcase.

"I'll see if I can find someone who is interested," he said. "If there's anything in it that we can use, it will be a feather in my cap."

"I don't care who uses it," I said, "just so long as somebody hangs."

"It's that good—or bad—is it?"

"So I've been told."

I have no idea where he took the evidence first, or who evaluated it; but it was a month before I got any response. Then my lawyer friend dropped in one night and casually invited me up to his place to play a few records after the Pampas closed. We left singly, but arrived at his apartment within a few minutes of each other. After a drink and one side of a new Shearing disc, there was a knock on his door.

Two crew-cut collegians only a few years older than my host came in and were introduced as FBI agents. One of them did most of the talking and the other most of the listening.

"This is a good picture of you, Meaghan," the agent said, examining the jacket of my latest LP album. "Better than ours." He grinned pleasantly and sat down facing me.

240

"Thank you," I said. "I posed for this one."

"You posed for the other one, but the sports shirt is more becoming than your marine blouse."

"More comfortable, too," I said. "Not that I was painfully uncomfortable at Quantico."

"Not even when consorting with the enemy?" He laughed genially.

"You mean Madame Vladishenka?"

"That's the one."

"Well, I guess I spoke too soon. Am I branded as a subversive?"

"Only by a few sports writers. Your Russian girl friend is as clean as a whistle."

"You know all about me, don't you?" I said. I wondered how far back they had gone.

"That's our business. Now, what do you know about the file our friend here turned over to us?"

"No more than you do. Not as much—I've never seen inside that suitcase."

"What was your reason for bringing it in?" The banter was all gone from his voice.

"Somebody ruined my father's trucking business—killed a number of men. I want to see justice done."

"You want to see Justice done in, you mean." He risked the pun, but no humor showed in his eyes or around his mouth.

"Yes."

"Then you do know something of the bag's contents."

"I was told a little."

"By whom?"

"By the person who got the evidence for me," I said.

"Who was that?"

"Another interested party."

"You aren't talking, are you?" He relaxed for a moment and

chuckled. His partner remained grim, studying every expression that crossed my face.

"I'm telling you all I know."

"Or want to know?"

"Yes. I was told that the less I knew, the less likelihood there was of my getting hurt."

"And you still don't want to get hurt?" He even knew about the Johnny Fox show.

"No," I said.

"Do you have confidence in the source you are shielding?"

"Complete confidence," I said.

He too studied me carefully before he spoke again.

"Would you be willing to testify if called?" he asked at last.

"How could I? I don't know a thing about it." Then I laughed. "On the other hand how could I refuse if I'm called?"

"That's a good question." Again he chuckled. "You could take the Fifth."

"Can't you verify the material through other sources?"

"Possibly. Will you tell us whose files were rifled for this evidence?"

I hesitated for a moment before answering. But I assumed they could find out if they did not already know.

"Tommy Kaufman's," I said.

Both agents nodded simultaneously. Whether they had substantiated facts or surmises I never knew.

"O.K., Meaghan," my interlocuter said, "there's a lot in that bag. We'll spread it around where it will do the most good. We'll know pretty soon how it's standing up."

With that they thanked me and left. I do not know how soon I expected results, or what I expected in the way of results. I got word to Ella that her evidence had been delivered. She answered and gave her address as Frank Conrad and Associates. She said that she was working in a clinic outside New York but she described the place as fabulous, a veritable country club. She did not, however, give a very clear account of the nature of her work, other than to hint at mysteries involving depth surveys and motives and inhibitions—all jargon to me.

In July I rejoined Lola at the Profile Club in Philadelphia. She was as wonderful as ever and helped keep my mind off developments in Washington. We moved on to Cleveland in August. During our first week there I got a short note from Ella.

> We're doing fine, Big Brother. We're in the headlines.
>
> Love,
> ELLA

The next day I went to the library and looked up recent issues of newspapers to see what she meant. I found nothing that I could identify positively, ignorant of the evidence as I was; but papers for August 3, 4, and 5, did carry accounts of a roundup of narcotics peddlers in New York. Aniello Santagata and Settimo Accardi were arrested as the alleged leaders. The names of half a dozen others led me to assume that the raid was what Ella had referred to in her letter, though I dared not write and ask her.

During the fall I received similar notices from Ella, usually after some of Avolo's countrymen had been hauled in on narcotics or racketeering charges. I began to see a pattern, or at least a thread of continuity running through the incidents. Things moved too slowly though, it seemed to me. I wrote Ella, somewhat petulantly I suppose, that I hoped she knew what she was talking about in her game of cat and mouse.

> You dear [she wrote], you really didn't open our bag of tricks, did you? It's much better that you didn't. Pandora that I am, I could never have resisted the temptation. That's what I like about my present job. We're really snooping here, right into the libido. I'm becoming quite expert in preparing briefs for our legal counsel on things they never

dreamed of—or rather have dreamed of all their lives but never admitted. I work with psychologists and psychiatrists and sociologists and anthropologists—experts who know all about everybody. Who knows? I may even understand me one of these days—or you. From the subliminal to the ridiculous!

But back to you, you can take my word for it, you are playing a good game, short yardage so far but enough for first downs. That's my big brother out there.

Love,
ELLA

After reading her letters I still knew no more about what Ella was doing than I knew about what we were doing jointly; but it was encouraging to learn that she thought our poisoned plant was bearing fruit. I felt hope rising again that I might save Mama yet, save her for me—although the best Ella could do for Daddy was to avenge his ruin. I trusted Ella. I was sure that Ricardo was on his way out. It was good that we could work together for the same end, if from somewhat different motivation. The vision of a home with me and Mama and Ella together again began to take on its earlier clarity. Ella had said that she wanted to come back home. We could all grow old together, intimately, happily.

Lola sensed the change in me, and fostered it.

"You perkin' up some now, Rusty, boy," she said. "You comin' alive, like you got a new gal or somp'n. Have you, boy?"

"Nobody but you, Lola," I said.

She cackled and tousled my hair. We were rehearsing for a new album of hers, *Songs for Sun Bathers*, to be released in the spring. We were doing well with her records. Everybody loved them. Mine, while meeting with consistent critical acclaim, and being featured on juke boxes in and around Chicago, were not nearly so popular. I was being typed as a musician's musician, as Lola might well claim to be, but I lacked the universality of

244

her appeal. I could not work both sides of the street, as she could. I held my place among the critics' Top Ten, however, even if I seldom rated so high with the disc jockeys; and I was improving during those early months of 1956.

With spring we headed west again, to the mountains—to Denver. Captain Hammer was still there and I visited him as soon as I was settled.

He was looking much better than he had looked the last time I had seen him. His face was fuller, his hands stronger. He was wearing glasses and turning the pages of a book on a stand laid across the arms of his wheel chair when I found him in his usual place on the sun deck. I told him that he was looking well.

"Thanks, Rusty," he said. "How are you?" He laid his glasses aside.

"Fine."

"And Ella?"

"All right the last time I saw her, almost a year ago."

"What is she doing now?" he asked.

"Search me," I said. "She's working for Frank Conrad and Associates in New York."

"Motivational research," he said. "Depth surveys."

"Yes, that's it—from the subliminal to the ridiculous, she said." I sat down, half facing him.

"Well, it's good to hear that she can take that attitude toward it," he said with a chuckle and then turned grave. "She's really learning the rules before joining up."

"Captain Hammer," I said, "what are you talking about? You two were way over my head when she was here. What's it all about?"

"It's all about us—you and me and Ella—all of us."

"All right, what about us? Out with it."

Captain Hammer closed his book and placed it and his reading stand on a book cart beside his chair. The cart was loaded with volumes.

"We have a choice," he began, in the tone he had often used with me back at Highcastle. "At least we think we have—it's long been a moot question in philosophy and theology—though Ella's present outfit is trying to prove that we haven't.

"We have the choice of merely looking at the face of things, and being reasonably happy, or of peering into the essence and living in despair.

"Ella knows that. She knew it when we met. Maybe she's always known it. She knows the difference between form and substance, and she's in the process of learning a great deal more where she is now." The prospect saddened him.

"What is this 'joining up' business?" I asked. I remembered their use of that phrase.

"It's following the trend set by a preponderant majority of the people living in our time—to accept appearances and to hell with the rest.

"Accept the face of religion, whether it's Bishop Sheen's Pomp and Circumstance or Billy Graham's Sawdust Trail—but don't under any conditions analyze its tenets or its real implications.

"Assume sincerity, as Dale Carnegie counsels, whether you feel it or not, and find Dr. Peale's peace of mind by justifying whatever you are doing or have done or want to do, simply by following the basic principle that positive thinking makes it so. Be firm and hard-headed in your errors.

"Accept the union label as a guarantee of superior craftsmanship, be it in murder, mayhem, or manufacturing. Call death insurance life insurance, as it's printed on the face of your policy.

"Conform to the whims of nine old men because they constitute a court and the word of a court is the law of the land. Speak glibly of the cold war while the atmosphere around you becomes hotter by the minute with strontium 90.

"Join up, Rusty. Do these things and neither life nor death

246

will hold any terrors for you. Stay outside the pale and get lost—beat—angry. Do you understand, now that I've spelled it out for you?"

"Yes, sir," I said.

"That's your choice—Ella's choice. Face or essence, form or substance." He paused; and when I made no comment, he frowned and continued, "A picture, they tell me, is worth a thousand words. Look at one. Look at me!"

I looked at his face—tanned, rugged, virile, and for the moment smiling. His eyes even held an expectant twinkle as he laid aside the blanket spread over his lap. His legs were all gone—just stumps enough for him to sit on, his pajama legs pinned up into neat little bundles.

"One more center slice of Hammer's Premium Ham and I'm through," he said as he replaced his blanket. "My wounds have no more chance of healing than the sores on our body politic."

He was still smiling, bitterly.

"You will notice that I did not look down," he said. "I prefer to look at my face in a mirror. I'm taking care of it, as you remarked when you shook my hand a few minutes ago."

I had learned not to say, "I'm sorry." Ella had taught me that.

"When you write Ella, tell her I've joined up," he said. "Will you do that?"

"Yes, if you want me too, if you're sincere."

"Sincere is a dirty word, Rusty. Madison Avenue has ruined it. Just tell her that I mean it."

"And do you really mean it?"

"I certainly do. I am not long for this world. I never was for it. I've lived in despair. I will not die in despair." The determination in his voice was strong, strong enough to speak for the despair in which he had lived.

"Can you join up?" I asked.

"Why not? I know better, but millions who know better are long-time members in good standing. If they can, I can. What

247

do you think I am, half a man?" He dropped his hands where his lap should have been.

"No, sir," I said. "I will not mistake form for substance—not in your case, sir."

"Thanks, Rusty. I appreciate that the way you meant it. Now carry it on. Don't be fooled by what I have seemed to be. I'm in earnest now. I don't know why we're here, but we *are* here. I will grant that we're supposed to be here. If we are to survive, life must be tolerable. To make life tolerable we must accept the illusions. *Ergo* it was meant that we should accept them.

"Even Plato insisted that phenomena are all that most of us can ever know—noumena are beyond us. I bow to the divine will. I will that my will be made subservient." He made a token bow.

I could not tell whether he was serious or not. I think he was. I hope he was. I should hate to think that he died in despair. I visited him frequently during my stay in Denver. We talked of other things after that, of my football career, of his—I went back twenty years in the newspaper files to read of his exploits so I could relive them with him, as I go back now to visit those many green isles in my own life before the furies got me. We left Denver in July, and Captain Hammer was dead when I passed that way again.

After an ominous lull, both in the newspapers and in Ella's letters, things began to look up again. One morning in September I opened a San Francisco newspaper and saw Justice Ricardo's name in the headlines. The boss had at last been subpoenaed by a Senate investigating committee. According to the story it was a big thing the Republicans were trying to pull off before the general elections in November. Rumor had it that several agencies of the government working together had compiled a formidable mass of evidence. It was hinted that they had held it back and reinforced it to make an airtight case and to stage a big show at just the right moment.

248

It was a show that I wanted to see. I doubted that I would be called as a witness, but I wanted to be present when Justice was "done in," as the FBI agent had put it. My appetite for his blood was further whetted by a telegram from Ella.

FOURTH QUARTER   WE ARE AHEAD AND WE HAVE THE BALL

ELLA

After that I *had* to go back East. I told Lola before our last show. She had some recording commitments, which made me somewhat hesitant to mention my leaving her.

"How is Pokey doing now?" I asked.

"He's outa jail, back at work, doin' awright, I guess." She backed up to me to have her fresh dress zipped.

"Do you think he'd like to rejoin you, Lola? I mean, after all, I'm just substituting for him."

"You mean they gona git that Mistuh Justice and give yo' mammy back to you, don't you, Rusty, boy?" She could read the newspapers even if she could not read music. She turned and faced me.

I could not lie to her.

"Yes, Lola," I said, "that's it. I want to go back East for the fireworks."

"Awright, Rusty. I always told you you could leave me whenevah things started workin' out yo' way. Looks like it's that time." Her eyes were big and soft.

"I hate to leave you, Lola; but you're the whole show. You don't really need me."

"I'll git by. Ol' Lola's been 'round a long time. I ain't nevah had nobody could back me up the way you do, honey, but I reckon me an' ol' Pokey kin make a livin'." Her laugh was throaty, indulgent. "You run 'long home. Tell yo' mammy that I took good care of you."

249

"I will," I said. "No one will ever know how well you took care of me."

"I'll know, Rusty, boy. I'll know." She knew everything.

I wired Paul Ade immediately to get me a booking in Washington. The best he could do was a club date in Philadelphia. So when we finished our engagement in San Francisco, Lola and I split up and I flew East. Of course I was not actually in Washington but I was near enough to get there in a hurry if anything broke.

And I was near enough, as was everyone else in the country, to witness Justice Ricardo's performance on television. For hours on end I watched the chairman of the Senate committee put questions to Ricardo, and I heard him drone repeatedly, "I decline to answer on the grounds that it might tend to incriminate me." I heard Justice linked with vice in all its forms—gambling, extortion, organized prostitution, racketeering, the narcotics traffic. Always he hid behind the Fifth Amendment. After three days, during which he did not even resort to counsel since he made only the one pat answer, he began to grow arrogant and contemptuous. As his confidence grew his smile became more irritating than his voice. I seethed inside at his effrontery.

Then the committee prepared to adjourn over the week end.

"Mr. Ricardo," the chairman said in closing, "you have evaded every question we have asked so far. I promise you that when this committee reconvenes next Tuesday you will be confronted with such an array of witnesses and such a preponderance of evidence that you will never smile again so long as you live."

"Ain't nobody going to talk, Senator," Ricardo said condescendingly. "Ain't nothing to talk about. We're just wasting time and taxpayers' money."

Through sheer force of habit I continued to watch the television screen or to listen to the radio right on over the week end.

250

Although nothing official could be expected before Tuesday, the air was full of rumor and conjecture. I listened to dozens of radio and TV commentators make their guesses, backed by hints of secret documents and scores of witnesses already in custody or under subpoena.

By Sunday evening my interest in the commentators' padded palaver began to pall. I was lying down when the networks suddenly came alive with a news flash. The excited voice of an announcer cut into a scheduled musical program.

"We interrupt this program to give you a special news bulletin which has just come over the wire. Less than ten minutes ago, Justice Ricardo's moll, mouthpiece, and three of his henchmen were killed in a crash near Plymouth, Indiana. They were en route to Washington. That's all we have right now, folks. Stay tuned to this station for details."

I stayed tuned to that station until I heard the names: Tommy Kaufman, Nestra Bercelli, Rocco Panzica, Pietro (Pete) Baroni, and Rafael Mazarro. The announcer continued.

"All of these except Tommy Kaufman were subpoenaed to appear before the Senate committee Tuesday morning.

"Kaufman, Chicago's best-known criminal lawyer, has defended Ricardo and many other clients allegedly connected with Ricardo in criminal activities. Presumably he was on his way to act as counsel for the other members of the party.

"The automobile in which they were riding collided with a butane truck a few miles west of Plymouth, Indiana, on Highway 30. The truck exploded, mangling the victims beyond recognition, but the occupants of the car are known because they have been under surveillance for several days, and were observed by highway patrolmen only a few minutes before the crash.

"The driver of the butane truck, who gave his name as Mario Meli of Hammond, Indiana, said that he had pulled off onto a side road and left his truck for a minute. He stated that the

251

brakes must have given way, allowing the tank to roll back into the path of the oncoming automobile. He considers it a miracle that he escaped injury.

"Police are holding Meli for investigation. Preliminary searches have revealed no police record so far, though Chicago police say the crash has all the earmarks of a gang killing. Ironically enough, a source close to the present Senate investigation says that Ricardo and two of the victims of the crash, Baroni and Mazzaro, have been linked with the systematic destruction of a trucking firm in Texas by tactics similar to those employed in this crash, if the collision proves to have been intentional."

The announcer elaborated on his story but added nothing new. No one did the rest of that night. I could not sleep. I could not even turn off the radio. I was held by it, held to it for hours, trying to get just one more bit of news. Sometime after midnight I received a wire from Ella.

STAY RIGHT WHERE YOU ARE DON'T GO ANYWHERE
MAMA SAYS SO I AM COMING
ELLA

The first ray of hope. Good old Ella. She really came through when I needed her most. If *Mama said so*, obviously Mama was alive. I was sure that Rocco Panzica was the man I had known as her chauffeur, but it did not follow necessarily that he *always* drove her. I could see the reasoning of the police. The men were using her car. It would be natural to suppose that she was in it when it collided with the truck. I could imagine what the explosion had been like. There would have been nothing left to identify. So the police were guessing.

The woman in the car—if there had been one—was not Mama. She would never have been served with a subpoena. There would have been no reason for serving her. I finally relaxed as I felt my blood warming up again. Soon I would see Ella, then Mama. This gang killing would finish Justice Ricardo, whatever the other evidence might be. I drank a nightcap and dozed off a little while before dawn.

I was up again by the time the morning paper was dropped outside my door. It was full of the accident, a rehash of the story related the night before, with pictures of the crash—or rather of a big hole in the highway where the explosion had occurred. There was a box calling attention to other stories on page three.

When I turned to page three, I saw first a big picture of Mama, a recent one and a not very good one. Beneath it was a brief explanation.

The notorious Nestra Bercelli, alleged long-time mistress of Justice Ricardo, and operator of the glamorous Priscilla Smart Model Agency of Chicago, reputed to be the most exclusive and most profitable call-girl service in the country, who was killed in the crash near Plymouth, Indiana, late yesterday afternoon.

There followed a lengthy story of Mama's supposed operations and a purported biography based, so far, on scanty information. The smears, the damning innuendoes, the hedging use of "alleged" and "believed" and "thought to be," angered me as much as Ricardo's hiding behind the Fifth Amendment had done a few days earlier. I boiled and fumed as I read.

After I had finished with Justice Ricardo I had other things to do. I would see that Mama sued every stinking one of the weaseling reporters who wrote a word about her and every paper and news service that carried the story. I was glad that she was alive to defend herself and clear her name. Her very existence would show the wiseacres how wrong they could be. I was still frothing when Ella called me on a house telephone to report that she was downstairs.

I told her to come on up, and I started to shave and make myself presentable. She took time to buy newspapers and cigarettes; so I was partially dressed by the time she knocked on my door.

"Isn't it horrible?" she asked as she embraced me.

"Yes," I said. "How can they do such a thing?" I **was** thinking of the reporters.

"They can do anything," Ella said. "They are as vicious as any animal in the jungle. Look what they did to Daddy."

I let go of her and looked at her closely for the first time. The furies were taking their toll. She had cried all night.

"How is Mama?" I asked.

"How is Mama?" she looked at me blankly, then suspiciously.

"You wired that she said for me to stay here. How is she? Where is she?" I was getting impatient. My voice was rising.

"Oh, no, Rusty! Mama was in that car. The reports are correct. Don't you know that? Can't you believe it? *Won't* you believe it?"

"But you said—" Ella's insistence that Mama was dead killed something in me. I trusted Ella, but now I could not believe she was telling the truth. I refused to listen to her or speak to her. Yet the conversation went on.

I suddenly became detached. There was a period of total blackness. I died too. But gradually I came back or, if not back, nearer than I had been. I was a presence in that room, one of three. I experienced the eerie sensation that I remembered from dreams in which I was dead and attending my own funeral, looking into the coffin at the body I had once inhabited. There my body was with Ella, or Mama, or Madame Bercelli. I was confused. Nothing seemed real.

"Mama left a letter with Uncle Tony, to be opened if anything like this should ever happen. She was prepared for it." Ella's voice came from far away, like the voice of a ghost on the radio, through a filter.

254

"How did you know?" I was startled to hear my own voice, filtered and far away. It seemed to be issuing from a zombie immanent in my own body (or was it Daddy's body?), towering above Ella or Mama or Madame Bercelli, and glowering at her viciously.

"Uncle Tony called me as soon as he was sure. Mama sent money regularly to him to put into a strongbox for us. There's a lot. I don't know how much.

"Then there was this letter, a long one. It said for all of us to keep out of it, stay away from her funeral. She said for me to come to you and tell you, wherever you were, and stay with you. I've come.

"She even explained how we could get our money and use it without paying taxes on it or letting anyone know we had it."

"I don't want any money. Do you have the letter?"

"No. I wouldn't dare carry it around. It's back in the safe-deposit box in Jersey City. But she told us how much she loved us and she said for me to kiss you for her. I haven't." She kissed me. Again I had the feeling that she was kissing some-one else, a dead man, a zombie. His face was rigid, immobile, cold, but I could feel his sensations, her warm lips on his.

"So Mama was expecting it?"

"Everybody in the rackets is expecting it," she said.

"In the rackets?" I was shocked and angry at her insinuations. "You don't believe those stories about Mama, do you?"

Ella dropped wearily onto my bed. She gave me one miserable glance and lowered her eyes.

"They're true, Rusty," she said softly. "All true. I found that out too, while I was in Chicago."

"Then you deliberately did this to Mama. *We* did this to her. We've killed her."

"Well, look what she did to Daddy." Ella flared up.

"Just what did she do to Daddy?"

"Ruined him," Ella said. "Who do you think was behind the whole plot to destroy him?"

"Justice Ricardo." I tried to control my voice, to get it out of the filter, out of the land of ghosts.

"Justice Ricardo could have picked any one of a thousand truck lines—much larger ones than Daddy's—to have made an example of." She had her voice under control too. "He could have broken a big company just as easily and made a much bigger impression on the industry. Why, then, do you suppose he destroyed Rapid Petroleum Transit?"

"Because he was jealous of Daddy."

"Don't be naïve, Rusty. Mama knew Justice Ricardo before she ever left Sicily. She went to him deliberately, knowing exactly what she was doing." She looked up, but seeing the expression on my face she quickly changed her tone and added, "She did it for us, in the beginning, just as Daddy made his mistakes in our interest.

"But Mama vowed to get even with Daddy for taking Gina. When the time was ripe, she did it—and how!"

"And now you've avenged him. You've killed her. God damn you, Ella!" The demon that had possessed my body slapped her. I cringed as though someone had struck Mama.

"Oh, no, no, Rusty." She looked up like a hurt animal. She put her hand to her burning cheek. I felt sorry for her. "Don't do this to me. Don't curse me. We're all we've got now. We mustn't let anything come between *us*."

"Not even murdering Mama? You brought in the evidence and I—I spread it around where it would do the most good." I hid my eyes behind my hands. I was blinded momentarily to all except a vision of Mama pursued and struck down by one of Daddy's tank trucks.

"Rusty, there wasn't one word about Mama in that entire file. I saw to that." Ella's voice was farther away than ever, and thinner. "Believe me. I popped off just now. I've got the

256

furies. Forget what I said about Mama. It *was* Justice Ricardo who ruined Daddy. The evidence was against him, not Mama. Honest, Rusty. I tried to keep her out of it."

"But you knew that Mama might become involved when investigations began." I opened my eyes at the sound of my voice. "You should have known that. You're the smartest one in the family. Remember?"

Ella hid her face. She hid Mama from me too. She was just a woman then—any woman.

"It—it was a risk I had to take," she said. "I took risks myself. So did you. I risked Mama. It's not my fault that she was vulnerable."

"But it's your fault that she's dead. Yours—and mine."

I began pacing the floor.

"How could you even risk it?" I asked. "Loving Mama as you do, knowing how much I loved her. She was everything to us."

I stopped in front of the woman and glared down at her.

"Mama's the only person or thing I ever loved in this world," I said threateningly. "I ought to kill you."

"You don't love the Madame Nestra Bercelli who was killed Sunday." She held her eyes steady as she spoke. "You love an image of Mama that hasn't had any real existence for ten years. You don't even know what Mama was like. All you know is what she looked like."

I slapped her again. She never even flinched, but I felt her pain. My own cheek smarted from the blow.

"Nestra Bercelli is no more Mama than that drunken Bozo we saw in Jersey City is Daddy," she went on calmly, though tears were streaming down her cheeks. "Our Mama and Daddy have been dead for years, both of them. They could never have done these things to us. We're all there is left, and now two strangers are coming between us. I can't stand it. I'm glad Madame Bercelli is dead, too."

257

I hit her again. No, it was not I; it was someone else. She made no response whatever. She did not even feel it. He might not have been punishing her. He might have been beating Madame Bercelli for destroying Mama. How could Mama have gone to Justice Ricardo seeking a lover? He slapped the woman a fourth time.

"Beat me, Rusty," she said, smiling. "Daddy used to spank me, and then love me more than ever. I used to tease him into spanking me, just so he would love me more.

"Go ahead; beat me, but love me afterwards."

"Get up and get out of here," I said. "I've never loved you. I never will. I never want to see you again."

"I can't leave," she pleaded. "We're one. We're twins. We should never have been separated. Mama should have had only one of us."

"God damn it, get up," I said. I grabbed her by the arm and lifted her from the bed. She offered no resistance as I hustled her to the door, screaming at her, "Get out of here. Get out of my life. I can't bear the sight of you."

She hung onto me and managed to kiss me once before I shoved her out into the hall and slammed the door behind her. She had been soft and pliable in my arms even as I abused her. She was hysterical. She was crazy. So was I, I guess. I don't remember.

CHORUS

O.K. So THE GREAT Rusty Meaghan had flipped his wig. Is that bad? He still walked among us. We were free to spin his discs. He fell in with hi-fi sessions devoted entirely to his music. He dug it. He picked us up on what he was doing and how he was doing it. He remembered when the tunes were taped, where he was at the time. He remembered everything up to that scene in his hotel room in Philadelphia after his mother's death.

He bugged us more than ever. In spite of his life story, he was calm and serene. Somewhere, somehow, he had fallen out, way out, beyond any other cat we knew. He still had something wonderful to lay on us. We sounded a hundred opinions, made a thousand guesses.

Teresina dogged him everywhere he went, however. She must have sensed that both Kurt and Clara were after him, and she wasn't about to relinquish her claim. If he ever came back, he would come back to her. Still he bugged her as much as he bugged the rest of us. He had a secret.

"It must be in his Sacred Writings," Foulard sounded. "They're blue, I'm sure, Brittany-sky blue."

Word spread. Cats began hiking in from all over. They listened in on hi-fi sessions. They too fell under Rusty's spell— he sounded so hip in those séances. But there was no more truth-talk from him. He had searched all he knew.

Except the Sacred Writings, we kept reminding ourselves— and Teresina. The situation grew tense again. Monkeys began clawing, pot was burning constantly, sex was going insane—whatever the kick, it was magnified. Petty crime picked up in the city, and fuzz began crowding in on our colony. By sheer force of numbers we finally prevailed upon Teresina to ask Rusty if he would read to us from his Sacred Writings.

"I'd be glad to," he said graciously. Like he was the most accommodating cat in the colony.

We all sighed. Our out-of-town guests pressed us to spread the word. Still more swarmed in, until it became obvious that the warehouse was the only joint that would hold the crowd. Dick Ferguson, who had decided after all that he could not put the phallus in the right place until he learned Rusty's secret, made arrangements to open the warehouse for us on Sunday afternoon.

That seemed cool. We ought to hold our reading from the Sacred Writings on somebody's Sabbath. There was reverence in that, real reverence. Indeed it was a subdued, pious congregation of cats that filled the warehouse that Sunday afternoon. Some of us had even bathed. At least one wore a collar and tie.

Rusty Meaghan looked like a little boy scrubbed for Sunday school, and at the same time like a true Elder of the Faith as he took his place behind Kurt's lectern and opened the service in our—

SANCTUARY, 1958

I AM INDEBTED to Captain Hammer, my departed mentor, for leading me to the gods of our time. This wisdom has come to me at various times and places, sometimes mystically, under circumstances which I cannot recall, sometimes in surroundings which are etched clearly in my memory.

I shall tell you as much as I can about the conditions under which these revelations have been made clear to me. I shall not quote directly, but I believe my interpretations are correct and will be acceptable to you. I will speak informally from my notes.

First I shall give you my gleanings from the Book of Carnegie. It is clear in my mind, as is the journey upon which I picked it up. I do not know why I was making the journey. My first image is the inside of a taxicab. I was riding from somewhere to the B. and O. Railroad station in Philadelphia.

By the time I reached the depot the early morning sun was flooding Chestnut Street with a glare that blinded me. It was the first sunshine I had seen for weeks. I could not endure it; so I hurried inside to the newsstand and bought the most expensive pair of dark sunglasses that were on display. After putting them on, I felt better.

From the morning newspapers, I learned that it was Monday, November 5, 1956. The headlines all had to do with tomorrow's general elections. I was not interested. Mechanically I drifted to a ticket window.

"Good morning," an agent greeted me cheerfully. "Where to?"

His question put me into a near panic. I had no idea where I was going.

"Just a minute," I said, hastily feeling my breast pocket. "I've forgotten something. I'll be back." Sane, normal people frequently forget things. The agent should have known that.

He smiled at me tolerantly as I wheeled and hurried out onto the sidewalk. I walked west on Chestnut to the bridge over the Schuylkill and loitered there until I regained my composure. Then I returned casually to the station. I was more careful that time.

I went to study the bulletin board. There was a train leaving within the hour for Cincinnati and St. Louis, with connections for points west, including Denver. Denver looked good. I might have a talk with Captain Hammer. Anyway I would have ample time on the way to decide, and I could always catch another train out of Denver if I changed my mind.

So I approached the ticket window the second time with confidence. No one could have told that I had had any trouble reaching a decision—and people were looking at me. I could feel their eyes. I went back to the same agent. He would be expecting me. I did not want to disappoint him. He might think I was crazy.

"One way to Denver," I said, before he had time to speak. "Pullman all the way—lower."

"Lower, one way to Denver," he repeated happily. He was glad that I was back. I felt better, too—safer with his approval.

He made up my ticket and put it into an envelope.

"Thank you," I said.

I went back to the newsstand. My Pullman seat was waiting for me, but the day would be long. It was the days that I dreaded most. I would need something to fill those daylight hours. I thumbed through some magazines but ended up buying a paper-bound copy of Dale Carnegie's *How to Win Friends and Influence People*. It might be well if I became interested in those pursuits. Captain Hammer had mentioned Dale Carnegie as one of the gods of our time. I would have a chance to find out what he had been talking about, just in case I should ever want to appeal to the gods.

As soon as my train was called I went aboard. My seat was on the left. I preferred it that way. With my music case beside me, I settled back and opened my book at Lowell Thomas's introduction, "A Short Cut to Distinction." I could hear Captain Hammer—or Ella—reducing that to "A Short Cut to Extinction." I learned from Mr. Carnegie's own preface that it was an *action* book, backed up by Herbert Spencer's solemn pronouncement that the great aim of education was not knowledge but action.

No wonder Captain Hammer had been depressed the last time I saw him. After his active life had been destroyed he had spent his time seeking knowledge. Obviously he did not belong in this world—he had been uneducated, or diseducated, by the loss of his legs. He was no longer a man of action; *ergo*, as he would have said, no longer educable.

I skipped the part on handling people. That was the last thing I wanted to do, now that Mama was dead. The formulae for making people like me were a little more inviting. I would not object to being WELCOME ANYWHERE, if I decided to live; but I doubted my becoming GENUINELY INTERESTED IN PEOPLE, and at the moment I found it hard to SMILE. I skipped on to the NUTSHELL, which seemed to be the ultimate in short cuts to hypocrisy. However, I tried to keep an open mind.

The most impressive piece of wisdom I ran into was the fact that the only way to win an argument is to avoid it. I laid the book aside so I might savor that morsel. It made sense. I was pretty sure that I had taken the train to avoid some kind of an argument with somebody—Ella, or Paul Ade, or myself. So far I had not faced up to the issue, the issue being: Was I or was I not a matricide, the most loathsome creature in anybody's world?

My musings were interrupted by the entrance of my traveling companion, a bald, pink, round little man wearing rimless spectacles and encumbering himself with three sample cases in addition to his suitcase. He asked my permission to sit in the seat he had already paid for and bustled around helping the porter stow his baggage. At last he lit on the seat facing me and folded his wings over his prosperous belly, but only for a moment. As soon as I glanced at him a second time he unfolded again.

"Clark is my name," he said, offering his hand. "Harold J. Clark, greeting cards."

"Meaghan," I said. "Rusty Meaghan, sharps and flats."

"Oho, I get it, a musician." He laughed heartily. "How is the music business these days?"

"Looking up." I hoped that was an acceptable expression.

"Our whole economy is looking up," he said seriously, sincerely. "Whichever way the election goes tomorrow, we're headed for a boom—a healthy boom. I don't care how you vote, Meaghan. I've cast an absentee ballot. You on your way home from somewhere?"

"Yes."

"That's good. Your mom and pop will be happy to see you."

The air brakes hissed and our car eased into motion. My companion looked at his watch.

"Out on time," he said—as if that mattered to me.

"See you're improving yourself," he continued as we gathered speed.

"What?" I asked. I was listening to the trucks on the rails beneath us.

264

"Your book." He indicated the Carnegie capsule on the seat beside me.

"Oh," I said. "Yes. I just put it down."

"Mind if I look it over?"

"No." I handed him the volume.

"I memorized it, ten, fifteen years ago," he said as he reached eagerly for the book. "But I like to reread it now and then. Wonderful, inspiring. Revolutionized human relations. Great man, Dale Carnegie."

"Real great," I said. Silently I thanked the great man for diverting his disciple's attention. Mr. Clark was already engrossed in the book, smiling his approval of familiar passages as he read.

I sank back into my seat and watched the brown Pennsylvania countryside roll by to the rhythm of the wheels. I was oblivious to the other passengers, almost in a coma, a state of catalepsy hanging on from the numb days or weeks I had spent I could not remember where. When Mr. Clark suggested lunch, I excused myself and bought an orange from the butch boy. I kneaded the orange for a long time, until it was soft inside, and then bit off the navel end and sucked the juice. I remembered the oranges that grew around Sarasota, which I had plucked myself and sucked on as a child. I remembered all of Sarasota, our house there—the little Spanish-style stucco on an inlet of Sarasota Bay—the palms, the tumbling mat in our back yard.

Before Mr. Clark returned I fortified myself with *Look* and *Life,* big picture books that I could hide behind. He respected my ramparts, or he was too deeply interested in further self-improvement to bother me with his conversation. Still I thought night would never come. But it did. I welcomed Mr. Clark's suggestion that we have a drink in the club car. We had several; at least I had three Martinis while he sipped on a bourbon and ginger ale.

We both ended up with healthy appetites. After dinner I suggested that we return to the club car while the porter readied our berths. I was eager for the seclusion of my lower, but I did not dare risk sitting in the Pullman until bedtime. My impatience would have aroused suspicion if I had had to wait in the car with the other passengers while berths were being prepared. The people would have been watching me. Martinis soothed my nerves; so I preferred to drink in the club car for an hour or so.

"Your eyes been bothering you long, son?" Mr. Clark asked. "I see you wear those dark glasses all the time."

"Strain," I said.

"Music, huh?"

"Yes. I'm taking a little time off."

"Pain?" he asked.

"No. I'm feeling no pain."

"That's what I mean. You're downing those Martinis pretty fast."

"I have trouble sleeping on a train," I said. "Just thought I'd relax before turning in."

"I see," he said. "Spend most of my time on a train. Sleep like a baby."

The solid food I had eaten for dinner gave my stomach a little trouble, but I managed to keep it down until we returned to our Pullman. Mr. Clark was almost as sickening. He was fussy. The time he took in the lounge, brushing his teeth and dressing for bed, irritated me almost beyond endurance. In time, however, he climbed the ladder to his upper and bade me a cheery good night.

My berth was delicious. Because of fatigue and delay—and possibly the Martinis—I lay down in a state of semiconscious exhaustion. The intimacy, the warmth, the familiarity of my snug little haven closed in on me and shut out the people who had been staring at me, the memories that had been plaguing me, the fears that had been disturbing me all day. Mama's presence was nearer than it had been at any time since Ella unleashed her furies on me. It pervaded the berth, permeated my being, crept into the dark fearsome caverns of my mind. Now the selective factor, whatever it is, chose only those images most welcome to me and filled my consciousness with contentment. For hours I lay in the lush bed of reverie, lulled by the cradling rhythm of the Pullman car, before finally dozing off into dream-rich euphoria.

We lost Mr. Clark sometime early in the morning. Friend-winner and people-influencer that he was, he departed without disturbing me. I was awakened once by light streaming through my window, but I pulled down the shade and reveled again in hours of half-slumber, until the porter became so insistent in his inquiries that I finally relinquished my berth and went into the lounge to dress. It was almost noon before I was settled again in my seat.

With day an admitted reality, my doubts returned. No one claimed Mr. Clark's seat, and no one came visiting; but the attention of the other passengers was upon me. They gave no overt signs, but I could tell. I wondered if they knew who I was, if they had learned my secret. I listened for any one of them to mention matricide. No one did. They were all very cagey. So was I. I was on to them. I kept my distance, and they respected it. They might have been a little afraid of me. I suspected that they considered me insane.

We were late into St. Louis. I missed my west-bound connection and had several hours' lay-over there. I walked to town. I was safe. People were too deeply interested in the elections to notice me. Only one person spoke to me—a mousy, middle-aged woman, who sold me Norman Vincent Peale's *The Power of Positive Thinking for Young People*. That was another one of the Sacred Writings of our time. It was important.

"We don't have the regular adult edition," she said apologeti-

267

cally. "We can't keep it in stock. But you're really quite young. You'll be inspired by this."

I agreed to accept it. I did feel young that day. I had felt like a baby all night.

"Have you ever heard Dr. Peale?" she asked while she wrapped the book—she insisted on wrapping it.

"No," I said.

"Well, I have. I've been to his church in New York. I remember a sermon on how to be a better person—by thought replacement. Just study our thoughts and decide whether they are creative or destructive. If we are not satisfied with ourselves we can replace our destructive thoughts with creative ones and be better persons. It's helped me so much. I am a much better person than I used to be."

I paid her and continued to listen while she counted my change. I had no choice.

"I remember another sermon, too," she said, "about how to be hopeful. You just practice being hopeful the way people practice playing golf or playing the pipe organ. I have practiced hope several hours every day since I heard him say that— and I'm so full of hope now."

She handed me my change and smiled wistfully as I thanked her. Unquestionably she was a better person and full of hope, even for me.

My own hopes were soon dashed. I hoped for a Martini but I found that I could not buy a drink until after the polls closed; so I went back to the depot and started to read my book.

After a pep chapter urging me to trust myself—which was indeed a task for me to undertake—I ventured on to seek the power that resides in a quiet mind. Of course I had to quit worrying.

I remembered Captain Hammer saying, "Not to worry is to be an idiot," but he admitted that he did not belong in this world.

268

Dr. Peale prescribed emptying the mind—practice emptying the mind just as one practices hope or golf or music—which seemed to me about as short and direct a route to idiocy as anyone could wish for, but I did not trust my own reason just then. It was as simple as swinging a baseball bat, "easy like," he said. The advice sounded about right for teen-agers—empty the mind before it has much in it, while the job requires less effort. I learned that visualizing the word "serenity" was also of great potency. There were further instructions, too, on sitting and standing and walking and thinking of sunsets and moonlight and noonday woods, as well as some more words to add to "serenity" in one's meditation on symbols. I felt equal to those assignments. Surely Captain Hammer had been wrong about the difficulty of adapting to our world. It was a snap, a surprisingly mild life-adjustment program.

When my train was called I went aboard at once. We were well on our way by the time the bar in the club car opened. Sitting alone, I was privileged to drink myself into a solitary stupor, barely within hearing of the political discussions and election prophecies going on around me. The din of voices came from far off, indistinct, unimportant, meaningless. Who cared? Mr. Clark had said that our economy would boom regardless of the outcome of the election.

The long-delayed Martinis made dinner unnecessary. I sat where I was until my early bedtime. Then I approached my berth tingling with the anticipation of another night of bliss. I heard all the old lullabies again, relived the scenes brought back by my twin jinn—I liked that, twin jinn, Noilly Prat and Gordon. I was appreciative and grateful for their services. My eyes were wet when I finally closed them, the better to see the images and feel the presence sharing my berth with me.

With daylight again I forced myself to get up early and to eat breakfast. I had decided to call on Captain Hammer, now that I had learned some of the mysteries of the gods. I could intel-

269

ligently discuss with him the Sacred Writings of Peale and Carnegie. Consequently, I was alert and eager when the train pulled into Denver.

Even before I made reservations at a hotel I telephoned the VA hospital to see if I could call on Captain Hammer the next morning or afternoon. It was then that I learned he was dead. I could not believe the news. I was beginning not to believe in death at all.

The more I thought about it the more thoroughly I was convinced that the voice on the telephone had lied to me. The VA hospital was run by bureaucrats, and bureaucrats are notoriously incompetent—Captain Hammer had told me that many times. I could think of only one thing to do, go and find out in person; so I took a taxi out to the hospital and went to the information desk myself.

The attendant also told me that Captaim Hammer was dead. He had been taken from Fort Logan Veterans Administration Hospital to Fort Logan National Cemetery. Since the two were adjacent I asked where he was buried and had the taxi driver take me there. I found the marker. It said that Captain Hammer was dead.

Denver had been the nearest thing to a destination I had had when I bought my railroad ticket. Now I had nowhere to go. I felt silly when the cabbie asked me where to.

"The public library," I said. One can always go to the public library. On the long ride from Fort Logan back to the Civic Center I wondered why I was going there. I did some fast thinking on the way, made foolproof plans so the librarians would not think I was crazy.

First I read the newspapers—a Democratic Congress and a Republican President. I thought that was nice and friendly. Mr. Clark had said that it did not matter who won the election —so both sides had won. Of further interest was the fact that Justice Ricardo had been assassinated—shot in a barber chair in broad daylight—by persons unknown. I would have liked to know them.

The library still had three hours to go before closing time. I was afraid to stop reading. People would begin staring at me. One must read when one accepts the hospitality of a public library; so I turned again to the Sacred Writings.

I asked first for the Book of Sheen. From *Peace of Soul* I learned that Our Blessed Lord preferred nasty people to nice people, that He voiced no condemnation against Mary Magdalene or the thief but against their accusers, no invective against badness but against self-righteous goodness. I was pleased to find out that sin was not the negation of a code but the rejection of a loved one, an outrage against love. All of this made me feel good. It fit in with Mr. Carnegie's admonition for people to understand me instead of condemning me. I had broken a code—I had killed my mother—but I had not rejected her or ceased to love her. I was blameless.

The Book of Overstreet was equally comforting. Mr. Overstreet urged me to substitute an insight into authentic human relations for silly class prejudices and to free myself from the half-truths of the crowd and think as a reasonable member of the human race.

Turning from *About Ourselves* to Mr. Overstreet's *A Guide to Civilized Loafing,* which seemed to be addressed more particularly to me at the moment, I was heartened by his encouragement to survey the world and choose what I wanted and mold and re-create my choices into something that would move into areas of happy experience. By exploring, in my loneliness, ways that are intimately my own I could find keenest delights as well as peace and serenity.

Mr. Overstreet proved to be great, real great. My environment was not just what I saw, he said. It had emerged from something different into what it was now. Beneath its outer appearances (we were on home ground now) I would find

271

warm stirrings which I had never guessed were there. Three gateways to the happy life would open to me if I would only live in the past, explore the present, and visualize the future.

I had really been on the beam for the last few weeks, especially the last two nights in my Pullman berth. I had been living in the past and exploring the present. My weakness lay in visualizing the future. I had a new opportunity, however, to do as I pleased, which Mr. Overstreet ventured to call civilized. I was free to enter into an order of life in which I could call my soul my own.

A librarian came by and whispered to me, "Closing time."

I looked up. There was only one other patron in the reading room, a mustached, tousled-haired old man at the same table with me. He looked up too.

"I'll take your books," the librarian said. She was kind and motherly. Now that we had stopped reading she raised her voice ever so slightly. "I hope you have found peace of mind, young man. Aren't these books inspirational?"

"Peace of mind?" The boor across the table from me snorted contemptuously. "If man had found peace of mind we'd still be living in caves, dying of plagues, and enslaving our neighbors. The minute you find peace of mind, young man, you're through, finished, kaput!" He stalked out of the library as noisily as he could.

"Don't mind him," the librarian said softly. "I imagine he was disappointed in love or something."

"I don't mind him," I said. "Good night."

"Good night."

Outside again I was lost again. I was lost for a long time. I have no idea how long a time, or where I spent the time. I did have the beginnings of my Sacred Writings, however, to sustain me.

I have continued to run away from arguments, as Mr. Carnegie would have me do. I practice emptying my mind constantly according to the admonitions of Dr. Peale, and in the Book of Sheen I find forgiveness for every wrong I do or have done. I have found comfort too in the approved evil done by the AEC, and in the revocation of ancient laws and customs by acts recorded in the Book of Judges, as I call my collection of Supreme Court decisions. I practice hope, too. Who knows but that the next supreme decree will absolve me of all my guilt as earlier ones have exonerated traitors and seditionaries?

I now turn to my notes on the Book of Graham—

CHORUS

LIKE IT was too much, even for the cats assembled in the warehouse. Like our Rusty Meaghan, our widely heralded shaman, was turning out to be squarer than a TV spectacular. He had sold us out. The visiting cats started the rumble. They began throwing beer cans at Rusty, then at members of our own select company. A few switch blades appeared from somewhere and the joint started jumping. It was a real gasser.

Then the fuzz descended upon us. They had been crowding us for over a week. Like they don't dig us from juvenile delinquents. Whenever there's JD trouble anywhere they fall in on us. And there was trouble in the sanctuary that Sunday afternoon. The fuzz busted over a hundred of us, cats and chicks alike, as many as they could haul in their paddy wagons, and put the rest under don't-leave-town notice.

All, that is, except Teresina and Rusty Meaghan. When we passed Teresina's shop (we being in the paddy wagon) there was Teresina open for business as usual, and Rusty nowhere to be seen. Like Teresina can smell fuzz clear across town; so she and Rusty had cut out at the first hint of a rumble.

After we got out of slam we called on Teresina. Like she was in the scene from in front. We all sounded her, where was Rusty?

"Gone. Copped out," she said. "Like you don't expect him to stick around after that rumble you creeps laid on for him, do you?"

275

"You creeps!" Foulard said. "Jesus Christ, Teresina, you set up the whole scene. Sacred Writings, Zen—four-square cornpone!"

"I told you the Sacred Writings were his. I never read them. Anyway what's the drag? So Rusty flipped his wig. Don't we all?"

"Like from in front Barbarossa was this or that," Foulard reminded us. "He's *that*—in spades."

Kurt wasn't quite so bitter. Since the rumble, he had begun to wonder whether he was his mother or his father. He was quoting about as much Bible as poetry. Apropos of something about Rusty he said,

"And be ye not conformed to this world: but be ye transformed by the renewing of your mind that ye may prove what is the good and acceptable and perfect will of God."

"Yeah, I dig you," Paul Patterson said. "Like we're drug because Rusty didn't conform to us any more than we conform to squareville. Like some of us spades won't be happy until all the white people turn black. Like, man, there's no bigotry like antibigotry, no prejudice like good, strong, militant, fanatic tolerance."

"I still think I could fill that empty mind of his with some real cool ideas," Clara said dreamily.

His Presence was still with us. Like that's the way it is with all cults, all religions. The gods have always come and gone. They're never here now. Like they trod this earth once. They walked among us. Then the bull or the boar or the mob tore them up, but the true believers say they'll be back with us in the spring. Like the women find the body's gone but piously predict that it will be back in time for the ritual of the rutting season.

That's how things stood when this slick chick blew in from

the East looking for Rusty. She was the kind of doll that the square hucksters use to peddle everything from lingerie to influence. She was the cover girl, the pin-up, the model, the sex motif of square merchandising. A gorgeous, sun-suited brunette, she wheeled up in front of Teresina's shop in a red Italian short and started sounding all of us, "Where is Rusty?"

Teresina had never heard of him. Neither had Clara. Kurt was evasive too; but Dick Ferguson, who was still bugged by his phallic placement problem, had a suggestion. When this chick started swinging her long brown legs deeper into the district she ran into Dick and he said, "Like maybe he's making it in a pad I know up the beach a piece."

"Can you take me there?" the chick sounds Dick. "I have my car parked down by the pier."

Dick knew that, as we all did. But like it was a two-seater, and Kay is a little bit square in her loveways. She's a good provider, too; so Dick did some fast creative thinking.

"Like I don't know how to get there by land," he said. "Like if we rented a motorboat I could find it."

We dug him. We rounded up a large enough shore party to keep the heat off and showed the chick where she could rent a motor launch. With Dick at the tiller we roared away from the pier and headed north. Four of us rode in the boat. Kurt, hating to see horsepower go to waste, borrowed a pair of water skis and trailed along behind on a leash. In a short while Dick throttled back—so slow that Kurt lost way and sank into the water—and turned to starboard. We headed into a shallow inlet and beached the launch before a small Spanish-style stucco cottage set in a grove of palm trees.

The place, Teresina's beach pad, appeared to be empty; but we went on up to the cottage anyway. The door was open.

"Rusty!" the chick called.

There was no answer.

"Rusty!" She went on inside.

277

We followed her, all except Kurt, who held back to let his swim trunks drip dry.

The pad was square-furnished, spinet piano and all, a picture right out of *American Home*. Teresina was two of everything, a real hetero-psyche. We followed the chick through the living room and into the bedroom.

It was a shrine. On a flower stand against a blank wall was a pin-up picture of this very doll, in something less than her present scanty sun suit, with a vase of wild flowers on each side.

"Rusty's here," the chick said. "There's Mama's picture."

Kurt moaned behind us. He dug the scene at a glance. We all did. That was the picture Rusty had fought over at High-castle, and this chick was Ella. We could see how it would shake Kurt up—Clara, too, and probably Teresina.

"Rusty!" Ella called again, louder than ever, and started back into the living room.

Rusty entered the front door. He had really copped out, shaved off his beard.

"Hello, Mama," he said softly.

"I'm Ella."

"Oh. Hello, Ella. Hi, cats."

"Hi," we said as the brother and sister clenched in a family reunion.

Like it was awkward. Like it should have been a big scene. But Rusty was as unruffled as if he had been expecting all of us, including Ella. Like nothing bugged him. He was still way out, untouched by our level of reality.

"Sit down," he said when Ella let go of him, partially at least.

We sat on the floor. The Meaghan twins settled on a piece of patio furniture and began devouring each other with hungry eyes.

"How have you been?" Ella asked.

"Fine," Rusty said. "And you?"

"Worried. Where have you been?"

"Here. I was in Philadelphia. You saw me there."

"That was over a year ago. Where else?"

"Here."

"How long have you been here?"

Rusty looked at us, and for the first time those Brittany-sky blue eyes began to seem troubled.

"How long has he been here?" Ella addressed her question to us.

"Two months, three months," Dick said and shrugged his shoulders.

"Where did he come from?"

We shook our heads. No one knew.

"He was on a train to Denver on election day in 1956," Kurt said helpfully. "He told us that in a truth-talk."

"Truth-talk?" Ella frowned.

"Search," Foulard explained.

"Talk truth-talk to me, Rusty," she said, turning again to her brother.

"Maybe this will help him remember," Foulard said and fished a reefer out of his jeans. He lit it and offered it to Rusty.

Rusty took it, puffed once, and passed it to Ella. She took a drag and coughed violently. Then she sniffed the stick and handed it back to Rusty.

"Madison Avenue never heard of that brand," she said in disgust.

"They've heard of it, miss," Dick said. "They just don't advertise it."

"I can readily see why. It's marijuana, isn't it?"

"Sure. It makes him remember, makes for the truth-talk."

"Help him, Ella," Kurt said. He was striving manfully to head off another attack of hysteria. "Tell him something you know. Help him remember."

Rusty eased off the settee and sat cross-legged on the floor. Ella joined him.

"Do you remember when Paul came to see you?" she asked.

"Paul Ade?"

"Yes, about the concert for the Gold Star Mothers?"

"Gold Star Mothers. Concert. Yes, I seem to remember the concert."

"Paul arranged it, in Philadelphia,"

"Oh yes, it was in—"

PHILADELPHIA, 1956

A FEW MINUTES before eight, I took the elevator to the ballroom. The hall was already full, buzzing with womantalk. I skirted the audience to one of the screens which had been set up on each side of the bandstand. As I ducked behind it I almost bumped into a man about my own age, wearing earphones and tinkering with the dials on an Ampex tape recorder.

"Hi, Rusty," he said.

"Hi."

"Baldwin is the name, no relation to Liberace's piano."

"Glad to know you," I said. "A fine piece of equipment you've got there."

"Yeah," he said. "Cost a fortune, but it's paying out. Next to their heroic sons, nothing is dearer to these women than the sound of their own voices."

"Have you been taping the entire convention?"

"Every word. Do it all the time. It's a living."

"You can skip my performance."

"Not a chance. This is what I'm hired for. Anyway I've got all your records. I'm not about to miss the chance to get a tape of my own."

"O.K." I shrugged.

"Say, Rusty. What are you doing here? These dames won't dig you."

"Paul sent me," I said.

"Now, Gold Star Mothers," the program chairman was saying, "let's quiet down for the feature performer of our meeting. Mr. Meaghan is here, in the wings."

Baldwin turned his attention to his clocks. I straightened up and smoothed my dress suit. It was eight o'clock, time for my test.

The program chairman was a big, busty woman in her early sixties. Her voice was strong—built on many chairmanships, I was sure.

"Mr. Meaghan is an ex-marine, a brave warrior, like our own heroic sons, but more fortunate. And we, too, are fortunate to have him with us this evening. He has played all over the United States and has made a number of records for Pan-Orpheus—many of which we are all familiar with."

Her last statement was open to doubt, but I had no time to dwell on it.

"Now, may I present Mr. Alfred Meaghan, Junior."

"Oh, brother!" Baldwin said under his breath.

I was mad. There was nothing like that in my contract. It was too late now, but Paul Ade was in for it. He was through as my agent, if I should have any further need for one.

I walked to the piano and bowed. The women—gray-haired, blue-haired, some Korean Gold Stars with natural hair—applauded loudly. I smiled as I looked them over, but I hated them. There was not one there who looked anything like Mama. They were not mothers. They had no right to be there, to be alive, with sons dead and buried, like Mama, and me left behind, like them.

But I would play. I would show them. I would join them. I would be a hypocritical Grade-A Bastard.

I raised my hand for silence. They all quieted down expectantly. I strode over to the microphone.

"Dear Gold Star Mothers," I said, "it is fitting that I come here tonight and play for you. I might be called a Gold Star Son. My mother lost her life, too, in the service of her country."

282

She had indeed been on her way to testify before a Senate committee, all in the line of duty.

The house came down. Tears dropped on orchids everywhere, and on motherly bosoms, and on elaborate evening gowns of every shade and hue. Bastardy can be beautiful.

There was a microphone on a short boom over the keyboard. The house quieted again as I sat down.

"I shall play 'Liebestraum' first," I said into the mike. A thousand breaths sighed at once. "After that you may call your selections from where you are. I will play what you want to hear."

"Liebestraum" came out as creamy as Miracle Whip, and it was lapped up just as hungrily. The applause was deafening. I could have anticipated the requests as they came from every part of the ballroom. "Clair de Lune," "Moonlight Sonata," "The Swan," "Rhapsody by Candlelight," "Chant d'Amour," "The Rosary," "Stardust," on and on, *ad nauseam*. There was not a Rusty Meaghan arrangement in the lot. I was glad that I was out of practice—the clinkers sounded more convincing. Sometimes, though, I found myself playing the music in its original, reasonably difficult form. I had to concentrate to simplify it to the level that was expected. But I worked at it, personality and all. The only thing missing was the candelabra.

The women kept me playing for two hours. At fifteen hundred dollars an hour I could contain my rage. They got their money's worth. After my last encore I was still able to smile when the Gold Star Mothers swamped me. My wrists ached. My fingers were numb. My chest was tight. But I played the game. The mothers mothered me, kissed me, mussed up my clothes, tousled my hair. They loved me. Flash bulbs were popping all around. My face was headed for a multitude of dressing tables.

"What shall we call you?" one of them asked. "Al or Alfred?"

"Just call me Junior," I said, still baring my teeth in an

283

expression that might have passed for a smile. "My own dear mother always called me that." I asked Mama's forgiveness.

When the storm was over, I caught a glimpse of Paul Ade in the back of the house, waiting for me. Well, I really wanted to see him now, for one brief moment, just long enough to deliver my old Highcastle right to his jaw. Unfortunately two dear mothers escorted me to the elevator. Paul got into the car with us. I did not offer to shake hands.

"Oh, Mr. Ade," the program chairman said, "Junior was just as good as you said he would be. Wasn't he wonderful?"

"Great, real great," Paul said with a big show of sincerity.

My right was firmly in the grasp of a quiet, ninety-pound mite of a mother, for whom I did feel a momentary affection, or pity, or something. She let go of me when we reached the lobby, and they all said good night to me and my manager.

I restrained myself until we got back to my room. "They paid me in cash," Paul said.

"Good. I'll take mine now." I did not ask him to sit down or offer him a drink.

He counted out the money, took his cut, and gave me the rest.

"Now, about some regular work," he began.

"In the morning," I said.

"Yeah, I guess you do need a little rest."

"I need a lot of rest."

"O.K.," he said and turned to leave. "No hard feelings."

"Nothing but. I may kill you some day."

He laughed uncertainly at my threat as he edged out of my room.

That is all I remember.

284

CHORUS

"THAT'S ALL you remember?" Ella asked. Her eyes were pleading. She might have been a Gold Star Mother, from the adoration on her face.

"Yes, that's all." Rusty furrowed his brow and tried. Like he always tried to please.

"That's when we lost you. We've all been looking for you—Paul, Lola, Gina—Daddy."

"How are Gina and Daddy?"

"Gina's doing fine. Daddy—Daddy's dead, Rusty. He fell down a flight of stairs in a second-story hotel in Cleveland."

"Too bad. I wish I'd known."

"As I said, we tried to find you. When Paul went back to your hotel room the morning after your concert, you were gone. We couldn't trace you. And you don't know where you've been?"

"Denver?" he asked brightly, trying to be helpful.

"Yes. The VA hospital thought you had been there, but they weren't sure." She turned to us and asked, "Will someone bring the large envelope I left in the boat?"

"Sure," Dick said and ran after it.

"Mama left us some money," Ella said.

"You told me that in Philadelphia."

"Yes, I know. Well, Paul Ade was disgusted with you. I bought you—bought your contract from him, after Daddy died. I've been managing you ever since."

"Managing me? I haven't done anything. I haven't played since Mama died."

"You played the Gold Star concert."

"Oh, yes—that."

"And you played for us once," Kurt said. "Crazy, man, crazy. Way out. You're still with it."

Rusty was really bugged now. He no longer looked like the old Barbarossa—with his beard gone and his eyes beginning to cloud up.

Dick returned with the envelope.

"This it, miss?" he asked.

"Yes, thank you. Look, Rusty."

Ella opened the envelope and took out a gaudily jacketed LP album. There was Rusty, red curls, freckles, pearly teeth and all, smiling at three Gold Star Mothers—in color and hi-fi.

ALFRED MEAGHAN, JR.
GOLD STAR ALBUM

it said in big gold caps.

"Where did you get that, Ella?" Rusty asked in dismay.

"We made it, four sides, from the tape that Baldwin kid made in Philadelphia. It's all there, your concert, your patter, everything."

"You can't do this," Rusty said.

"The hell we can't," Ella said. "We've done it. You're under contract to me and you're under contract to Sol Meyer. Pan-Orpheus has sold a million of these at nine-ninety-five a throw and they are still pressing them as fast as they can. It's the biggest concert recording since *Benny Goodman at Carnegie Hall.*"

"But Ella—" His expression was more sorrowful than angry —reproving.

"Oh, Rusty," Ella said. She was crying. "Come back. We can be together again forever. You can have anything you want.

286

Your own TV show. One-night stands at your own price. We can live together, travel together, just like old times. Like Mama and Daddy starting out together again. We're just like them. We can *be* Mama and Daddy."

A quick sob escaped Kurt. He whined, then giggled nervously.

Ella came back to us in a hurry.

"Will one of you bring my car out here?" she asked. "And then one of you come back in the boat and pick him up?"

"I'll drive it out," Foulard said.

"We'll come back for him," Dick said.

With that we all got up and cut out for the boat. Ella gave us fifty dollars.

"Later, cats," Rusty called after us.

"Later," we said.

Kurt was too stoned out to ride his water skis back to the pier. He all but flipped his wig on the way.

"If Mumsy had only had a girl child," he kept repeating. "If she'd only had twins, a boy and a girl, instead of me. If only I had a sister like Ella, with so much of Mumsy in her. Like she's Rusty's mama all over again."

We couldn't quiet him down, not even after we got him back to his pad, not until someone hustled a fix for him. The big dose of heroin relaxed him and he looked positively sublime as he smiled in euphoria, even while big tears rolled down his cheeks.

STROPHE

Both Foulard and Dick reported that when they went back to the pad on the beach Rusty was already playing Teresina's spinet piano.

"He was with it," Dick said. "Swinging way out. Crazy, man, crazy!"

"Not entirely," Foulard said. "Some of it was schmalz all the way. Like when Rusty swings, he swings wide, but he swings both ways."

The three chicks—Clara, Kay, and Teresina—made one pilgrimage to the shrine, in a motorboat.

"There they were," Teresina said enviously, "practicing accrobatics on the beach."

"They were beautiful to watch," Kay said. "As graceful as a nymph and faun at play. When we swung in close, they waved to us and dived into the surf, happy as babies." Her eyes sparkled.

"If you ask me," Clara said, meeting the issue squarely, "that sister of his is a shameless hussy."

Like we seldom watch TV, but we did rent a few sets to catch the first Alfred Meaghan, Jr., Show in the fall.

"Rusty Meaghan is one cat," Foulard said, "and Alfred Meaghan, Jr., is another. Like from in front, it's always been this or that, a bundle of opposites."

"Barbarossa is another," Teresina remembered wistfully.

Like Barbarossa walked among us. Rusty still cuts far-out discs. Al and Ella are the darlings of squareville these days. Like somebody is always commercializing somebody else's idols.

Maybe it was one big shuck. Maybe not. We're still searching it. Like whenever two or three of us are gathered together in some pad or espresso house, there Barbarossa is in the midst of us.

288